THE QUEEN PEDAUQUE

Turn to the end of this volume
for a complete list of titles
in the Modern Library

The
QUEEN PEDAUQUE

ANATOLE FRANCE

Translated by JOS. A. V. STRITZKO

Introduction by JAMES BRANCH CABELL

THE MODERN LIBRARY
PUBLISHERS : NEW YORK

Books by Anatole France
in THE MODERN LIBRARY

Manufactured in the United States of America
Bound for THE MODERN LIBRARY *by* H. Wolff

CONTENTS

INTRODUCTION

WHAT one first notes about *The Queen Pédauque* is the fact that in this ironic and subtle book is presented a story which, curiously enough, is remarkable for its entire innocence of subtlety and irony. Abridge the "plot" into a synopsis, and you will find your digest to be what is manifestly the outline of a straightforward, plumed romance by the elder Dumas.

Indeed, Dumas would have handled the "strange surprising adventures" of Jacques Tournebroche to a nicety, if only Dumas had ever thought to have his collaborators write this brisk tale, wherein d'Astarac and Tournebroche and Mosaïde display, even now, a noticeable something in common with the Balsamo and Gilbert and Althotas of the *Mémoires d'un Médecin*. One foresees, to be sure, that, with the twin-girthed Creole for guide, M. Jérôme Coignard would have waddled into immortality not quite as we know him, but with somewhat more of a fraternal resemblance to the Dom Gorenflot of *La Dame de Monsoreau;* and that the blood of the abbé's death-wound could never have bedewed the book's final pages, in the teeth of Dumas' economic unwillingness ever to despatch any character who was "good for" a sequel.

And one thinks rather kindlily of *The Queen Pédauque* as Dumas would have equipped it. . . Yes, in reading here, it is the most facile and least avoidable of mental exercises to prefigure how excellently Dumas would have contrived this book,—somewhat as in the reading of Mr. Joseph Conrad's novels a many of us are haunted by the sense that the Conrad "story" is, in its essential beams and stanchions, the sort of thing which W. Clark Russell used to put together, in a rather different way, for our illicit perusal. Whereby I only mean that such seafaring was illicit in those aureate days when, Cleveland being consul for the second time, your geography figured as the screen of fictive reading-matter during school-hours.

One need not say that there is no question, in either case, of "imitation," far less of "plagiarism"; nor need one, surely, point out the impossibility of anybody's ever mistaking the present book for a novel by Alexandre Dumas. Ere Homer's eyesight began not to be what it had been, the fact was noted by the observant Chian, that very few sane architects commence an edifice by planting and rearing the oaks which are to compose its beams and stanchions. You take over all such supplies ready hewn, and choose by preference time-seasoned timber. Since Homer's prime a host of other great creative writers have recognised this axiom when they too began to build: and "originality" has by ordinary been, like chess and democracy, a Mecca for little minds.

Besides, there is the vast difference that M. Anatole France has introduced into the Dumas theatre some preeminently un-Dumas-like stage-business: the characters, between assignations and combats, toy amorously with ideas. That is the difference which at a stroke dissevers them from any helter-skelter character in Dumas as utterly as from any of our clearest thinkers in office.

It is this toying, this series of mental *amourettes,* which incommunicably "makes the difference" in almost all the volumes of M. France familiar to me, but our affair is with this one story. Now in this vivid book we have our fill of color and animation and gallant strangenesses, and a stir of characters who impress us as living with a poignancy unmastered as yet by anybody's associates in flesh and blood. We have, in brief, all that Dumas could ever offer, here utilised not to make drama but background, all being woven into a bright undulating tapestry behind an erudite and battered figure,—a figure of odd medleys, in which the erudition is combined with much of Auto-lycus, and the unkemptness with something of à Kempis. For what one remembers of *The Queen Pédauque* is l'Abbé Jérôme Coignard; and what one remembers, ultimately, about Coignard is not his crowded career, however opulent in larcenous and lectual escapades and fisticuffs and broached wineflasks, but his religious meditations, wherein a merry heart does, quite actually, go all the way.

Coignard I take to be a peculiarly rare type of man (there is no female of this species), the type that is genuinely interested in religion. He stands apart. He halves little with the staid majority of us, who sociably contract our sacred tenets from our neighbors like a sort of theological measles. He halves nothing whatever with our more earnest-minded juniors who—perennially dis-covering that all religions thus far put to the test of nominal practice have, whatever their paradisial *entrée,* resulted in a deplorable earthly hash—perennially run yelping into the shrill agnosticism which believes only that one's neighbors should not be permitted to believe in anything.

The creed of Coignard is more urbane. "Always bear in mind that a sound intelligence rejects everything that is contrary to reason, except in matters of faith, where it is necessary to believe blindly." Your opinions are thus all-important, your physical conduct is largely a matter of taste, in a philosophy which ranks affairs of the mind immeasurably above the gross accidents of matter. Indeed, man can win to heaven only through repentance, and the initial step toward repentance is to do something to repent of. There is no flaw in this logic, and in its clear lighting such abrogations of parochial and transitory human laws as may be suggested by reason and the consciousness that nobody is looking, take on the aspect of divinely appointed duties.

Some dullard may here object that M. France—attestedly, indeed, since he remains unjailed—cannot himself believe all this, and that it is with an ironic glitter in his ink he has recorded these dicta. To which the obvious answer would be that M. France (again like all great creative writers) is an ephemeral and negligible person beside his durable puppets; and that, moreover, to reason thus is, it may be precipitately, to disparage the plumage of birds on the ground that an egg has no feathers. . . . Whatever M. France may believe, our concern is here with the conviction of M. Coignard that his religion is all-important and all-significant. And it is curious to observe how unerringly the abbé's thoughts aspire, from no matter what remote and low-lying starting-point, to the loftiest niceties of religion and the high thin atmosphere of ethics. Sauce spilt upon the good man's collar is but a reminder of the influence of clothes upon our moral being, and of how terrifyingly is the destiny of each person's soul dependent upon such trifles; a glass of light white wine leads not, as we are nowadays taught to believe, to instant ruin, but to edifying considerations of the life and glory of St. Peter; and a pack of cards suggests, straightway, intransigent fine points of martyrology. Always this churchman's thoughts deflect to the most interesting of themes, to the relationship between God and His children, and what familiary etiquette may be necessary to preserve the relationship unstrained. These problems alone engross Coignard unfailingly, even when the philosopher has had the ill luck to fall simultaneously into drunkenness and a public fountain, and retains so notably his composure between the opposed assaults of fluidic unfriends.

What, though, is found the outcome of this philosophy, appears a question to be answered with wariness of empiricism. None can deny that Coignard says when he lies dying: "My son, reject, along with the example I gave you, the maxims which I may have proposed to you during my period of lifelong folly. Do not listen to those who, like myself, subtilise over good and evil." Yet this is just one low-spirited moment, as set against the preceding fifty-two high-hearted years. And the utterance wrung forth by this moment is, after all, merely that sentiment which seems the inevitable bedfellow of the moribund,—"Were I to have my life over again, I would live differently." The sentiment is familiar and venerable, but its truthfulness has not yet been attested.

To the considerate, therefore, it may appear expedient to dismiss Coignard's trite winding-up of a half-century of splendid talking, as just the infelicitous outcropping, in the dying man's enfeebled condition, of an hereditary foible. And when moralising would approach an admonitory forefinger to the point that Coignard's manner of living brought him to die haphazardly, among preoccupied strangers at a casual wayside inn, you do, there is no questioning it, recall that a more generally applauded manner of living has been known to result in a more competently arranged-for demise, under the best churchly and legal auspices, through the rigors of crucifixion.

So it becomes the part of wisdom to waive these mundane riddles, and to consider instead the justice of Coignard's fine epitaph, wherein we read that "living without worldly honors, he earned for himself eternal glory." The statement may (with St. Peter keeping the gate) have been challenged in paradise, but in literature at all events the unhonored life of Jérôme Coignard has clothed him with glory of tolerably longeval looking texture. It is true that this might also be said of Iago and Tartuffe, but then we have Balzac's word for it that merely to be celebrated is not enough. Rather is the highest human desideratum twofold,— *D'être célèbre et d'être aimé*. And that much Coignard promises to be for a long while.

James Branch Cabell

Dumbarton Grange,
July, 1921.

THE QUEEN PEDAUQUE

THE QUEEN PÉDAUQUE

CHAPTER I

Why I recount the singular Occurrences of my Life

I INTEND to give an account of some odd occurrences in my life. Some have been exquisite, some queer. Recollecting them, I am myself in doubt if I have not dreamed them. I have known a Gascon cabalist, of whom I could not say that he was wise, because he perished miserably, but he delivered sublime discourses to me, on a certain night on the Isle of Swans, speeches[1] I was happy enough to keep in my memory, and careful enough to put into writing. Those speeches referred to magic and to occult sciences, with which people were very much infatuated in my days.

Everyone speaks of naught else but Rosicrucian mysteries.[2] Besides I do not myself expect to gain great honour by these revelations. Some will say that everything is of my own invention, and that it is not the true doctrine, others that I only said what one had already known. I own that I am not very learned in cabalistic lore, my master having perished at the beginning of my initiation.

[1] The original manuscript, written in a fine hand, of the eighteenth century, bears the sub-heading "Vie et Opinions de M. l'Abbé Jérôme Coignard" [*The Editor*].

[2] This writing dates from the second half of the eighteenth century [*The Editor*].

But, little as I have learned of his craft, it makes me vehemently suspect that all of it is illusion, deception and vanity.

I think it quite sufficient to repudiate magic with all my strength, because it is contrary to religion. But still I believe myself to be obliged to explain concerning one point of this false science, so that none may judge me to be more ignorant than I really am. I know that cabalists generally think that Sylphs, Salamanders, Elves, Gnomes and Gnomides are born with a soul perishable like their bodies and that they acquire immortality by intercourse with the magicians.[1] On the contrary my cabalist taught me that eternal life does not fall to the lot of any creature, earthly or aerial. I follow his sentiment without presuming myself to judge it.

He was in the habit of saying that the Elves kill those who reveal their mysteries, and he attributes the death of M. l'Abbé Coignard, who was murdered on the Lyons road, to the vengeance of those spirits. But I know very well that this much lamented death had a more natural cause. I shall speak freely of the air and fire spirits. One has to run some risk in life and that with Elves is an extremely small one.

I have zealously gathered the words of my good teacher M. l'Abbé Jérôme Coignard, who perished as I have said. He was a man full of knowledge and godliness. Could his soul have been less troubled he would have

[1] This opinion is especially supported in a little book of the Abbé Montfaucon de Villars, "Le Comte de Gabalis au Entretiens sur les sciences secrètes et mystérieuses suivant les principes des anciens mages ou sages cabbalistes," of which several editions are extant. I only mention the one published at Amsterdam (Jacques Le Jeune, 1700, 18mo, with engravings), which contains a second part not included in the original edition [*The Editor*].

been the equal in virtue of M. l'Abbé Rollin, whom he far surpassed in extent of knowledge and penetration of intellect.

He had at least the advantage over M. Rollin that he had not fallen into Jansenism during the agitation of a troubled life, because the soundness of his mind was not to be shaken by the violence of reckless doctrines, and before Him I can attest to the purity of his faith. He had a wide knowledge of the world, obtained by the frequentation of all sorts of companies. This experience would have served him well with the Roman histories he, like M. Rollin, would doubtless have composed should he have had time and leisure, and if his life could have been better matched to his genius. What I shall relate of this excellent man will be the ornament of these memoirs. And like Aulus Gellius, who culled the most beautiful sayings of the philosophers into his "Attic Nights," and him who put the best fables of the Greeks into the "Metamorphoses," I will do a bee's work and gather exquisite honey. But I do not flatter myself to be the rival of those two great authors, because I draw all my wealth from my own life's recollections and not from an abundance of reading. What I furnish out of my own stock is good faith. Whenever some curious person shall read my memoirs he will easily recognise that a candid soul alone could express itself in language so plain and unaffected. Where and with whomsoever I have lived I have always been considered to be entirely artless. These writings cannot but confirm it after my death.

CHAPTER II

My Home at the *Queen Pédauque* Cookshop—I turn the Spit and
learn to read—Entry of Abbé Jérôme Coignard

MY NAME is Elme Laurent Jacques Ménétrier. My
father, Léonard Ménétrier, kept a cookshop at the
sign of *Queen Pédauque,* who, as everyone knows, was
web-footed like the geese and ducks.

His penthouse was opposite Saint Benoît le Bétourné
between Mistress Gilles the haberdasher at the *Three
Virgins* and M. Blaizot, the bookseller at the sign of
Saint Catherine, not far from the *Little Bacchus,* the gate
of which, decorated with vine branches, was at the corner
of the Rue des Cordiers. He loved me very much, and
when, after supper, I lay in my little bed, he took my
hand in his, lifted one after the other of my fingers,
beginning with the thumb, and said:

"This one has killed him, this one has plucked him,
this one has fricasseed him and that one has eaten him,
and the little *Riquiqui* had nothing at all. Sauce, sauce,
sauce," he used to add, tickling the hollow of my hand
with my own little finger.

And mightily he laughed, and I laughed too, dropping
off to sleep, and my mother used to affirm that the smile
still remained on my lips on the following morning.

My father was a good cookshop-keeper and feared God.
For this he carried on holidays the banner of the Cooks'
Guild, on which a fine-looking St Laurence was embroidered, with his grill and a golden palm. He used to say
to me:

4

"Jacquot, thy mother is a holy and worthy woman."

He liked to repeat this sentence frequently. True, my mother went to church every Sunday with a prayer-book printed in big type. She could hardly read small print, which, as she said, drew the eyes out of her head.

My father used to pass an hour or two nightly at the tavern of the *Little Bacchus;* there also Jeannette the hurdy-gurdy player and Catherine the lacemaker were regular frequenters. And every time he returned home somewhat later than usual he said in a soft voice, while pulling his cotton night-cap on:

"Barbe, sleep in peace; as I have just said to the limping cutler: 'You are a holy and worthy woman.' "

I was six years old when, one day, readjusting his apron, with him always a sign of resolution, he said to me:

"Miraut, our good dog, has turned my roasting-spit during these last fourteen years. I have nothing to reproach him with. He is a good servant, who has never stolen the smallest morsel of turkey or goose. He was always satisfied to lick the roaster as his wage. But he is getting old. His legs are getting stiff; he can't see, and is no more good to turn the handle. Jacquot, my boy, it is your duty to take his place. With some thought and some practice, you certainly will succeed in doing as well as he."

Miraut listened to these words and wagged his tail as a sign of approbation. My father continued:

"Now then, seated on this stool, you'll turn the spit. But to form your mind you'll con your horn-book, and when, afterwards, you are able to read type, you'll learn by heart some grammar or morality book, or those fine maxims of the Old and New Testaments. And that because the knowledge of God and the distinction between good and evil are also necessary in a working position, certainly of but trifling importance but honest as mine is, and which was my father's and also will be yours, please God."

And from this very day on, sitting from morn till night, at the corner of the fireplace, I turned the spit, the open horn-book on my knees. A good Capuchin friar, who with his bag came a-begging to my father, taught me how to spell. He did so the more willingly as my father, who had a consideration for knowledge, paid for his lesson with a savoury morsel of roast turkey and a large glass of wine, so liberally that by-and-by the little friar, aware that I was able to form syllables and words tolerably well, brought me a fine "Life of St Margaret," wherewith he taught me to read fluently.

On a certain day, having as usual laid his wallet on the counter, he sat down at my side, and, warming his naked feet on the hot ashes of the fireplace, he made me recite for the hundredth time:

> "Pucelle sage, nette et fine,
> Aide des femmes en gésine
> Ayez pitié de nous."

At this moment a man of rather burly stature and withal of noble appearance, clad in the ecclesiastical habit, entered the shop and shouted out with an ample voice:

"Hello! host, serve me a good portion!" With grey hair, he still looked full of health and strength. His mouth was laughing and his eyes were sprightly, his cheeks were somewhat heavy and his three chins dropped majestically on a neckband which, maybe by sympathy, had become as greasy as the throat it enveloped.

My father, courteous by profession, lifted his cap and bowing said:

"If your reverence will be so good as to warm yourself near the fire, I'll soon serve you with what you desire."

Without any further preamble the priest took a seat near the fire by the side of the Capuchin friar.

Hearing the good friar reading aloud:

> "Pucelle sage, nette et fine,
> Aide des femmes en gésine,"

he clapped his hands and said:

"Oh, the rare bird! The unique man! A Capuchin who is able to read! Eh, little friar, what is your name?"

"Friar Ange, an unworthy Capuchin," replied my teacher.

My mother, hearing the voices from the upper room, descended to the shop, attracted by curiosity.

The priest greeted her with an already familiar politeness and said:

"That is really wonderful, mistress; Friar Ange is a Capuchin and knows how to read."

"He is able to read all sorts of writing," replied my mother.

And going near the friar, she recognised the prayer of St Margaret by the picture representing the maiden martyr with a holy-water sprinkler in her hand.

"This prayer," she added, "is difficult to read because the words of it are very small and hardly divided, but happily it is quite sufficient, when in labour-pains, to apply it like a plaster on the place where the most pain is felt and it operates just as well, and rather better, than when it is recited. I had the proof of it, sir, when my son Jacquot was born, who is here present."

"Do not doubt about it, my good dame," said Friar

Ange. "The orison of St Margaret is sovereign for what you mentioned, but under the special condition that the Capuchins get their Maundy."

In saying so, Friar Ange emptied the goblet of wine which my mother had filled up for him and, throwing his wallet over his shoulder, went off in the direction of the *Little Bacchus*.

My father served a quarter of fowl to the priest, who took out of his pocket a piece of bread, a flagon of wine and a knife, the copper handle of which represented the late king on a column in the costume of a Roman emperor, and began to have his supper.

But having hardly taken the first morsel in his mouth he turned round on my father and asked for some salt, rather surprised that no salt cellar had been presented to him offhand.

"So did the ancients use it," he said, "they offered salt as a sign of hospitality. They also placed salt cellars in the temples on the tablecloths of the gods."

My father presented him with some bay salt out of the wooden shoe which was hung on the mantelpiece. The priest took what he wanted of it and said:

"The ancients considered salt to be a necessary season-ing of all repasts, and held it in so high esteem that they metaphorically called salt the wit which gives flavour to conversation."

"Ah!" said my father, "high as the ancients may have valued it, the excise of our days puts it still higher."

My mother, listening the while she knitted a woollen stocking, was glad to say a word:

"It must be believed that salt is a good thing, because the priests put a grain of it on the tongues of the babies held over the christening font. When my Jacques felt the salt on his tongue he made a grimace; as tiny as he was he already had some sense. I speak, Sir Priest, of my son Jacques here present."

The priest looked on me and said:

"Now he is already a grown-up boy. Modesty is painted on his features and he reads the 'Life of St Margaret' with attention."

"Oh!" exclaimed my mother, "he also reads the prayer for chilblains and that of 'St Hubert,' which Friar Ange has given him, and the history of that fellow who has been devoured, in the Saint Marcel suburb, by several devils for having blasphemed the holy name of our Lord."

My father looked admiringly on me, and then he murmured into the priest's ear that I learned anything I wanted to know with a native and natural facility.

"Wherefore," replied the priest, "you must form him to become a man of letters, which to be, is one of the honours of mankind, the consolation of human life and a remedy against all evils, actually against those of love, as it is affirmed by the poet Theocritus."

"Simple cook as I am," was my father's reply, "I hold knowledge in high esteem, and am quite willing to believe that it also is, as your reverence says, a remedy for love. But I do not think that it is a remedy against hunger."

"Well, perhaps it is not a sovereign ointment," replied the priest; "but it gives some solace, like a sweet balm, although somewhat imperfect."

As he spoke Catherine the lacemaker appeared on the threshold, with her bonnet sideways over her ear and her neckerchief very much creased. Seeing her, my mother frowned and let slip three meshes of her knitting.

"Monsieur Ménétrier," said Catherine to my father, "come and say a word to the sergeants of the watch. If you do not, they doubtless will lock up Friar Ange. The good friar came to the *Little Bacchus,* where he drank two or three pots without paying for them, so as not to go contrary to the rules of St Francis, he said. But the worst of it is, that he, seeing me in company under the arbour, came near me to teach me a new prayer. I told him it was not the right moment to do so, and he insisting on it, the limping cutler, who was sitting by me, tore his beard rather roughly. Friar Ange threw himself on the cutler, who fell to the ground, and by his fall upset the table and pitchers.

"The taverner, running up, seeing the table knocked over, the wine spilt, and Friar Ange with one foot on the cutler's head, swinging a stool with which he struck anyone approaching him, this vile taverner swore like a real devil and called for the watch. Monsieur Ménétrier, do come at once and take the little friar out of the watch's clutches. He is a holy man, and quite excusable in this affair."

My father was inclined to oblige Catherine, but for this once the lacemaker's words had not the effect she expected. He said plainly that he could not find any excuse for the Capuchin, and that he wished him to get a good punishment by bread and water in the darkest corner of the cellars of the convent, of which he was the shame and disgrace.

He warmed up in talking:

"A drunkard and a dissipated fellow, to whom I give daily good wine and good morsels and who goes to the tavern to play the deuce with some ill-famed creatures, depraved enough to prefer the company of a hawking cutler and a Capuchin friar to that of honest sworn tradesmen of the quarter. Fie! fie!"

Therewith he suddenly stopped his scoldings and looked sideways on my mother, who, standing up at the entry to the staircase, pushed her knitting needles with sharp little strokes.

Catherine, surprised by this unfriendly reception, said drily:

"Then you don't want to say a good word to the taverner and the sergeant?"

"If you wish it, I'll tell them to take the cutler and the friar."

"But," she replied, and laughed, "the cutler is your friend."

"Less mine than yours," said my father sharply. "A ragamuffin and a humbug, who hops about——"

"Oh!" she exclaimed, "that's true, really true, that he hops. He hops, hops, hops!"

And she left the shop, shaking with laughter.

My father turned round to the priest, who was picking a bone:

"It is as I had the honour to say to your reverence! For each reading and writing lesson that Capuchin friar gives to my child, I pay him with a goblet of wine and a fine piece of meat, hare, rabbit, goose, or a tender poulet or a capon. He is a drunkard and evil liver!"

"Don't doubt about that," said the priest.

"But if ever he dares to come over my threshold again, I'll drive him out with a broomstick."

"And you'll do well by it," said the priest; "that Capuchin is an ass, and he taught your son rather to bray than to talk. You'll act wisely by throwing into the fire that 'Life of St Catherine,' that prayer for the cure of chilblains and that history of the bugbear, with which that monk poisoned your son's mind. For the same price you paid for Friar Ange's lessons, I'll give him my own; I'll teach him Latin and Greek, and French also, that language which Voiture and Balzac have brought to perfection. And in such way, by a luck doubly singular and favourable, this Jacquot Tournebroche will become learned and I shall eat every day."

"Agreed!" said my father. "Barbara, bring two goblets. No business is concluded without the contracting parties having a drink together as a token of agreement. We will drink here. I'll never in my life put my legs into the *Little Bacchus* again, so repugnant have that cutler and that monk become to me."

The priest rose and, putting his hands on the back of his chair, said in a slow and serious manner:

"Before all, I thank God, the Creator and Conserver of all things, for having guided me into this hospitable house. It is He alone who governs us and we are compelled to recognise His providence in all matters human, notwithstanding that it is foolhardy and sometimes incongruous to follow Him too closely. Because being universal He is to be found in all sorts of encounters, sublime by the conduct which He keeps, but obscene or ridiculous for the part man takes in it and which is the only part where they appear to us. And therefore one must not shout, in the manner of Capuchin monks and goody-goody women, that God is to be seen in every trifle. Let us praise the Lord; pray to Him to enlighten me in the teachings I'll give to that child, and for the rest let us rely on His holy will, without searching to understand it in all its details."

And raising his goblet, he drank deeply.

"This wine," he said, "infilters into the economy of the human body a sweet and salutary warmth. It is a liquor worthy to be sung at Teos and at the Temple by the princes of bacchic poets, Anacreon and Chaulieu. I will anoint with it the lips of my young disciple."

He held the goblet under my chin and exclaimed:

"Bees of the Academy, come, come and place yourselves

in harmonious swarms on the mouth of Jacobus Tournebroche, henceforth consecrated to the Muses."

"Oh! Sir Priest," said my mother, "it is a truth that wine attracts the bees, particularly sweet wine. But it is not to be wished that those nefarious flies should place themselves on the mouth of my Jacquot, as their sting is cruel. One day in biting into a peach a bee stung me on the tongue, and I had to suffer fiendish pains. They would be calmed only by a little earth, mixed up with spittle, which Friar Ange put into my mouth in reciting the prayer of St Comis."

The priest gave her to understand that he spoke of bees in an allegorical sense only. And my father said reproachfully :

"Barbe, you're a holy and worthy woman, but many a time I have noticed that you have a peevish liking to throw yourself thoughtlessly into serious conversation like a dog into a game of skittles."

"Maybe," replied my mother. "But had you followed my counsels better, Léonard, you would have done better. I may not know all the sorts of bees, but I know how to manage a home and understand the good manners a man of a certain age ought to practise, who is the father of a family and standard-bearer of his guild."

My father scratched his ear, and poured some wine for the priest, who said with a sigh:

"Certainly, in our days, knowledge is not as much honoured in our kingdom of France, as it had been by the Romans, although degenerated at the time when rhetoric brought Eugenius to the Emperor's throne. It is not a rarity in our century to find a clever man in a garret without fire or candle. *Exemplum ut talpa*—I am an example."

Thereafter he gave us a narration of his life, which I'll

report just as it came out of his own mouth—that is, as near it as the weakness of my age allowed me to hear distinctly and hereafter keep in my memory. I believe I have been able to restore it after the confidences he gave me at a later time, when he honoured me with his friendship.

CHAPTER III

The Story of the Abbé's Life

"A S YOU see me," he said, "or rather as you do not see me, young, slender, with ardent eyes and black hair, I was a teacher of liberal arts at the College of Beauvais under Messrs Dugué, Guérin, Coffin and Baffier. I had been ordained, and expected to make a big name in letters. But a woman upset my hopes. Her name was Nicole Pigoreau and she kept a bookseller's shop at the *Golden Bible* on the square near the college. I went there frequently to thumb the books she received from Holland and also those bipontic editions illustrated with notes, comments and commentaries of great erudition. I was amiable and Mistress Pigoreau became aware of it, which was my misfortune.

"She had been pretty, and still knew how to be pleasing. Her eyes spoke. One day the Cicero, Livy, Plato and the Aristotle, Thucydides, Polybius and Varro, the Epictetus, Seneca, Boethius and Cassiodorus, the Homer, Æschylus, Sophocles, Euripides, Plautus and Terence, the Diodorus of Sicily and Dionysius of Halicarnassus, St John Chrysostom and St Basil, St Jerome and St Augustine, Erasmus, Saumaise, Turnebe and Scaliger, St Thomas Aquinas, St Bonaventure, Bossuet dragging Ferri with him, Lenain, Godefroy, Mézeray, Maimbourg, Fabricius, Father Lelong and Father Pitou, all the poets, all the historians, all the fathers, all the doctors, all the theologians, all the humanists, all the compilers, assembled high and low on the walls, became witnesses to our kisses.

" 'I could not resist you,' she said to me; 'don't conceive a bad opinion of me.'

"She expressed her love for me in singular raptures. Once she made me try on neck and wrist bands of fine lace, and finding them suit me well she insisted on my accepting them. I did not want to. But on her becoming irritated by my refusal, which she considered an offence against love, I finally consented to accept them, afraid to offend her.

"My good fortune lasted till I was to be replaced by an officer. I became spiteful over it, and in the ardour of avenging myself I informed the College Regents that I did not go any longer to the *Golden Bible,* for fear of seeing there expositions rather offensive to the modesty of a young clerical. To say the truth, I had not to congratulate myself on this contrivance. Madame Pigoreau, becoming aware of my sayings, publicly accused me of having robbed her of a set of lace neck and wrist bands. Her false complaint reached the ears of the College Regents, who had my boxes searched; therein was found the garment, a matter of considerable value. I was expelled from college and had, like Hippolyte and Bellerophon, to put up with the wiles and wickedness of woman.

"Finding myself in the streets with my few rags and my copybooks, I ran great risk of starving, when, dressed in my clerical suit, I recommended myself to a Huguenot gentleman, who employed me as secretary and dictated to me libels on our religion."

"Ah!" exclaimed my father, "that was wrong of your reverence. An honest man ought not to lend his hand to such abominations. And as far as I am concerned, although ignorant, and of a working condition, I cannot bear the smell of Colas' cow."

"You're quite right, my host," continued the priest.

"It is the worst point in my life. The very one I am most sorry for. But my man was a Calvinist. He employed me to write against Lutherans and Socinians only; these he could not stand at all, and, I assure you, he compelled me to treat them worse than ever it was done at the Sorbonne."

"Amen," said my father. "Lambs graze together while wolves devour one the other."

The priest continued his narrative:

"Besides, I did not remain for long with that gentleman, who made more fuss about the letters of Ulric von Hutten than of the harangues of Demosthenes, and in whose house water was the only drink. Afterwards I followed various callings, but all without success. I became a pedlar, a strolling player, a monk, a valet, and at last, by resuming my clerical garb, I became secretary to the Bishop of Séez and edited the catalogue of the precious MSS. contained in his library. This catalogue consists of two volumes in folio, which were placed in his gallery, bound in red morocco, with his crest on and the edges gilded. I venture to say it was a good work.

"It would have depended on myself alone to get old and grey in studies and peace with the right reverend prelate, but I became enamoured of the waiting-maid of the bailiff's lady. Do not blame me severely. Dark she was, buxom, vivacious, fresh. St Pacomus himself would have loved her. One day she took a seat in the stage coach to travel to Paris in quest of luck. I followed her. But I did not succeed as well as she did. On her recommendation I entered the service of Mistress de Saint Ernest, an opera dancer, who, aware of my talents, ordered me to write after her dictation a lampoon on Mademoiselle Davilliers, against whom she had some grievance. I was a pretty good secretary, and well deserved the fifty crowns she had promised me. The book was printed at Amsterdam by Marc-Michel Rey, with an allegoric frontispiece, and Mademoiselle Davilliers received the first copy of it just when she went on the stage to sing the great aria of Armida.

"Anger made her voice hoarse and shaky. She sang false and was hooted. Her song ended, she ran as she was, in powder and hoop petticoats, to the Intendant of the Privy Purse, who could not refuse her anything. She fell on her knees before him, shed abundant tears and shouted for vengeance. And soon it became known that the blow was struck by Mistress de Saint Ernest.

"Questioned, hard pressed, sharply threatened, she denounced me as the author, and I was put into the Bastille, where I remained four years. There I found some consolation in reading Boethius and Cassiodorus.

"Since then I have kept a public scrivener's stall at the Cemetery of the Saints Innocent, and lend to servant girls in love a pen, which should rather have described the illustrious men of Rome and commented on the writings of the holy fathers. I earn two farthings for every love letter, and it is a trade by which I rather die than live. But I do not forget that Epictetus was a slave and Pyrrho a gardener.

"Just now, unexpectedly, I have been paid a whole crown for an anonymous letter. I have not had anything to eat for two days. Therefore I at once looked out for a cookshop. From outside in the street I perceived your illuminated sign and the fire of your chimney throwing joyful flaming lights on the windows. On your threshold I smelt delicious odours. I came in, and now, my dear host, you have the history of my life."

"I have become aware that it is the life of a good man," said my father, "and with the exception of Colas' cow

there is hardly anything to complain of. Give me your
hand! We are friends, what's your name?"

"Jérôme Coignard, doctor of divinity, master of arts."

CHAPTER IV

The Pupil of M. Jérôme Coignard—I receive Lessons in Latin, Greek and Life

THE marvellous in the affairs of mankind is the concatenation of effects and causes. M. Jérôme Coignard was quite right in saying: "To consider that strange following of bounds and rebounds wherein our destinies clash, one is obliged to recognise that God in His perfection is in want neither of mind nor of imagination nor comic force; on the contrary He excels in imbroglio as in everything else, and if after having inspired Moses, David and the Prophets He had thought it worth while to inspire M. le Sage or the interluders of a fair, He would dictate to them the most entertaining harlequinade." And in a similar way it occurred that I became a Latinist because Friar Ange was taken by the watch and put into ecclesiastical penance for having knocked down a cutler under the arbour of the *Little Bacchus*. M. Jérôme Coignard kept his promise. He gave me lessons and, finding me tractable and intelligent, he took pleasure in instructing me in the ancient languages.

In but a few years he made me a tolerably good Latinist.

In memory of him I have conceived a gratitude which will not come to an end but with my life. The obligation I am under to him is easily to be conceived when I say that he neglected nothing to shape my heart and soul, together with my intellect. He recited to me the "Maxims of Epictetus," the "Homilies of St Basil" and the "Consolations of Boethius." By beautiful extracts he opened to me the philosophy of the Stoics, but he did not make it appear in its sublimity without showing its inferiority to Christian philosophy. He was a subtle theologian and a good Catholic. His faith remained whole on the ruins of his most beloved illusions, of his most cherished hopes. His weaknesses, his errors, his faults, none of which he ever tried to dissemble or to colour, have never shaken his confidence in the Divine goodness. And to know him well, it must be known that he took care of his eternal salvation on occasions when, to all appearance, he cared the least about it. He imbued me with the principles of an enlightened piety. He also endeavoured to attach me to virtue as such, and to render it to me, so to say, homely and familiar by examples drawn from the life of Zeno.

To make me acquainted with the dangers of vice, he went for arguments to the nearest fountain-head, confessing to me that by having loved wine and women too much, he had lost the honour of taking the professor's chair of a college in long gown and square cap.

To these rare merits he joined constancy and assiduity, and he gave his lessons with an exactitude hardly to be expected of a man given as he was to the freaks of a strolling life, and always carried away by a luck less doctoral than picaresque. This zeal was the effect of his kindness and also of his liking of that good St James's Street, where he found occasion to satisfy equally the appetites of his body and intellect. After having given me, during a succulent repast, some profitable lesson, he indulged in a stroll to the *Little Bacchus* and the *Image of St Catherine*, finding in that narrow piece of ground that which was his paradise—fresh wine and books.

He became a constant visitor of M. Blaizot the bookseller, who received him well, notwithstanding that he only used to thumb the books without ever making the smallest purchase. And it was quite marvellous to see my good teacher in the most remote part of the shop, his nose closely buried in some little book recently arrived from Holland, suddenly raising his head to discourse, as it might happen, with the same abundant and laughing knowledge, on the plans of an universal monarchy attributed to the late king, or, it may be, to the *aventures galantes* of a financier with a ballet girl. M. Blaizot was never tired of listening to him. This M. Blaizot was a little old man, dry and neat, in flea-coloured coat and breeches and grey woollen stockings. I admired him very much, and could not think of anything more glorious than, like him, to sell books at the *Image of St Catherine*.

One recollection of mine gave to M. Blaizot's shop quite a mysterious charm. It was there, I was still very young, I saw for the first time the nude figure of a female. I can see her now. It was an Eve in an illustrated Bible. Her stomach was rather big, her legs were rather short, and she held converse with a serpent in a Dutch landscape. The proprietor of this engraving inspired me with a consideration which grew afterwards when I took, thanks to M. Coignard, a great liking for books.

At the age of sixteen I knew Latin pretty well, and also a little Greek. My good teacher said to my father:

"Do you not think, my dear host, that it is rather an indecency to let a young Ciceronian go about dressed as a scullion?"

"I never thought of it," replied my father.

"It is true," said mother, "that it would be suitable to give our son a dimity vest. He is of an agreeable appearance, has good manners and is well taught. He will do honour to his dress."

For a moment my father remained thoughtful and then he asked if it would be quite suitable for a cook to wear a dimity vest. But M. Coignard reminded him that, being suckled by the Muses, I would never become a cook, and that the time was not far off when I should wear a clerical neckband.

My father sighed, thinking that never would I be the banner-bearer of the Guild of Parisian Cooks, and my mother became quite glittering with pleasure and pride at the idea of her son belonging to the Church.

The first effect my dimity vest produced was to give me a certain confidence in myself, and to encourage me to get a more complete idea of women than the one I had from the Eve of M. Blaizot. I reasonably thought first on Jeannette the hurdy-gurdy player, and on Catherine the lacemaker, both of whom I saw pass our shop twenty times a day, showing when it rained, a fine ankle and a tiny foot, the toes of which turned from one stone to the other. Jeannette was not so pretty as Catherine. She was somewhat older and less well dressed. She came from Savoy and did her hair *en marmotte,* with a checked kerchief covering her head. But her merit was, not to stick to ceremony and to understand what was wanted of her without being spoken to. This character agreed well with my timidity. One evening under the porch of St Benoît le Bétourné, where there are stone seats all round, she taught me what till then I had not known, but which she had known for a long time.

But I was not so grateful to her as it should have been my duty to be, and thought of nothing else but to bring the science she had taught me to others, prettier ones. As an excuse for my ingratitude I ought to say that Jeannette the hurdy-gurdy player did not value her lessons any higher than I did myself, and that she willingly gave them to every ragamuffin of the district.

Catherine was of more reserved manners. I stood in awe of her and did not dare to tell her how pretty I considered her to be. She made me doubly uncomfortable by making game of me and not losing a single occasion of jeering at me. She teased me by reproaching my chin for being hairless. I blushed over it and wished to be swallowed by the earth. On seeing her I affected a sullen mien and chagrin. I pretended to scorn her. But she was really too pretty for my scorn to be true.

CHAPTER V

My Nineteenth Birthday—Its Celebration and the Entrance of
M. d'Asterac

O N THAT night, the night of Epiphany and the nineteenth anniversary of my birth, the sky poured
down with the melting snow a cold ill-humour, penetrating
to the bone, while an icy wind made the signboard of the
Queen Pédauque grate, a clear fire, perfumed by goose
grease, sparkled in the shop and the soup steamed in the
tureen on the table; round which M. Jérôme Coignard, my
father and myself were seated. My mother, as was her
habit, stood behind her husband's chair, ready to serve
him. He had already filled the priest's dish when, through
the suddenly open door, we saw Friar Ange, very pale, the
nose red, the beard soaked. In his surprise my father
elevated the soup ladle up to the smoked beams of the
ceiling.

My father's surprise was easily explained. Friar
Ange, after his fight with the cutler, had at first disappeared for a lapse of six months, and now two whole
years had passed without his giving any sign of life. On
a certain day in spring he went off with a donkey laden
with relics, and, worse still, he had taken with him
Catherine dressed as a nun. Nobody knew what had
become of them, but there was a rumour at the *Little
Bacchus* that the little friar and the little sister had had
some sort of difference with the authorities between Tours
and Orleans. Without forgetting that one of the vicars

of St Benoît shouted everywhere, and like one possessed, that that rascal of a Capuchin had stolen his donkey.

"What," exclaimed my father, "this rogue does not lie in a dungeon? There is then no more justice in this kingdom."

But Friar Ange recited the *Benedicite* and made the sign of the cross over the soup-tureen.

"Hola!" continued my father. "Peace to all cant, my beautiful monk! Confess that you have passed in an ecclesiastical prison at least one of the two years that your Beelzebub-face has not been seen in our parish. James Street has been more honest for your absence and the whole quarter of the town more respectable. Look on that fine Olibrius, who goes into the fields with the donkey of someone and the girl of everyone."

"Maybe," replied Friar Ange, eyes on the ground and hands in his sleeves. "Maybe, Master Léonard, you have Catherine in mind. I have had the happiness to convert her to a better life, so much and so well that she ardently wished to follow me, and the relics I was carrying, and to go with me on some nice pilgrimage, especially to the Black Virgin of Chartres! I consented under the condition that she clad herself in ecclesiastical dress, which she did without a murmur."

"Hold your tongue!" replied my father, "you are a dissipated fellow. You have no respect for your cloth. Return to where you came from and look, if you please, in the street, if Queen Pédauque is suffering from chilblains."

But my mother made the friar a sign to sit down under the chimney-mantel, which he softly did.

"One has to forgive much to Capuchins," said the abbé, "because they sin without malice."

My father begged of M. Coignard not to speak any

more of the breed, the name alone of which burnt his ears.

"Master Léonard," said the priest, "philosophy conducts the soul to clemency. As far as I am concerned I willingly give absolution to knaves, rogues and rascals and all the wretched. And more, I owe no grudge to good people, though in their case there is much insolence. And if, Master Léonard, like myself, you should have been familiar with respectable people, you would know that they are not a rap better than the others, and are often of a less agreeable companionship. I have been seated at the third table of the Bishop of Séez and two attendants, both clad in black, were at my sides: constraint and weariness."

"It must be acknowledged," said my mother, "that the servants of his Grace had some queer names. Why did he not call them Champagne, Olive or Frontin as is usual?"

The priest continued:

"It's true, certain persons get easily accustomed to the inconveniences to be borne by living with the great. There was at the second table of the bishop a very polite canon who kept on ceremony till his last moment. When the news of his bodily decline reached the bishop he went to his room and found him dying. 'Alas,' said the canon, 'I beg your Grace's pardon to be obliged to die before your eyes.' 'Do, do! Don't mind me,' said the bishop with the utmost kindness."

At this moment my mother brought the roast and put it on the table with a movement of homely gravity which caused my father some emotion; with his mouth full he shouted:

"Barbe, you're a holy and worthy woman."

"Mistress," said my dear teacher, "is as a fact to be

compared to the strong women of the scripture. She is a godly wife."

"Thank God!" said my mother, "I have never been a traitor to the faithfulness I owe unto Léonard Ménétrier, my husband, and I reckon well, now that the most difficult part is passed, not to fail him till my last hour is come. I wish he would keep his faith to me as I keep mine to him."

"Madam, when first I looked on you I could see you to be an honest woman," replied the priest, "because I have experienced near you a quietude more connected with heaven than with this world."

My mother, who was simple-minded, but not stupid, understood very well what he wanted to say, and replied that if he had known her twenty years ago, he would have found her to be quite another than she had become in this cookshop, where her good looks had vanished with the fire of the spit and the fumes of the dishes. And as she was touched she mentioned that the baker at Auneau had found her to be so much to his liking that he had offered her cakes every time she passed his shop. "Besides," she added angrily, "there is neither girl nor woman ugly enough to be incapable of doing wrong if she had a fancy to do it."

"This good woman is right," said my father. "I remember when I was a prentice at the cookshop of the *Royal Goose* near the Gate of St Denis, my master, who was then the banner-bearer of the guild, as I myself am to-day, said to me: 'I'll never be a cuckold, my wife is too ugly.' This saying gave me the idea to attempt what he thought to be impossible. I succeeded at my first attempt, one morning when he went to La Vallée. He spoke the truth, his wife was very ugly, but high spirited and grateful."

At this anecdote my mother broke out and said that such things ought not to be told by a father to his wife and son, if he wanted to have their respect.

M. Jérôme Coignard, seeing her become red with anger, changed the conversation with kindly meant ability. He addressed himself abruptly to Friar Ange, who, hands in his sleeves, sat humbly at the corner of the fireside:

"Little friar, what kind of relics did you carry on the second vicar's donkey's back in company with Sister Catherine? Was it your small clothes you gave the devotees to kiss, in the manner of some grey friars, of whom Henry Estienne has narrated the adventures?"

"Ah! your reverence," meekly said Friar Ange with the expression of a martyr suffering for truth, "it was not my small clothes, it was a foot of St Eustache."

"I should have taken my oath on it, if it would not be a sin to do so," exclaimed the priest, brandishing the drumstick of a fowl. "Those Capuchins turn out saints utterly ignored by good authors, who work on ecclesiastical history. Neither Tillemont nor Fleury speak of that St Eustache to whom a church is consecrated, very wrongly, at Paris, when so many saints recognised by writers well deserving to be believed, are still waiting for a similar honour. The 'Life of St Eustache' is a tissue of ridiculous fables; the same is the case of that of St Catherine, who has never existed except in the imagination of some wicked Byzantine monk. But I do not want to attack her too hardly, as he is the patroness of men of letters, and serves as a signboard to the bookshop of that good M. Blaizot, which is the most delectable abode in this world."

"I also had," continued quickly the little friar, "a rib of St Mary the Egyptian."

"Ah! Ah!" shouted the priest, throwing the chicken

bone across the room, "concerning this one, I do consider her to be very, very holy, as during her lifetime she gave a fine example of humility."

"You know, madam," he said and took mother's sleeve, "that St Mary the Egyptian, going on pilgrimage to the sepulchre of our Lord, was stopped by a deep flowing river, and not possessing a single farthing to pay for the passage on the ferry-boat she offered to the boatmen her own body as a payment. What do you say to that, my good mistress?"

First of all my mother asked if the story was quite true. After she had been assured that the matter had been printed in a book and painted on a stained window in the Church of La Jussienne she believed it.

"I think," she said, "that one has to be as holy as she was to do the like without committing a sin. I must say that I should not like to do it."

"As far as I am concerned," said the priest, "I approve of the conduct of that saint, quite in accord with the most subtle doctors. It is a lesson for honest women stubborn in too much pride of their haughty virtue. Thinking well over it there is some sensuality in prizing too highly the flesh and guarding excessively what one ought to despise. There are some matrons to be met with who believe they have a treasure and who visibly exaggerate the interest God and the angels may have in them. They believe themselves to be a kind of natural Holy Sacrament. St Mary the Egyptian was a better judge. Pretty and divinely shaped as she was, she considered that it would be all too proud of her flesh to stop in the course of a holy pilgrimage for a paltry indifferent reason which is no more than a piece of mortification and far from being a precious jewel. She humbled herself, madam, and entered by using so admirable a humility the road of penitence, where she accomplished marvellous works."

"Your reverence," said my mother, "I do not understand you. You are too learned for me."

"That grand saint," said Friar Ange, "is painted in a state of nature in the chapel of my convent, and by the grace of God all her body is covered with long and thick hair. Reproductions of this picture have been printed, and I'll bring you a fully blessed one, my dear madam."

Tenderly touched, my mother passed the soup-tureen to him, behind the back of my teacher. And the holy friar, seated on the cinder board, silently soaked his bread in the savoury liquid.

"Now is the moment," said my father, "to uncork one of those bottles which I keep in reserve for the great feasts, which are Christmas, Twelfth Night, and St Laurence's Day. Nothing is more agreeable than to drink a good wine quietly at home secure of unwelcome intruders."

Hardly had these words been uttered when the door was opened and a tall man in black entered the shop in a squall of snow and wind exclaiming:

"A Salamander! A Salamander!"

And without taking notice of anyone he bent over the grate, rummaging in the cinders with the end of his walking stick, very much to the detriment of Friar Ange, who coughed fit to give up the ghost, swallowing the ashes and coal-dust thrown into his soup plate. And the man in black still continued to rummage in the fire, shouting, "A Salamander! I see a Salamander!" while the stirred-up flames made the shadow of his bodily form tremble on the ceiling like a large bird of prey.

My father was surprised and rather annoyed by the manners of the visitor. But he knew how to restrain himself. And so he rose, his napkin under his arm, and

went to the fireplace, bending to the hearth, both his
fists on his thighs.

When he had sufficiently considered the disordered fireplace, and Friar Ange covered with ashes, he said:

"Your lordship will excuse me. I cannot see anything
but this paltry monk, and no Salamander.

"Besides," my father went on, "I have but little regret
over it. I have it from hearsay that it is an ugly beast,
hairy and horned, with big claws."

"What an error!" replied the man in black. "Salamanders resemble women, or, to speak precisely, nymphs,
and they are perfectly beautiful! But I feel myself
rather a simpleton to ask you if you're able to see this one.
One has to be a philosopher to see a Salamander, and I
do not think philosophers could be found in this kitchen."

"You may be mistaken, sir," said the Abbé Coignard.
"I am a Doctor of Divinity and Master of Arts. I have
also studied the Greek and Latin moralists, whose
maxims have strengthened my soul in the vicissitudes of
my life, and I have particularly applied Boethius as an
antidote for the evils of existence. And here near me is
Jacobus Tournebroche, my disciple, who knows the
sentences of Publius Syrus by heart."

The stranger turned his yellow eyes on the priest, eyes
strangely marked over a nose like the beak of an eagle,
and excused himself with more courtesy than his fierce
mien led one to expect, for not having at once recognised
a person of merit, and further he said:

"It is very likely that this Salamander has come for
you or your pupil. I saw it very distinctly in passing along the street before this cookshop. She would
appear better if the fire were fiercer; for this reason it
is necessary to stir the fire vigorously when you believe
a Salamander to be in it."

At the first movement the stranger made to rummage again in the fire, Friar Ange anxiously covered the soup-tureen with a flap of his frock and shut his eyes.

"Sir," said the Salamander-man, "allow your young pupil to approach the fireplace to say if he does not see something resembling a woman hovering over the flames."

At this very moment the smoke rising under the slab of the chimney bent itself with a peculiar gracefulness, and formed rotundities quite likely to be taken for well-arched loins by a rather strangely strained imagination. Therefore I did not tell an absolute lie by saying that, maybe, I saw something.

No sooner had I given this reply than the stranger, raising his huge arm, gave me a straight hander on the shoulder so powerful that I thought my collar-bone was broken. But at once he said to me, with a very sweet voice and a benevolent look:

"My child, I have been obliged to give you so strong an impression that you may never forget that you have seen a Salamander, which is a sign that your destiny is to become a learned man, perhaps a magician. Your face also made me surmise favourably of your intelli-gence."

"Sir," said my mother, "he learns anything he wants to know and he'll be a priest if it pleases our Lord."

M. Jérôme Coignard added that I had profited in a certain way by his lessons, and my father asked the stranger if his lordship would not be disposed to eat a morsel.

"I am not in want of anything," said the stranger, "and it's easy for me to go without any food for a year or longer because of a certain elixir the composition of which is known only to the philosophical. This faculty is not confined to myself alone, it is the common property of all wise men, and it is known that the illustrious Cardan went without food during several years without being incommoded by it. On the contrary his mind became singularly vivacious. But still I'll eat what it pleases you to offer me, simply to please you."

And he took a seat at our little table without any ceremony. At once Friar Ange also noiselessly pushed his stool between mine and that of my teacher and sat on it to receive his portion of the partridge pie my mother was dishing up.

The philosopher having thrown his cape over the back of his seat, we could see that he wore diamond buttons on his coat. He remained thoughtful. The shadow of his nose fell on his mouth and his hollow cheeks went deep into his jaws. His gloomy humour took possession of the whole company. No other noise was audible but the one made by the little friar munching his pie.

Suddenly the philosopher said:

"The more I think it over, the more I am convinced that yonder Salamander came for this lad." And he pointed his knife at me.

"Sir," I replied, "if the Salamanders are really as you say, this one honours me very much, and I am truly obliged to her. But, to say the truth, I have rather guessed than seen her, and this first encounter has only awakened my curiosity without giving me full satisfaction."

Unable to speak at his ease, my good teacher was suffocating. Suddenly, breaking out very loud, he said to the philosopher:

"Sir, I am fifty-one years old, a master of arts and a doctor of divinity. I have read all the Greek and Latin authors, who have not been annihilated either by time's injury or by man's malice, and I have never seen a

Salamander, wherefrom I conclude that no such thing exists."

"Excuse me," said Friar Ange, half suffocated by partridge pie and half by dismay; "excuse me! Unhappily some Salamanders do exist and a learned Jesuit father, whose name I have forgotten, has discoursed on their apparition. I myself have seen, at a place called St Claude, at a cottager's, a Salamander in a fireplace close to a kettle. She had a cat's head, a toad's body and the tail of a fish. I threw a handful of holy water on the beast, and it at once disappeared in the air, with a frightful noise like sudden frying and I was enveloped in acrid fumes, which very nearly burnt my eyes out. And what I say is so true that for at least a whole week my beard smelt of burning, which proves better than anything else the maliciousness of the beast."

"You want to make game of us, little friar," said the abbé. "Your toad with a cat's head is no more real than the Nymph of that gentleman, and it is quite a disgusting invention."

The philosopher began to laugh, and said Friar Ange had not seen the wise man's Salamander. When the Nymphs of the fire meet with a Capuchin they turn their back on him.

"Oh! Oh!" said my father, bursting out laughing, "the back of a Nymph is still too good for a Capuchin."

And being in a good humour, he sent a mighty slice of the pie to the little friar.

My mother placed the roast in the middle of the table, and took advantage of it to ask if the Salamanders are good Christians, of which she had her doubts, as she had never heard that the inhabitants of fire praised the Lord.

"Madam," replied my teacher, "several theologians of the Society of Jesus have recognised the existence of a

people of incubus and succubus who are not properly
demons, because they do not let themselves be routed by
an aspersion of holy water and who do not belong to the
Church Triumphant; glorified spirits would never have
attempted, as has been the case at Perouse, to seduce the
wife of a baker. But if you wish for my opinion, they
are rather the dirty imaginations of a sneak than the
views of a doctor.

"You must hate and bewail that sons of the Church,
born in light, could conceive of the world and of God a
less sublime idea than that formed by a Plato or a Cicero
in the night of ignorance and of paganism. God is less
absent, I dare say, from the Dream of Scipio than from
those black tractates of demonology the authors of which
call themselves Christians and Catholics."

"Sir," replied the priest, "I found a very old MS. of
Cicero spoke with effluence and facility, but he was but a
commonplace intellect, and not very learned in holy
sciences. Have you ever heard of Hermes Trismegistus
and of the Emerald Table?"

"Sir," replied the priest, "I found a very old MS. of
the Emerald Table in the library of the Bishop of Séez,
and I should have marvelled over it one day or another,
but for the chamber-maid of the bailiff's lady who went
to Paris to make her fortune and who made me ride in
the coach with her. There was no witchcraft used, Sir
Philospher, and I only succumbed to natural charms:

> 'Non facit hoc verbis; facie tenerisque lacertis
>   Devovet et flavis nostra puella comis.' "

"That's a new proof," said the philosopher, "women
are great enemies of science, and the wise man ought to
keep himself aloof from them."

"In legitimate marriage also?" inquired my father.

"Especially in legitimate marriage," replied the philosopher.

"Alas!" my father continued to question, "what remains to your poor wise men when they feel disposed for a little fun?"

The philosopher replied:

"There remains for them the Salamanders."

At these words Friar Ange raised a frightened nose over his plate and murmured:

"Don't speak like that, my good sir; in the name of all the saints of my order, do not speak like that! And do not forget that the Salamander is naught but the devil, who assumes, as everyone knows, the most divergent forms, pleasant now and then when he succeeds in disguising his natural ugliness, hideous sometimes when he shows his true constitution."

"Take care on your part, Friar Ange," replied the philosopher, "and as you're afraid of the devil, don't offend him too much and do not excite him against you by inconsiderate tittle-tattle. You know that this old Adversary, this powerful Contradictor, has kept, in the spiritual world, such a power, that God Almighty Himself reckons with him. I'll say more, God, who was in fear of him, made him His business man. Be on your guard, little friar, the two understand one another."

In listening to this speech, the poor Capuchin thought he heard and saw the devil himself, whom the stranger resembled, pretty near, by his fiery eyes, his hooked nose, his black complexion and his long and thin body. His soul, already astonished, became engulfed in a kind of holy terror, feeling on him the claws of the Malignant, he began to tremble in all his limbs, hastily put in his wide pockets all the decent eatables he could get hold of.

rose gently and reached the door by backward steps, muttering exorcisms all the while.

The philosopher did not take any notice of this. He took from his pocket a little book covered with horny parchment, which he opened and presented to my dear teacher and myself. It contained an old Greek text, full of abbreviations and ligatures which at first gave me the effect of an illegible scrawl. But M. Coignard, having put on his barnacles and placed the book at the necessary distance, began to read the characters easily; they looked more like balls of thread that had been unrolled by a kitten than the simple and quiet letters of my St John Chrysostom, out of which I studied the language of Plato and the New Testament. Having come to the end of his reading he said:

"Sir, this passage is to be translated as: *Those of the Egyptians who are well informed study first the writings called epistolographia, then the hieratic, of which the hierogrammatists make use, and finally the hieroglyphics.*"

And then taking off his barnacles and shaking them triumphantly he continued:

"Ah! Ah! Master Philosopher, I am not to be taken as a greenhorn. This is an extract of the fifth book of the *Stromata*, the author of which, Clement of Alexandria, is not mentioned in the martyrology, for different reasons, which His Holiness Benedict XI. has indicated, the principal of which is, that this Father was often erroneous in matters of faith. It may be supposed that this exclusion was not sensibly felt by him, if one takes into consideration what philosophical estrangement had during his lifetime inspired this martyr. He gave preference to *exile* and took care to save his persecutors a crime, because he was a very honest man. His style of writing was not elegant; his genius was lively, his morals were pure, even austere. He had a very pronounced liking for allegories and for lettuces."

The philosopher extended his arm, which seemed to me to be remarkably elongated as it reached right over the whole of the table, to take back the little book from the hands of my learned tutor.

"It is sufficient," he said, pushing the *Stromata* back into his pocket. "I see, reverend sir, that you understand Greek. You have well translated this passage, at least in a vulgar and literal sense. I intend to make your and your pupil's fortune; I'll employ both of you to translate at my house the Greek texts I have received from Egypt."

And turning towards my father, he continued:

"I think, Master Cook, you will consent to let me have your son to make him a learned man and a great one. Should it be too much for your fatherly love to give him entirely to me, I would pay out of my own pocket for a scullion as his substitute in your cookshop."

"As your lordship understands it like that," replied my father, "I shall not prevent you doing good to my son."

"Always under the condition," said my mother, "that it is not to be at the expense of his soul. You'll have to affirm on your oath to me that you are a good Christian."

"Barbe," said my father, "you are a holy and worthy woman, but you oblige me to make my excuses to this gentleman for your want of politeness, which is caused less, to say the truth, by the natural disposition, which is a good one, than by your neglected education."

"Let the good woman have her say," remarked the philosopher, "and let her be reassured; I am a very religious man."

"That's right!" exclaimed my mother. "One has to worship the holy name of God."

"I worship all His names, my good lady. He has more

han one. He is called Adonaï, Tetragrammaton, Jehovah, Otheres, Athanatos and Schyros. And there are many more names."

"I did not know," said my mother. "But what you say, sir, does not surprise me; I have remarked that people of condition have always more names than the lower people. I am a native of Auneau, near the town of Chartres, and I was but a child when the lord of our village left this world for another. I remember very well when the herald proclaimed the demise of the late lord, he gave him nearly as many names as you find in the All Saints litany. I willingly believe that God has more names than the Lord of Auneau had, as His condition is a much higher one. Learned people are very happy to know them all. And if you will advance my son Jacques in this knowledge I shall, my dear sir, be very much obliged to you."

"Well, the matter is understood," said the philosopher, "and you, reverend sir, I trust it will please you to translate from the Greek, for salary, let it be understood."

My good tutor, who was collecting all this while the few thoughts in his brain which were not already desperately mixed up with the fumes of wine, refilled his goblet, rose and said:

"Sir Philosopher, I heartily accept your generous offer. You are one of the splendid mortals; it is an honour, sir, for me to be yours. If there are two kinds of furniture I hold in high esteem, they are the bed and the table. The table, filled up by turns with erudite books and succulent dishes, serves as support to the nourishment both of body and spirit; the bed propitious for sweet repose as well as for cruel love. He certainly was a divine fellow who gave to the sons of Deucalion bed and table. If I find with you, sir, those two precious pieces of furniture, I'll follow your name, as that of my benefactor, with immortal praise, and I'll celebrate you in Greek and Latin verses of all sorts of metres."

So he said, and drank deeply.

"That's well," replied the philosopher. "I'll expect both of you to-morrow morning at my house. You will follow the road to St Germain till you come to the Cross of the Sablons, from that cross you'll count one hundred paces, going westward, and you'll find a small green door in a garden wall. You'll use the knocker which represents a veiled figure having a finger in her mouth. An old follower will open the door to you; you'll ask to see M. d'Asterac."

"My son," said my good tutor, pulling my coat sleeve, "put all that in your memory, put cross, knocker, and the rest, so that we'll be able to find, to-morrow, the enchanted door. And you, Sir Mæcenas——"

But the philosopher was gone. No one had seen him leaving.

CHAPTER VI

Arrival at the Castle of M. d'Asterac and Interview with the
Cabalist

ON THE following day at an early hour we walked,
my tutor and I, on the St Germain road. The snow
which covered the earth under the russet light of the sky,
rendered the atmosphere dull and heavy. The road was
deserted. We walked in wide furrows between the walls
of orchards, tottering fences and low houses, the windows
of which looked suspiciously on us. And, after having left
behind two or three tumbledown huts built of clay and
straw, we saw in the middle of a disconsolate heath the
Cross of the Sablons. At fifty paces farther commenced a
very large park, closed in by a ruined wall, wherein was
the little door, and on it the knocker representing a hor-
rible-looking figure with a finger in her mouth. We recognised it easily as the one the philosopher had described,
and used the knocker.

After some rather considerable time, an old servant
opened it and made us a sign to follow him across the
untidy park. Statues of nymphs, who must have seen
the boyhood of the late king, secreted under tree ivy their
gloominess and mutilations. At the end of an alley, the
sloughs of which were covered with snow, stood a castle
of stone and brick, as morose as the one of Madrid, which,
oddly covered by a high slate roof, looked like the castle
of the Sleeping Beauty in the wood.

Following the silent valet, M. Coignard whispered
to me:

"I confess, my son, that this lodging has no smiling appearance. It shows the ruggedness wherein the customs of Frenchmen were still immured in the time of King Henry IV., and it drives the soul to gloom and nearly to melancholy by the state of forlornness in which unhappily it has been left. How much sweeter it would be to climb the enchanted hillocks of Tusculum with the hope of hearing Cicero discourse of virtue, under the firs and pines of his villa so dear to the philosopher! And have you not observed, my boy, that all along yonder road neither taverns nor hostels are to be met with, and that it would be necessary to cross the bridge and go up the hill to the Bergères to get a drink of fresh wine? There is thereabout a hostel of the *Red Horse,* where, if I remember well, Madame de St Ernest took me once to dinner in the company of her monkey and her lover. You can't imagine, Tournebroche, how excellent the victuals are there. The *Red Horse* is as well known for its morning dinners as for the abundance of horses and carriages which it has on hire. I convinced myself of it when I followed to the stables a certain wench who seemed to be rather pretty. But she was not; it would be a truer saying to call her ugly. But I illuminated her with the colours of my longings. Such is the condition of men when left to themselves; they err wretchedly. We are all abused by empty images; we go in chase of dreams and embrace shadows. In God alone is truth and stability."

Meanwhile we ascended, behind the old servant, the disjointed flight of steps.

"Alas!" said my tutor, "I begin to regret your father's cookshop, where we ate such good morsels while explaining Quintilian."

After having scaled the first flight of large stone stairs, we were introduced into a saloon, where M. d'Asterac was occupied with writing near a big fire, in the midst of Egyptian coffins of human form raised against the walls, their lids painted with sacred figures and golden faces with long glossy eyes.

Politely M. d'Asterac invited us to be seated and said:

"Gentlemen, I expected you. And as you have both kindly consented to do me the favour of staying with me, I beg of you to consider this house as your own. You'll be occupied in translating Greek texts I have brought back with me from Egypt. I have no doubt you will do your best to accomplish this task when you know that it is connected with the work I have undertaken, to discover the lost science by which man will be re-established in his original power over the elements. I have no intention of raising the veil of nature and showing you Isis in her dazzling nudity; but I will entrust you with the object of my studies without fear that you'll betray the mystery, because I have confidence in your integrity and also in the power I have to guess and to forestall all that may be attempted against me and to dispose for my vengeance of secret and terrible forces. From the defaults of a fidelity, of which I do not doubt; my power, gentlemen, assures me of your silence.

"Know then that man came out of Jehovah's hands with that perfect knowledge he has since lost. He was very powerful and very wise when he was created, that's to be seen in the books of Moses. But it's necessary to understand them. Before all it is clear that Jehovah is not God, but a grand Demon, because he has created this world. The idea of a God both perfect and creative is but a reverie of a barbarity worthy of a Welshman or a Saxon. As little polished as one's mind may be one cannot admit that a perfect being tags anything to his own perfection, be it a hazelnut. That's common sense;

God has no understanding, as he is endless how could he understand? He does not create, because he ignores time and space, which are conditions indispensable to all constructions. Moses was too good a philosopher to teach that the world was created by God. He took Jehovah for what he really is—for a powerful Demon, or if he is to be called anything, for the Demiurgos.

"It follows that Jehovah, creating man, gave him knowledge of the visible and the invisible world. The fall of Adam and Eve, which I'll explain to you another day, had not fully destroyed that knowledge of the first man and the first woman, who passed their teachings on to their children. Those teachings, on which the domination of nature relies, have been consigned to the book of Enoch. The Egyptian priests have kept the tradition which they fixed with mysterious signs on the walls of the temples and the coffins of the dead. Moses, brought up in the sanctuary of Memphis, was one of the initiated. His books, numbering five, perhaps six, contain like very precious archives the treasures of divine knowledge. You'll discover there the most beautiful secrets if you have cleared them of the interpolations which dishonour them; one scorns the literal and coarse sense, to attach oneself to the most subtle. I have penetrated to the largest part, as it will appear to you also later on. Meanwhile, the truth, kept like virgins in the temples of Egypt, passed to the wizards of Alexandria, who enriched them still more and crowned them with all the pure gold bequeathed to Greece by Pythagoras and his disciples, with whom the forces of the air conversed familiarly. Wherefore, gentlemen, it is convenient to explore the books of the Hebrews, the hieroglyphics of the Egyptians and those treatises of the Greeks which are called Gnostic precisely because they possessed knowledge. I reserve for myself, as is quite

equitable, the most arduous part of this extensive work.
I apply myself to decipher those hieroglyphics which the
Egyptians used to inscribe in the temples of their gods
and on the graves of their priests. Having brought over
from Egypt a great number of those inscriptions, I fathom
their sense by means of a key I was able to discover with
Clement of Alexandria.

"The Rabbi Mosaïde, who lives in retirement with me,
works on the re-establishment of the true sense of the
Pentateuch. He is an old man very well versed in magic,
who has lived seventeen years shut up in the crypt of the
Great Pyramid, where he read the books of Toth. Concerning yourselves, gentlemen, I intend to employ your
knowledge, in reading the Alexandrian MSS. which I
have collected myself in great numbers. There you'll find,
no doubt, some marvellous secrets, and I do not doubt that
with the help of these three sources of light—the Egyptian,
the Hebrew and the Greek—I'll soon acquire the means
I still want, to command absolutely nature, visible as
well as invisible. Believe me I shall know how to reward
your services by making you in some way participators
of my power.

"I do not speak to you of a more vulgar means to
recognise them. At the point I have reached in my
philosophical labours, money is for me but a trifle."

Arrived at this part of M. d'Asterac's discourse my
good tutor interrupted by saying:

"Sir, I'll not conceal from you that this very money,
which seems to be a trifle to you, is for myself a smarting
anxiety, because I have experienced that it is not easy to
earn some and remain an honest man or even otherwise.
Therefore I should be thankful for the assurance you
would kindly give on that subject."

M. d'Asterac, with a movement which seemed to remove

an invisible object, gave M. Jérôme Coignard the wished-for assurance; for myself, curious as I was of all I saw, I did not wish for anything better than to enter into a new life.

At his master's call, the old servant who had opened the door to us appeared in the study.

"Gentlemen," said our host, "I give you your liberty till dinner at noon. Meanwhile I should be very much obliged to you for ascending to the rooms I have had prepared for you, and let me know that there is nothing wanting for your comfort. Criton will conduct you."

Having assured himself that we were following him, silent Criton went out and began to ascend the stairs. He went up to the roof timbers, then, having taken some steps down a long passage, he indicated to us two very clean rooms where fires sparkled. I could never have believed that a castle as shattered on the outside, the front of which showed nothing but cracked walls and dark windows, was as habitable in some of its inner parts. My first care was to know where I was. Our rooms looked on the fields, the view from them embraced the marshy slopes of the Seine, extending up to the Calvary of Mont Valérien. Eyeing our furniture, I could see, laid out on my bed, a grey coat, breeches to match and a sword. On the carpet were buckle shoes neatly coupled, the heels joined and the points separated just as if they had of themselves the sentiment of a fine deportment.

I augured favourably of the liberality of our master. To do him honour, I dressed very carefully and spread abundantly on my hair the powder a box full of which I found on a small table. And very welcome were the laced shirt and white stockings I discovered in one of the drawers of the chest.

Having put on shirt, stockings, breeches, vest and coat,

I walked up and down my room with hat under the arm, hand on the guard of my sword, thinking all the time on the looking-glass, and regretting that Catherine, the lace-maker, could not see me in such finery.

In this way I was occupied for a little while, when M. Jérôme Coignard came into my room with a new neckband and very respectable clerical garb.

"Tournebroche," he exclaimed, "is it you, my boy? Never forget that you owe these fine clothes to the knowl-edge I have given you. They fit a humanist like yourself, as who says humanities says also elegance. But look on me and say if I have a good mien. In this dress I consider myself to be a very honest man. This M. d'Asterac seems to be tolerably magnificent. It's a pity he's mad. Wise he is in one way, as he calls his valet Criton, which means judge. And it's very true that our valets are the witnesses of all our actions. When Lord Verulam, Chancellor of England, whose philosophy I esteem but little, entered the great hall to be tried, his lackeys, who were clad with an opulence by which the copiousness of the Chancellor's household could be judged, rose to render him due honour. Lord Verulam said to them: 'Sit down, your rising is my falling.' As a fact, those knaves, by their extravagance, had pushed him to ruin and compelled him to do things for which he was indicted as a peculator. Tournebroche, my boy, always remember this misfortune of Lord Verulam, Chancellor of England and author of the 'Novum Organum.' But to return to that Sire d'Asterac, in whose service we are; it is a great pity that he is a sorcerer and given to cursed science. You know, my boy, I pride myself on my delicacy in matters of faith. I find it hard to serve a cabalist who turns our Holy Scriptures upside down under the pretext to understand them better that way. However, if he is, as his name and speech indicate, a

Gascon nobleman, we have nothing to be afraid of. A Gascon may make a contract with the devil and you may be sure that the devil will be done."

The dinner bell interrupted our conversation.

But while descending the stairs, my kind tutor said: "Tournebroche, my boy, remember, during the whole meal, to follow all my movements, to enable you to imitate them. Having dined at the third table of the Bishop of Séez, I know how to do it. It's a difficult art. It's harder to dine than to speak like a gentleman."

CHAPTER VII

Dinner and Thoughts on Food

WE FOUND in the dining-room a table laid for three, where M. d'Asterac made us take our places.

Criton, who acted as butler, served us with jellies, and thick soup strained a dozen times. But we could not see any joints. As well as we could, my kind tutor and myself tried to hide our surprise. M. d'Asterac guessed it and said:

"Gentlemen, this is only an attempt, and may seem to you an unfortunate one. I shall not persist in it. I'll have some more customary dishes served for you and I shall not disdain to partake of them. If the dishes I offer you to-day are badly prepared, it is less the fault of my cook than that of chemistry, which is still in its infancy. But they will at all events give you an idea of what will be in the future. At present men eat without philosophy. They do not nourish themselves like reasonable beings. They do not think of such. But of what are they thinking? Most of them live in stupidity and actually those who are capable of reflection occupy their minds with silly things like controversies and poetry. Consider mankind, gentlemen, at their meals since the far-away times when they ceased their intercourse with Sylphs and Salamanders. Abandoned by the genii of the air they grew heavy and dull in ignorance and barbarity Without policy and without art they lived, nude and miserable, in caverns, on the border of torrents or in the

50

trees of the forest. The chase was their only industry.
After having surprised or captured by quickness a timid
animal, they devoured that prey still palpitating.

"They also fed on the flesh of their companions and
infirm relatives; the first sepulchres of human beings were
living graves, famished and insensible intestines. After
long fierce centuries a divine man made his appearance:
the Greeks call him Prometheus. It cannot be doubted
that this sage had intercourse in the homes of the Nymphs
with the Salamander folks. He learnt of them and showed
to the unhappy mortals the art of producing and conserving fire. Of all the innumerable advantages that men
have drawn from this celestial present, one of the happiest
was the possibility of cooking food, and by this treatment,
to render it lighter and more subtle. And it's in a large
part due to the effect of a nourishment submitted to the
action of the flame that slowly and by degrees mankind
became intelligent, industrious, meditative and apt to
cultivate the arts and sciences. But that was only a first
step, and it is grievous to think that so many millions of
years had to pass before a second step was made. From
the time when our ancestors toasted beasts' quarters on
fires of brambles in the shelter of a rock, we have not
made any true progress in cooking, for sure, gentlemen,
you cannot put a higher value on the inventions of
Lucullus and that gross pie to which Vitellius gave the
name of Shield of Minerva than on our roasts, patties,
stews, our stuffed meats and all the fricassees which still
suffer from the ancient barbarity.

"At Fontainebleau, the king's table, where a whole stag
is dished up in his skin and his antlers, presents to the
eye of the philosopher a spectacle as rude as that of the
troglodytes, cowering round the smoking cinders, gnawing
horse bones. The brilliant paintings of the hall, the

guards, the richly clad officers, the musicians playing the
melodies of Lambert and Lulli in the gallery, the golden
goblets, the silver plate, the silken tablecloth, the Venetian
glass, the chased epergnes full of rare flowers, the heavy
candlesticks—they cannot change, cannot lend a dissimu-
lating charm to the true nature of this unclean charnel-
house, where men and women assemble over animal bodies,
broken bones and torn meats to gloat greedily over them.
Oh, what unphilosophical nourishment! We swallow with
stupid gluttony muscle, fat and intestines of beasts without
discerning in those substances such parts as are truly
adapted to our nourishment and those much more abundant
which we ought to reject; and we fill our stomach indis-
criminately with good and bad, useful and injurious.
That's the very point, where a separation is to be made,
and, if the whole medical faculty could boast of a chemist
and philosopher, we should no more be compelled to
partake of such disgusting feasts.

"They would prepare for us, gentlemen, distilled meats,
containing nothing but what is in sympathy and affinity
with our body. Nothing would be used but the quintes-
sence of oxen and pigs, the elixir of partridges and capons,
and all that is swallowed could be digested. I do not
give up all hope, gentlemen, of obtaining such results by
thinking somewhat deeper over chemistry and medicine
than I have had leisure to do up till now."

At these words of our host, M. Jérôme Coignard, raising
his eyes over the thin black broth in his plate, looked
uneasily at M. d'Asterac, who continued to say:

"But that would still be quite insufficient progress. No
honest man can eat animal flesh without disgust, and
people cannot call themselves refined as long as they keep
slaughter-houses and butchers' shops in their towns. But
the day will come when we shall know exactly the nourish

ing elements contained in animal carcasses, and it will become possible to extract those very same elements from bodies without life, and which will furnish an abundance of them. Those bodies without life contain, as a fact, all that is to be found in living beings, because the animal has been built up by the vegetable, which has itself drawn the substance out of the inert ground.

"Then people will feed on extracts of metal and mineral conveniently treated by physicians. I have no doubt but that the taste of them will be exquisite and the absorption salutary. Cookery will be done in retorts and stills and alchemists will be our cooks. Are you not impatient, gentlemen, to see such marvels? I promise them to you at a very near time. But you are not able at present to unravel the excellent effects that they will produce."

"In truth, sir, I do not unravel them," said my kind tutor, and had a long draught of wine.

"If such is the case," said M. d'Asterac, "listen to me for a moment. No more burdened with slow digestions, mankind will become marvellously active, their sight will become singularly piercing, and they will see the ships gliding on the seas of the moon. Their understanding will be clearer, their ways softer. They will greatly advance in their knowledge of God and nature.

"But it also seems necessary to look forward on all the changes which cannot fail to occur. Even the structure of the human body will be modified. It is an uncontradictable fact that without exercise all organs flatten and end by disappearing altogether. It has been observed that fishes deprived of light become blind. I myself have seen in Valais that shepherds who fed on curdled milk lost their teeth very early; some of them never had any at all. When men feed on the balms I have spoken of, their intestines will be shortened by ells and the volume of the stomach will shrink considerably."

"For once, sir," said my tutor, "you go too quickly and risk making a mess of it. I never considered it to be disagreeable when women get a little corporation, especially if all the remainder of her body is well proportioned. It's a kind of beauty I'm rather partial to. Do not transform it inconsiderately."

"No matter, we'll leave woman's body and flanks formed after the canons of the Greek sculptors. That will be to give you pleasure, reverend sir, and also in due consideration of the labours of maternity. It is true, I intend in that case also, to make several changes of which I'll speak to you on a future day. But to return to our subject. I have to acknowledge that all I have till now predicted is nothing but a preparatory measure for the real nourishment, which is that of the Sylphs and all aerial spirits. They drink light, which is sufficient to give to their bodies marvellous strength and subtility. It is their only potion, one day it will be ours also. Nothing more is to be done than to render the rays of the sun drinkable. I confess that I do not see with sufficient clearness the means to arrive at it, and I do foresee many encumbrances and great obstacles on the road. But whensoever some sage shall be able to do it, mankind will be the equal of Sylphs and Salamanders in intelligence and beauty."

My good tutor listened to these words, folded in himself, his head sadly lowered. He seemed to contemplate the changes to himself from the kind of food imagined by our host.

"Sir," he said after a while, "did you not speak at yonder cookshop of an elixir which dispenses with all kinds of food?"

"True, I did," replied M. d'Asterac, "but that liquor is only good for philosophers, and by that you may understand how restricted is the use of it. It will be better not to mention it."

One doubt tormented me. I asked leave of our host to submit it to him, certain that he would enlighten me at once. He allowed me to speak and I said:

"Sir, those Salamanders, who you say are so beautiful, and of whom, after your relation, I have conceived a charming idea, have they unhappily spoiled their teeth by light drinking, as the shepherds at Valais lost theirs by feeding only on milk diet? I confess I am rather uneasy about it."

"My son," replied M. d'Asterac, "your curiosity pleases me and I will satisfy it. The Salamanders have no teeth that we should call such. But their gums are furnished with two ranges of pearls, very white and very brilliant, lending to their smiles an inconceivable gracefulness. You should know that these pearls are light-hardened."

I said to M. d'Asterac that I was glad it was so and he continued:

"Men's teeth are a sign of ferocity. Once people are properly fed, their teeth will give way to some ornament similar to the pearls of the Salamander. Then it will become incomprehensible that a lover could, without horror and disgust, contemplate dogs' teeth in the mouth of his beloved."

CHAPTER VIII

The Library and its Contents

AFTER dinner our host conducted us to a vast gallery adjoining his study; it was the library. There were to be seen ranged on oaken shelves an innumerable army, or rather a grand assembly, of books in duodecimo, in octavo, in quarto, in folio, clad in calf, sheep, morocco leather, in parchment and in pigskin. The light fell through six windows on this silent assembly extended from one end of the hall to the other, all along the high walls. Large tables, alternated with globes and astronomical apparatus, occupied the middle of the gallery. M. d'Asterac told us to make choice of the place most convenient for our work.

My dear tutor, his head high, with look and breath inhaled all these books drivelling with joy.

"By Apollo!" he exclaimed, "what a splendid library! The Bishop of Séez's, over rich in works of canonical law, is not to be compared to this. There is no pleasanter abode in my opinion, actually the Elysian Fields as described by Virgil. At first sight I can discover such rare books and precious collections that I have my doubts, sir, if any other private library prevails over this, which is inferior in France only to the Mazarin and the Royal. I dare say, seeing all these Greek and Latin MSS. closely pressed together in this single corner, one may, after the Bodleian, the Ambrosian, the Laurentinian and the Vatican also name, sir, the Asteracian. Without flattering myself I may say that I smell truffles and books at a long distance and I consider myself from now, to be the equal of Peiresc, of Grolier and of Canevarius, who are the princes of bibliophiles."

"I consider myself to be over them," said M. d'Asterac quietly, "as this library is a great deal more precious than all those you have named. The King's Library is but an old bookshop in comparison with mine—that is, if you do not consider the number of books only and the quantity of blackened paper. Gabriel Naudé and your Abbé Bignon, both librarians of fame, are, compared to me, indolent shepherds of a vile herd of sheep-like books. I concede that the Benedictines are diligent, but they have no high spirit and their libraries reveal the mediocrity of the souls by whom they have been collected. My gallery, sir, is not on the pattern of others. The works I have got together form a whole which doubtless will procure me knowledge. My library is gnostic, œcumenic and spiritual. If all the lines traced on those numberless sheets of paper and parchment could enter in good order into your brain, you, sir, would know all, could do all, would be the master of Nature, the plasmator of things, you would hold the whole world between the two fingers of your hand as I now hold these grains of tobacco."

With these words he offered his snuff-box to my tutor.

"You are very polite," said M. Jérôme Coignard.

Letting his transported looks wander over the learned walls he continued:

"Between these third and fourth windows are shelves bearing an illustrious burden. There is the meeting place of Oriental MSS., who seem to converse together. I see ten or twelve venerable ones under shreds of purple and gold figured silks, their vestments. Like a Byzantine emperor, some of them wear jewelled clasps on their mantles, others are mailed in ivory plates."

"They are the writings of Jewish, Arabian and Persian cabalists," said M. d'Asterac. "You have just opened 'The Powerful Hand.'   Close to it you'll find 'The Open Table,' 'The Faithful Shepherd,' 'The Fragments of the Temple' and 'The Light of Darkness.'   One place is empty, that of 'Slow Waters,' a precious treatise, which Mosaïde studies at present.   Mosaïde, as I have already said to you, gentlemen, is in my house, occupied with the discovery of the deepest secrets contained in the scriptures of the Hebrews, and, over a century old as he is, the rabbi consents not to die, before penetrating into the sense of all cabalistic symbols.   I owe him much gratitude, and beg of you gentlemen, when you see him, to show him the same regard as I do myself.

"But let us pass that over and come to what is your special concern.   I thought of you, reverend sir, to transcribe and put into Latin some Greek MSS. of inestimable value.   I confide in your knowledge and in your zeal, and have no doubt that your young disciple cannot but be of great help to you."

And addressing me specially he said:

"Yes, my son, I lay great hopes on you.   They are based for a large part on the education you have received.   For, you have been brought up, so to say, in the flames, under the mantel of the chimney haunted by Salamanders.   That is a very considerable circumstance."

Without interrupting his speech, he took up an armful of MSS. and deposited them on the table.

"This," he said, showing a roll of papyrus, "comes from Egypt.   It is a book of Zosimus the Panopolitan, which was thought to be lost and which I found myself in a coffin of a priest of Serapis.

"And what you see here," he added, showing us some straps of glossy and fibrous leaves on which Greek letters traced with a brush were hardly visible, "are unheard-of revelations, due, one to Gophar the Persian, the other to John, the arch-priest of Saint Evagia.

"I should be very glad if you would occupy yourselves with these works before any others. Afterwards we will study together the MSS. of Synesius, Bishop of Ptolemy, of Olympiodorus and Stephanus, which I discovered at Ravenna, in a vault where they have been locked up since the reign of that ignoramus Theodosius who has been surnamed the Great."

As soon as M. d'Asterac was gone, my tutor sat down over the papyrus of Zosimus and, with the help of a magnifying glass commenced to decipher it. I asked him if he was not surprised by what he had just heard.

Without raising his head he replied:

"My dear boy, I have known too many kinds of persons and traversed fortunes too various to be surprised at anything. This gentleman seems to be demented, less because he really is so, but from his thoughts differing in excess from those of the vulgar. But if one listened to discourses commonly held in this world, there would be found still less sense than in those of that philosopher. Left to itself, the sublimest human reason builds its castles and temples in the air and, truly, M. d'Asterac is a pretty good gatherer of clouds. Truth is in God alone, never forget it, my boy. But this is really the book 'Jmoreth' written by Zosimus the Panopolitan for his sister Theosebia. What a glory and what a delight to read this unique MS. rediscovered by a kind of prodigy! I'll give it my days and night watches. How I pity, my boy, the ignorant fellows whom idleness drives into debauchery! What a miserable life they lead! What is a woman in comparison with an Alexandrian papyrus? Compare, if you please, this noble library with the

tavern of the *Little Bacchus* and the entertainment of this
precious MS. with the caresses given to a wench under
the bower; and tell me, my boy, where true contentment
is to be found. For me, a companion of the Muses, and
admitted to the silent orgies of meditation of which the
rhetor of Madama speaks with so much eloquence, I
thank God for having made me a respectable man."

CHAPTER IX

At Work on Zosimus the Panopolitan—I visit my Home and
hear Gossip about M. d'Asterac

DURING all the next month or six weeks, M. Coignard applied himself, day and night, just as he
had promised, to the reading of Zosimus the Panopolitan.
During the meals we partook of at the table of M.
d'Asterac the conversation turned on the opinions of the
gnostics and on the knowledge of the ancient Egyptians.
Being only an ignorant scholar I was of little use to my
good master. I did my best by making such researches
as he wanted me to make; I took no little pleasure in it.
Truly, we lived happily and quietly. At about the
seventh week, M. d'Asterac gave me leave to go and see
my parents at their cookshop. The shop appeared
strangely smaller to me. My mother was there alone and
sad. She cried aloud on seeing me fitted out like a
prince.

"My Jacques," she said, "I am very happy!"

And she began to cry. We embraced, then wiping
her eyes with a corner of her canvas apron she said:

"Your father is at the *Little Bacchus*. Since you left
he often goes there; in your absence the house is less
pleasant for him. He'll be glad to see you again. But
say, my Jacques, are you satisfied with your new position?
I regretted letting you go with that nobleman; I even
accused myself in confession to the third vicar of giving
preference to your bodily well-being over that of your
soul and not having thought of God in establishing you.
The third vicar reproved me kindly over it, and exhorted

me to follow the example of the pious women in the Scriptures, of whom he named several to me; but there are names there that I'll never be able to remember. He did not explain his meaning minutely as it was a Saturday evening and the church was full of penitents."

I reassured my good mother as well as I could and told her that M. d'Asterac made me work in Greek, which was the language in which the New Testament was written; this pleased her, but she remained pensive.

"You'll never guess, my dear Jacquot," she said, "who spoke to me of M. d'Asterac. It was Cadette Saint-Avit, the serving-woman of the Rector of St Benoît. She comes from Gascony, and is a native of a village called Laroque-Timbaut, quite near Saint Eulalie, of which M. d'Asterac is the lord. You know that Cadette Saint-Avit is elderly, as the waiting-woman of a rector ought to be. In her youth she knew, in her country, the three Messieurs d'Asterac, one of whom was captain of a man-of-war and has since been drowned. He was the youngest. The second was colonel of a regiment, went to war and was killed. The eldest, Hercules d'Asterac, is the sole survivor of the three brothers. It is the same one in whose service you are for your good, at least I hope so. He dressed magnificently in his youth, was liberal in his manners but of a sombre humour. He kept aloof from all public business and was not anxious to go into the king's service, as his two brothers had done and found in it an honourable end. He was accustomed to say that it was no glory to carry a sword at one's side, that he did not know of a more ignoble thing than the calling of arms, and that a village scavenger was, in his opinion, high over a brigadier or a marshal of France. Those were his sayings. I confess it does not seem to me either bad or malicious, rather daring and whimsical. But in some way they must be blameable, as Cadette Saint-Avit said that the rector of her parish considered them to be contrary to the order established by God in this world and opposed to that part of the Bible where God is given a name which means Lord of Hosts, and that would be a great sin.

"This M. Hercules had so little sympathy with the court that he refused to travel to Versailles to be presented to his Majesty according to his birthright. He said, 'The king does not come to me and I do not go to him,' and anyone of sense, my Jacquot, can understand that such is not a natural saying."

My good mother looked inquiringly and anxiously at me and went on:

"What more I have to inform you about, my dear Jacquot, is still less believable. However, Cadette Saint-Avit spoke of it as of a certainty. And so I will tell you that M. Hercules d'Asterac, when he lived on his estate, had no other care but to bottle the rays of the sun. Cadette Saint-Avit does not know how he managed it, but she is sure that after a time, in the flagons well corked and heated in water baths, tiny little women took form, charming figures and dressed like theatre princesses. You laugh, Jacquot; however, one ought not to joke over such things when one can see the consequence. It is a great sin to create in such a way creatures who cannot be baptised and who never could have a part in the eternal blessings. You cannot suppose that M. d'Asterac carried those grotesque figures to a priest in their bottles to hold them over the christening font. No godmother could have been found for them."

"But, my dear mamma," I replied, "the dolls of M. d'Asterac were not in want of christening, they had no participation in original sin."

"I never thought of that," said my mother. "And Cadette Saint-Avit herself did not mention it, although she was the servant of a rector. Unhappily she left Gascony when quite young, came to France and had no more news of M. d'Asterac, of his bottles and his puppets. I sincerely hope, my dear Jacquot, that he renounced his wicked works, which could not be accomplished without the help of the devil."

I asked:

"Tell me, my dear mother, did Cadette Saint-Avit, the rector's servant, see the bodies in the bottles with her own eyes?"

"No, my dear child; M. d'Asterac kept his dolls very secret and did not show them to anybody. But she heard of them from a churchman of the name of Fulgence, who haunted the castle, and swore he had seen those little creatures step out of their glass prisons and dance a minuet. And she had every reason to believe it. It is possible to doubt of what one sees, but you cannot doubt the word of an honest man, especially when he belongs to the Church. There is another misfortune with such secret practices, they are extremely costly and it is hard to imagine, as Cadette Saint-Avit said, what money M. Hercules spent to procure all those bottles of different forms, those furnaces and conjuring books wherewith he filled his castle. But after the death of his brothers he became the richest gentleman of his province, and while he dissipated his wealth in follies, his good lands worked for him. Cadette Saint-Avit rates him, with all his expenses, as still a very rich man."

These last words spoken, my father entered the shop. He embraced me tenderly and confided to me that the house had lost half its pleasantness in consequence of my departure and that of M. Jérôme Coignard, who was

honest and jovial. He complimented me on my dress
and gave me a lesson in deportment, assuring me that
trade had accustomed him to easy manners by the contin-
uous obligation he was under to greet his customers like
gentlemen, if as a fact they were only vile riff-raff. He
gave me, as a precept, to round off the elbows and to turn
my toes outward and counselled me, beyond this, to go and
see Léandre at the fair of Saint Germain and to adjust
myself exactly on him.

We dined together with a good appetite, and we
parted shedding floods of tears. I loved them well, both
of them, and what principally made me cry was that,
after an absence of six weeks only, they had already become somewhat strange to me. And I verily believe that
their sadness was caused by the same sentiment.

CHAPTER X

I see Catherine with Friar Ange and reflect—The Liking of
    Nymphs for Satyrs—An Alarm of Fire—M. d'Asterac in
    his Laboratory

WHEN I came out of the cookshop, the night was
    black. At the corner of the Rue des Ecrivains I
heard a fat and deep voice singing:

> "Si ton honneur elle est perdue
> La bell', c'est tu l'as bien voulu."

And soon I could see on the other side, whence the voice
sounded, Friar Ange, with wallet dangling on his
shoulder, holding Catherine the lacemaker round the
waist, walking in the shadow with a wavering and triumphal step, spouting the gutter water under his sandals in
a magnificent spirt of mire which seemed to celebrate
his drunken glory, as the basins of Versailles make their
fountains play in honour of the king. I put myself out
of the way against the post in the corner of a house door,
so as not to be seen by them, which was a needless precaution as they were too much occupied with one another.
With her head lying on the monk's shoulder, Catherine
laughed. A moonray trembled on her moist lips and in
her eyes, like the water sparkles in a fountain; and I
went my way, with my soul irritated and my heart
oppressed, thinking on the provoking waist of that fine
girl pressed by the arm of a dirty Capuchin.

"Is it possible," I said to myself, "that such a pretty
thing could be in such ugly hands? And if Catherine

despises me need she render her despisal more cruel by the liking she has for that naughty Friar Ange?"

This preference appeared singular to me and I conceived as much surprise as disgust at it. But I was not the disciple of M. Jérôme Coignard for nothing. This incomparable teacher had formed my mind to meditate. I recalled to myself the satyrs one can see in gardens carrying off nymphs, and reflected that if Catherine was made like a nymph, those satyrs, at least as they are represented to us, are as horrible as yonder Capuchin. And I concluded that I ought not to be so very much astonished by what I had just seen. My vexation, however, was not dissipated by my reason, doubtless because it had not its source there. These meditations got me along through the shadows of the night and the mud of the thaw to the road of Saint Germain, where I met M. Jérôme Coignard, who was returning home to the Cross of the Sablons after having supped in town.

"My boy," he said, "I have conversed of Zosimus and the gnostics at the table of a very learned ecclesiastic, quite another Peiresc. The wine was coarse and the fare but middling, but nectar and ambrosia floated through the discourse."

Then my dear tutor spoke of the Panopolitan with an inconceivable eloquence. Alas! I listened badly, thinking of that drop of moonlight which had this very night fallen on the lips of Catherine the lacemaker.

At last he came to a stop and I asked on what foundation the Greeks had established the liking of the nymphs for satyrs. My teacher was so widely learned that he was always ready to reply to all questions. He told me:

"That liking is based on a natural sympathy. It is lively but not so ardent as the liking of the satyrs for the nymphs, with which it corresponds. The poets have observed this distinction very well. Concerning it I'll narrate you a singular adventure I have read in a MS. belonging to the library of the Bishop of Séez. It was (I still have it before my eyes) a collection in folio, written in a good hand of last century. This is the singular fact reported in it. A Norman gentleman and his wife took part in a public entertainment, disguised, he as a satyr, she as a nymph. By Ovid it is known with what ardour the satyrs pursue the nymphs; that gentleman had read the 'Metamorphoses.' He entered so well into the spirit of his disguise that nine months after, his wife presented him with a baby whose forehead was horned and whose feet were those of a buck. It is not known what became of the father beyond that he had the common end of all creatures, to wit, that he died, and that beside that capriped he left another younger child, a Christian one and of human form. This younger son went to law claiming that his brother should not get a part of the deceased father's inheritance for the reason that he did not belong to the species redeemed by the blood of Jesus Christ. The Parliament of Normandy, sitting at Rouen, gave a verdict in his favour, which was duly recorded."

I asked my teacher if it was possible that a disguise could have such an effect on nature and if the shape of the child could follow that of a garment. M. Jérôme Coignard advised me not to believe it.

"Jacques Tournebroche, my son," he said, "remember always that a good mind repels all that is contrary to reason, except in matters of faith, wherein it is convenient to believe implicitly. Thank God! I have never erred about the dogmas of our very holy religion, and I trust to find myself in the same disposition in the article of death."

Conversing in this manner we arrived at the castle. The roof seemed in a red glow in the dark. Out of one in dark shadows. We heard the roaring of the fire, like fiery rain under the dense smoke wherewith the sky was veiled. We both believed the flames to be devouring the building. My good tutor tore his hair and moaned:

"My Zosimus, my papyrus, my Greek MSS.! Help! Help! my Zosimus!"

Running up the great lane over puddles of water reflecting the glare of the fire, we crossed the park buried in dark shadows. We heard the roaring of the fire, which filled the sombre staircase. Two at a time we ran up the steps, stopping now and again to listen whence came that appalling noise.

It appeared to us to come from a corridor on the third floor where we had never been. In that direction we fumbled our way, and seeing through the slits of a door the red brightness, we knocked with all our might on the panel. It opened at once.

M. d'Asterac, who opened the door, stood quietly before us. His long black figure seemed to be enveloped in flaming air. He asked quietly on what pressing business we were looking for him at so late an hour. There was no conflagration but a terrible fire, burning in a big furnace with reflectors, which as I have since learned are called athanors. The whole of the rather large room was full of glass bottles with long necks twined round glass tubes of a duck-beak shape, retorts, resembling chubby cheeks out of which came noses like trumpets, crucibles, cupels, matrasses, cucurbits and vases of all forms.

My dear old tutor wiping his face shining like live coals said:

"Oh, sir, we were afraid that the castle was alight like

straw. Thank God, the library is not burning. But are you practising the spagyric art, sir?"

"I do not want to conceal from you," said M. d'Asterac, "that I have made great progress in it, but withal I have not found the theorem capable of rendering my work perfect. At the moment you knocked at the door I was picking up the Spirit of the World, and the Flower of Heaven, which are the veritable Fountains of Youth. Have you some understanding of alchemy, Monsieur Coignard?"

The abbé replied that he had got some notions of it from certain books, but that he considered the practice of it to be pernicious and contrary to religion. M. d'Asterac smiled and said:

"You are too knowing a man, M. Coignard, not to be acquainted with the Flying Eagle, the Bird of Hermes, the Fowl of Hermogenes, the Head of a Raven, the Green Lion and the Phœnix."

"I have been told," said my good master, "that by these names are distinguished the philosopher's stone in its different states. But I have doubts about the possibility of a transmutation of metals."

With the greatest confidence M. d'Asterac replied:

"Nothing is easier, my dear sir, than to bring your uncertainty to an end."

He opened an old rickety chest standing in the wall and took out of it a copper coin, bearing the effigy of the late king, and called our attention to a round stain crossing the coin from side to side.

"That," he said, "is the effect of the stone, which has transmuted the copper into silver, but that's only a trifle."

He went back to the chest and took out of it a sapphire the size of an egg, an opal of marvellous dimensions and a handful of perfect fine emeralds.

"Here are some of my doings," he said, "which are proof enough that the spagyric art is not the dream of an empty brain."

At the bottom of the small wooden bowl lay five or six little diamonds, of which M. d'Asterac made no mention. My tutor asked him if they also were of his make, and, the alchemist having acknowledged it:

"Sir," said the abbé, "I should counsel you to show the curious those diamonds prior to the other stones by way of caution. If you let them look first at the sapphire, opal and the emeralds, you run the risk of a persecution for sorcery, because everyone will say that the devil alone was capable of producing such stones. Just as the devil alone could lead an easy life in the midst of these furnaces, where one has to breathe flames. As far as I am concerned, having stayed a single quarter of an hour, I am already half baked."

Letting us out, with a friendly smile M. d'Asterac spoke as follows:

"Well knowing what to think of the devil and the Other, I willingly consent to speak of them with persons who believe in them. The devil and the Other are, as it were, characters; one may speak of them just as of Achilles and Thersites. Be assured, gentlemen, if the devil is like what he is said to be, he does not live in so subtle an element as fire. It is wholly wrong to place so villainous a beast in the sun. But as I had the honour to say, Master Tournebroche, to the Capuchin so dear to your mother, I reckon that the Christians slander Satan and his demons. That in some unknown world there may exist beings still worse than man is possible, but hardly conceivable. Certainly, if such exist, they inhabit regions deprived of light, and if they are burning, it would be in ice, which, as a fact, causes the same smart-

ing pain, and not in illustrious flames among the fiery
daughters of the stars. They suffer because they are
wicked, and wickedness is an evil; but they can only
suffer from chilblains. With regard to your Satan,
gentlemen, who is a horror for your theologians, I do
not consider him to be despicable, if I judge him by all
you say of him, and, should he peradventure exist, I would
think him to be, not a nasty beast, but a little Sylph,
or at least a Gnome, and a metallurgist a trifle mocking
but very intelligent."

My tutor stopped his ears with his fingers and took
to flight so as not to hear anything more.

"What impiety, Tournebroche, my boy," he exclaimed,
when we reached the staircase. "What blasphemies!
Have you felt all the odium in the maxims of that
philosopher? He pushes atheism to a joyous frenzy,
which makes me wonder. But this indeed renders him
almost innocent, for being apart from all belief, he
cannot tear up the Holy Church like those who remain
attached to her by some half-severed, still bleeding limb.
Such, my son, are the Lutherans and the Calvinists, who
mortify the Church till a separation occurs. On the
contrary, atheists damn themselves alone, and one may
dine with them without committing a sin. That's to say,
that we need not have any scruple about living with M.
d'Asterac, who believes neither in God nor devil. But
did you see, Tournebroche, my boy, the handful of little
diamonds at the bottom of the wooden bowl?—the number
of which apparently he did not know, and which seemed
to be of pure water. I have my doubts about the opal
and the sapphires, but those diamonds looked genuine."
When we reached our chambers we wished each other a
very good-night.

CHAPTER XI

The Advent of Spring and its Effects—We visit Mosaïde

UP TILL springtime my tutor and myself led a regular and secluded life. All the mornings we were at work shut up in the gallery, and came back here after dinner as if to the theatre. Not as M. Jérôme Coignard used to say, to give ourselves in the manner of gentlemen and valets a paltry spectacle, but to listen to the sublime, if contradictory, dialogues of the ancient authors.

In this way the reading and translating of the Panopolitan advanced quickly. I hardly contributed to it. Such kind of work was above my knowledge and I had enough to do to learn the figure that the Greek letters make on papyrus. Sometimes I assisted my tutor by consulting the authors who could enlighten him in his researches, and foremost Olympiodorus and Plotinus, with whom since then I have remained familiar. The small services I was able to render him increased considerably my self-esteem.

After a long sharp winter I was on the way to become a learned person, when the spring broke in suddenly with her gallant equipage of light, tender green and singing birds; the perfume of the lilacs coming into the library windows caused me vague reveries, out of which my tutor called me by saying:

"Jacquot Tournebroche, please climb up that ladder and tell me if that rascal Manéthon does not mention a god Imhotep, who by his contradictions tortures one like a devil."

And my good master filled his nose with tobacco and looked quite content.

On another occasion he said:

"My boy, it is remarkable how great an influence our garments have on our moral state. Since my neckband has become spotted with different sauces I have dropped upon it I feel a less honest man. Now that you are dressed like a marquis, Tournebroche, does not the desire tickle you to assist at the toilet of an opera girl, and to put a roll of spurious gold pieces on a faro-table—in one word, do you not feel yourself to be a man of quality? Do not take what I say amiss, and remember that it is sufficient to give a coward a busby to make him hasten to become a soldier and be knocked on the head in the king's service. Tournebroche, our sentiments are composed of a thousand things we cannot detect for their smallness, and the destiny of our immortal soul depends sometimes on a puff too light to bend a blade of grass. We are the toy of the winds. But pass me, if you please, 'The Rudiments of Vossius,' the red edges of which I see stand out under your left arm."

On this same day, after dinner at three o'clock, M. d'Asterac led us, my teacher and myself, to walk in the park. He conducted us to the west, where Rueil and Mont Valérien are visible. It was the deepest and most desolate part. Ivy and grass, cropped by the rabbits, covered the paths, now and then obstructed by large trunks of dead trees. The marble statues on both sides of the way smiled, unconscious of their ruin. A nymph, with her broken hand near her mouth, made a sign to a shepherd to remain silent. A young faun, his head fallen to the ground, still tried to put his flute to his lips.

And all these divine beings seemed to teach us to despise the injuries inflicted by time and fortune. We followed the banks of a canal where the rainwater nourished the tree frogs. Round a circus rose sloping basins where pigeons went to drink. Arrived there we went by a narrow pathway driven through a coppice.

"Walk with care," said M. d'Asterac. "This pathway is somewhat dangerous, as it is lined by mandrakes which at night-time sing at the foot of the trees. They hide in the earth. Take care not to put your feet on them; you will get love sickness or thirst after wealth, and would be lost, because the passions inspired by mandrakes are unhappy."

I asked how it was possible to avoid the invisible danger. M. d'Asterac replied that one could escape it by means of intuitive divination, and in no other way.

"Besides," he added, "this pathway is fatal."

It went on in a direct line to a brick pavilion, hidden under ivy, which no doubt had served in time gone by as a guard house. There the park came to an end close to the monotonous marshes of the Seine.

"You see this pavilion," said M. d'Asterac; "in it lives the most learned of men. Therein Mosaïde, one hundred and twenty years old, penetrates, with majestic self-will, the mysteries of nature. He has left Imbonatus and Bartoloni far behind. I wanted to honour myself, gentlemen, by keeping under my roof the greatest cabalist since Enoch, son of Cain. Religious scruples have prevented Mosaïde taking his place at my table, which he supposes to be a Christian's, by which he does me too much honour. You cannot conceive the violence of hate, of this sage, of everything Christian. I had the greatest difficulty to make him dwell in the pavilion, where he lives alone with his niece, Jahel. Gentlemen, you shall

not wait longer before becoming acquainted with Mosaïde
and I will at once present both of you to this divine man."

And having thus spoken, M. d'Asterac pushed us inside
the pavilion, where between MSS. strewn all round was
seated in a large arm-chair an old man with piercing
eyes, a hooked nose, and a couple of thin streams of
white beard growing from a receding chin; a velvet cap,
formed like an imperial crown, covered his bald skull,
and his body, of an inhuman emaciation, was wrapped
up in an old gown of yellow silk, resplendent but dirty.

Right piercing looks were turned on us, but he gave
no sign that he noticed our arrival. His face had an
expression of painful stubbornness, and he slowly rolled
between his rigid fingers the reed which served him for
writing.

"Do not expect idle words from Mosaïde," said M.
d'Asterac to us. "For a long time this sage does not
communicate with anyone but the genii and myself. His
discourses are sublime. As he will never converse with
you, gentlemen, I'll endeavour to give you in a few words
an idea of his merits. First he has penetrated into the
spiritual sense of the books of Moses, after that into the
value of the Hebrew characters, which depends on the
order of the letters of the alphabet. This order has been
thrown into confusion from the eleventh letter forward.
Mosaïde has re-established it, which Atrabis, Philo,
Avicenne, Raymond Lully, P. de la Mirandola, Reuchlin,
Henry More and Robert Flydd have been unable to do.
Mosaïde knows the number of the gold which corresponds
to Jehovah in the world of spirits, and you must agree,
gentlemen, that that is of infinite consequence."

My dear tutor took his snuff-box in hand, presented it
civilly to us, took a pinch himself and said:

"Do you not believe, M. d'Asterac, that this sort of

knowledge is the very kind to bring one to the devil at the end of this transient life?

"After all, this sire Mosaïde plainly errs in his interpretation of the Holy Scriptures. When our Lord expired on the cross for the salvation of mankind the synagogue felt a bandage slip over her eyes, she staggered like a drunken woman and the crown fell from her head. Since then the interpretation of the Old Testament is confined to the Catholic Church, to which in spite of my many iniquities I belong."

At these words Mosaïde, like a goat god, smiled in a hideous manner, and said to my dear tutor, in a slow and musty voice sounding as from far away:

"The Masorah has not confided to thee her secrets and the Mischna has not revealed to thee her mysteries."

"Mosaïde," continued M. d'Asterac, "not only interprets the books of Moses but also that of Enoch, which is much more important, and which has been rejected by the Christians, who were unable to understand it; like the cock of the Arabian fable, who disdained the pearl fallen in his grain. That book of Enoch, M. Abbé Coignard, is the more precious because therein are to be seen the first talks the daughters of man had with the Sylphs. You must understand that those angels which as Enoch shows us had love connection with women were Sylphs and Salamanders."

"I will so understand, sir," replied my good master, "not wishing to gainsay you. But from what has been conserved of the book of Enoch, which is clearly apocryphal, I suspect those angels to have been not Sylphs but simply Phœnician merchants."

"And on what do you found," asked M. d'Asterac, "so singular an opinion?"

"I found it, sir, on what is said in that very book that

the angels taught the women how to use bracelets and necklaces, to paint the eyebrows and to employ all sorts of dyes. It is further said in the same book, that the angels taught the daughters of men the peculiar qualities of roots and trees, enchantments, and the art of observing the stars. Truly, sir, have not those angels the appearance of Syrians or Sidonians gone ashore on some half-deserted coast and unpacking in the shadow of rocks their trumpery wares to tempt the girls of the savage tribes? These traffickers gave them copper necklaces, armlets and medicines in exchange for amber, frankincense and furs. And they astonished these beautiful but ignorant creatures by speaking to them of the stars with a knowledge acquired by seafaring. That's clear, I think, and I should like to know in what M. Mosaïde could contradict me."

Mosaïde kept mute and M. d'Asterac, smiling again, said:

"M. Coignard, you do not reason so badly, ignorant as you still are of gnosticism and the Cabala. And what you say makes me think that there may have been some metallurgistic and gold-working Gnomes among the Sylphs who joined themselves in love with the daughters of men. The Gnomes, and that is a fact, occupied themselves willingly with the goldsmith's art, and it is probable that those ingenious demons forged the bracelets you believe to have been of Phœnician manufacture.

"But I warn you, you'll be at some disadvantage, sir, to compete with Mosaïde in the knowledge of human antiquities. He has rediscovered monuments which were believed to have been lost; among others, the column of Seth and the oracles of Sambéthé the daughter of Noah and the most ancient of the sybils."

"Oh!" exclaimed my tutor as he stamped on the powdery floor so that a cloud of dust whirled up. "Oh!

what dreams! It is too much, you make fun of me!
And M. Mosaïde cannot have so much foolery in his head,
under his large bonnet, resembling the crown of Charlemagne; that column of Seth is a ridiculous invention of
that shallow Flavius Josephus, an absurd story by which
nobody has been imposed upon before you. And the
predictions of Sambéthé, Noah's daughter, I am really
curious to know them; and M. Mosaïde, who seems to be
pretty sparing of his words, would oblige by uttering a
few by words of mouth, because it is not possible for him,
I am quite pleased to recognise it, to pronounce them by
the more secret voice in which the ancient sybils habitually
gave their mysterious responses."

Mosaïde, who seemed to hear nothing, said suddenly:
"Noah's daughter has spoken; Sambéthé has said:
'The vain man who laughs and mocks will not hear the
voice which goes forth from the seventh tabernacle, the
infidel walketh miserably to his ruin.'"

After this oracular pronouncement all three of us took
leave of Mosaïde.

CHAPTER XII

I take a Walk and visit Mademoiselle Catherine

IN THAT year the summer was radiant, and I had a longing to go walking. One day, strolling under the trees of the Cours-la-Reine with two little crowns I had found that very morning in the pocket of my breeches, and which were the first by which my goldmaker had shown his munificence, I sat down at the door of a small coffee-house, at a table so small that it was quite appropriate to my solitude and modesty. Then I began to think of the oddness of my destiny, while at my side some musketeers were drinking Spanish wine with girls of the town. I was not quite sure that Croix-des-Sablons, M. d'Asterac, Mosaïde, the papyrus of Zosimus and my fine clothes were not dreams, out of which I should wake to find myself clad in the dimity vest, back again turning the spit at the *Queen Pédauque*.

I came out of my reverie on feeling my sleeve pulled, and saw standing before me Friar Ange, his face nearly hidden by his beard and cowl.

"Monsieur Jacques Ménétrier," he said in a very low voice, "a lady, who wishes you well, expects you in her carriage on the highway, between the river and the Porte de la Conférence."

My heart began to beat violently. Afraid and charmed by this adventure, I went at once to the place indicated by the Capuchin, but at a quiet pace, which seemed to me to be more becoming. Arrived at the embankment I saw a carriage and a tiny hand on the door.

This door was opened at my coming, and very much surprised I was to find inside the coach Mam'selle Catherine, dressed in pink satin, her head covered with a hood of black lace, underneath which her fair hair seemed to sport.

Confused I remained standing on the step.

"Come in," she said, "and sit down near me. Shut the door if you please; you must not be seen. Just now in passing on the Cours I saw you sitting at the café. Immediately I had you fetched by the good friar, whom I had attached to me for the Lenten exercises, and whom I have kept since, because, in whatever position one may be, it is necessary to have piety. You looked very well, M. Jacques, sitting before your little table, your sword across your thighs and with the sad look of a man of quality. I have always been friendly disposed towards you and I am not of that kind of women who in their prosperity disregard their former friends."

"Eh! What? Mam'selle Catherine," I exclaimed, "this coach, these lackeys, this satin dress——"

"They are the outcome," she replied, "of the kindness of M. de la Guéritude, who is of the best set and one of the richest financiers. He has lent money to the king. He is an excellent friend whom, for all the world, I should not wish to offend. But he is not as amiable as you, M. Jacques. He has also given me a little house at Grenelle, which I will show you from the cellar to the garret. M. Jacques, I am mighty glad to see you on the road to fortune. Real merit is always discovered. You'll see my bedroom, which is copied from that of Mademoiselle Davilliers. It is covered all over with looking-glass and there are lots of grotesque figures. How is the old fellow your father? Between ourselves, he somewhat neglects his wife and his cookshop. It is very wrong of a man in his position. But let us speak of yourself."

"Let us speak of you, Mam'selle Catherine," said I. "You are so very pretty and it is a great pity you love the Capuchin." Nothing could be said against a government contractor.

"Oh!" she said, "do not reproach me with Friar Ange. I have him for my salvation only and if I would give a rival to M. de la Guéritude it would be——"

"Would be?"

"Don't ask me, M. Jacques; you're an ungrateful man, for you know that I always singled you out, but you do not care about me."

"Quite the contrary, Mam'selle Catherine. I smarted under your mockery. You sneered at my beardless chin. Many a time you have told me that I am but a ninny."

"And that was true, M. Jacques, truer than you believed it to be. Why could you not see that I had a liking for you?"

"Why, Catherine, you are so pretty as to make one fear. I did not dare to look at you. And one day I clearly saw that you were thoroughly offended with me."

"I had every reason for it, M. Jacques; you took that Savoyard in preference to me, that scum of the Port Saint Nicolas."

"Ah! be quite sure, Catherine, that I did not do so by wish or inclination, but only because she found ways and means energetic enough to vanquish my timidity."

"Oh! my friend, you may believe me, as I am the elder of us two, timidity is a great sin against love. But did you not see that that beggar had holes in her stockings and a seam of filth and mud, half-an-ell high, on the bottom of her petticoat?"

"I saw it, Catherine."

"Have you not seen, Jacques, how badly she is made and that really she is skinny?"

"I saw it, Catherine."

"And withal you loved that Savoyard she-monkey, you who have a white skin and distinguished manners!"

"I cannot understand it myself, Catherine. It must have been that at that moment my imagination was full of you. And it was your image only gave me the pluck and strength you reproach me with to-day. Imagine yourself, Catherine, my rapture to press you in my arms, yourself or only a girl who resembled you a little. Because I loved you desperately."

She took my hand and sighed, and in a tone of sadness I continued to say:

"Yes, I did love you, Catherine, and I could still love you except for that disgusting monk."

She cried out:

"What a suspicion! You offend me. It is a folly."

"Then you do not love the Capuchin?"

"Fie!"

As I did not consider it to be any use to press the subject further, I took her round the waist, we embraced, our lips met and all my being seemed to melt in voluptuousness.

After a short moment of luxurious confusion, she disentangled herself, her cheeks rosy, her eyes moistened, her lips half separated. It is from that day that I knew how much a woman is embellished and adorned by a kiss lovingly pressed on her mouth. Mine had made roses of the sweetest hue bloom on Catherine's cheeks and strewn into the flowery blue of her eyes drops of diamantine dew.

"You are a baby," she said, readjusting her hood. "Go! you cannot remain a moment longer. M. de la

Guéritude will be here at once. He loves me with an impatience which continually runs ahead of the meeting time."

Reading in my face how upset I was by this saying she spoke again with a quick vivacity:

"Listen, Jacques, he returns every night at nine to his old woman, who shrewish by age, cannot bear his infidelities since she herself is unable to pay him in the same coin and has become awfully jealous. Come to-night at half-past nine. I'll receive you. My house is at the corner of the Rue du Bac. You'll recognise it by its three windows on every floor and by its balcony covered with roses; you know I always did like flowers. Good-bye till to-night."

Caressingly she pushed me back, hardly able to hide the wish to keep me with her, then placing one finger over her mouth she whispered again:

"Till to-night."

CHAPTER XIII

Taken by M. d'Asterac to the Isle of Swans I listen to his Discourse on Creation and Salamanders

I REALLY do not know how it was possible to tear myself out of Catherine's arms. But it is a fact that in jumping out of her carriage I nearly fell on M. d'Asterac, whose tall figure leant against a tree on the roadside. Courteously I saluted him and showed the surprise I felt at this pleasant encounter.

"Chance," he said, "lessens as knowledge grows, for me it is suppressed. I knew, my son, that I had to meet you at this place. It is necessary for me to have a conversation with you already too long delayed. Let's go, if you please, in quest of solitude and quietness required by what I wish to tell you. Do not become anxious. The mysteries I desire to unveil before you are sublime, it is true, but pleasant also."

Having so spoken he conducted me to the bank of the Seine opposite the Isle of Swans, which rose out of the middle of the river like a ship built of foliage. There he made a sign to a ferryman, whose boat brought us quickly to the green isle, frequented only by invalids, who on fine days play there at bowls and drink their pint of wine. Night lit her first stars in the sky and lent a humming voice to the myriads of insects in the grass. The isle was deserted. M. d'Asterac sat down on a wooden bench at the end of an alley of walnut-trees, invited me to sit close to him and spoke:

"There are three sorts of people, my son, from whom
85

the philosopher has to hide his secrets. They are princes, because it would be imprudent to enlarge their power; the ambitious, whose pitiless genius must not be armed, and the debauchees, who would find in hidden sciences the means to satiate their evil passions. But I can talk freely to you, who are neither debauched—for I quite overlook the error you nearly gave way to in the arms of yonder girl—nor ambitious, having lived, till recently, contented to turn the paternal spit. Therefore I may disclose to you the hidden laws of the universe.

"It must not be believed that life is limited by narrow rules wherein it is manifested to the eyes of the profane. When they teach that creation's object and end was man, your theologians and your philosophers reason like the multiped of Versailles or the Tuileries, who believe the humidity of the cellars is made for their special use and that the remainder of the castle is uninhabitable. The system of the world, as Canon Copernicus taught in the last century, following the doctrines of Aristarchus of Samos and Pythagorean philosophers, is doubtless known to you, as there have actually been prepared some compendiums of them for the urchins of village schools and dialogues abstracted from them for the use of town children. You have seen at my house a kind of machine which shows it distinctly by means of a kind of clockwork.

"Raise your eyes, my son, and you'll see over your head David's chariot, drawn by Mizar and her two illustrious companions, circling round the pole; Arcturus, Vega of the Lyre, the Virgin's Sword, the Crown of Ariadne and its charming pearls. Those are suns. One single look on that world will make it clear to you that the whole of creation is the work of fire and that life, in its finest forms, is fed on flames.

"And what are the planets? Drops of a mixture of mind, a little mire and plenty of moisture. Behold the august choir of the stars, the assembly of the suns; they equal or excel ours in magnitude and power and after I have shown you on a clear winter's night, through my telescope, Sirius, your eyes and soul will be dazzled.

"Do you in good faith believe that Sirius Altair, Regulus, Aldebaran, all these suns are luminary only? Do you believe that this old Phœbus, who incessantly forces into space, wherein we are swimming, his inordinate surge of heat and light, has no other function but to light the earth and some other paltry and imperceptible planets? What a candle! A million times greater than the dwelling.

"I have to present to you first of all the idea that the universe is composed of suns and that the planets which may be in it are less than nothing. But as I foresee your wish to make an objection, I'll reply to it beforehand. The suns, you want to say, put themselves out in the course of centuries and by that also change into mud. No! is my reply; they keep themselves alive by means of comets which they attract and which fall on them. It is the dwelling of true life. The planets and this our earth are but the abode of ghosts. Such are the verities of which I have to convince you.

"Now that you understand, my son, that fire is the principal element, you'll easier comprehend what I wish to teach you and which is of greater importance than anything you may have learned up to now, or was even known to Erasmus, Turnebe or Scaliger. I do not speak of theologians like Quesnel or Bossuet who, between ourselves, I consider as the lees of human spirit, and who have no better understanding than a simple captain of guards. Don't let us hamper ourselves by despising those brains comparable in volume, as well as in construction, to wrens' eggs, but let us at once enter fully into the object of our conference.

"Whilst those earth-born creatures do not surpass a degree of perfection which, by beauty of form, has been attained by Antinoüs and by Madame de Parabère, and at which they alone have arrived by the faculty known to Democritus and myself; the beings formed by fire enjoy a wisdom and an intelligence of which we cannot possibly conceive the limit.

"Such is, my son, the nature of the glorious children of the suns; they know the laws of the universe just as we know the rules of chess, and the course of the stars does not trouble them any more than the moves on the chessboard of the king and the other men trouble us. Those genii create worlds in such spaces of the infinite where none at present exist, and organise them at their will. It distracts them momentarily from their principal business, which is to unite among themselves in unspeakable love. Only last night I turned my telescope on the Sign of the Virgin and saw on it a far-away vortex of light. No doubt, my son, that was the still unfinished work of one of those fire beings.

"Truly the universe has no other origin; far from being the effect of a single will, it is the result of the sublime freaks of a great many genii, recreating themselves by working on it each in his own turn and on his own side. That's what explains the diversity, the splendour and the imperfection. For the force and foresight of those genii, immense as they were, had still their limits. I should deceive you were I to say that a man, philosopher or magician, can have familiar intercourse with them.

"None of them gave me a direct manifestation of himself, and what I tell you of them is known to me by

induction only, and by hearsay. Certain as their existence is, I should not attempt to describe their habits and
their character. It is necessary to know when not to
know, my son, and I make it a point not to bring forward
other than perfectly well-observed facts.

"Let those genii, or rather demiurguses, abide in their
glory, and let us treat of illustrious beings who stand
nearer to us. Here, my son, is where one has to lend an
open ear.

"If in speaking of the planets I have given vent to a
feeling of disdain, it was that I only took into consideration the solid surface and shell of those little balls or tops
and the animals who sadly crawl on them. I should
have spoken in quite another tone, if in my mind I had
included with the planets the air and the vapours wherein
they are enveloped. For the air is an element in no way
of lesser nobility than fire, whence it follows that the
dignity and importance of the planets is in the air
wherein they are bathed. Those clouds, soft vapours,
puffs of wind, transparencies, blue waves, moving islets
of purple and gold which pass over our heads, are the
abode of adorable people. They are called Sylphs and
Salamanders, and are creatures infinitely amiable and
lovely. It is possible for us, and convenient, to form
with them unions, the delights of which are hardly
conceivable.

"The Salamanders are such that in comparison with
them the prettiest person at court or in the city is but an
ugly woman. They surrender themselves willingly to
philosophers. Doubtless you have heard of that marvel
by which M. Descartes was accompanied on his travels.
Some say that she was a natural daughter of his, that he
took with him everywhere; others think that she was an
automaton manufactured with inimitable art. As a fact

she was a Salamander, whom that clever man had taken
as his lady love. He never left her. During a voyage
in the Dutch Sea he took her with him on board, shut in
a box of precious wood lined with the softest satin. The
form of this box, and the precaution with which M. Descartes took care of it, drew the attention of the captain,
who, while the philosopher was asleep, raised the cover
and discovered the Salamander. This ignorant, rude
fellow imagined that such a marvellous creature was the
creation of the devil. In his dismay, he threw it into the
sea. But you will easily believe that the beautiful little
person was not drowned, and that it was no trouble to
her to rejoin M. Descartes. She remained faithful to
him during his natural life, and when he died she left
this world never more to return.

"I give you this example, chosen from many, to make
you acquainted with the loves between philosophers and
Salamanders. These loves are too sublime to be in need
of contracts, and you will agree that the ridiculous display usual at human weddings would be entirely out of
place at such unions. It would be indeed fine, if a
proctor in a wig and a fat priest put their noses together
over it! That sort of gentleman is good only to join
vulgar man to woman. The marriages of Salamanders
and sages have witnesses more august. The aerial people
celebrate them in ships which, moved by celestial breath,
glide, their sterns crowned with roses, to the sound of
harps, on invisible waves. But do not believe that, not
being entered in a dirty register in a shabby vestry, they
would be of little solidity and could be easily torn
asunder. They have for guarantors the spirits who gam-
bol on the clouds whence flashes the lightning and roars
the thunder. I reveal matters to you, my son, which
will be useful to you to know, because I conclude from

certain indications that your destiny is the bed of a Sala-mander."

"Alas! monsieur," I exclaimed, "this destiny alarms me, and I have nearly as many scruples as the Dutch captain who threw the lady love of Descartes into the sea. I cannot help thinking these aerial dames are demons. I should fear to lose my soul with them, for after all, sir, such marriages are against nature and in opposition to the divine law. Oh! why is not M. Jérôme Coignard, my good tutor, present to hear you! I am sure he would strengthen me by his valuable arguments against the delights of your Salamanders, sir, and your eloquence."

"The Abbé Coignard," said M. d'Asterac, "is an ad-mirable translator of Greek. But you must not want anything from him beyond his books. He has no philos-ophy. As far as you are in question, my son, you reason with the infirmity of ignorance, and the weakness of your arguments afflicts me. You say, those unions are against nature. What do you know about it? What means have you to gain knowledge of it? How is it possible to make a distinction between what is natural and what is not? Is the universal Isis known enough to discriminate between what is assisting her and what thwarts her? But to speak better still; nothing thwarts her and every-thing assists her, because nothing exists which does not enter into the functions of her organs and does not follow the numberless attitudes of her body. I beg of you to say, whence could enemies come to offend her? Nothing acts against her nor outside of her; the forces which seem to fight against her are nothing else but movements of her own life.

"The ignorant alone have assurance enough to decide if an action is natural or not. Let's admit their illusions for a moment and their prejudice, and let us feign to recognise the possibility of committing acts against nature. These acts, are they for that reason worse and condemnable? On this point I cannot but remember the vulgar opinion of moralists who represent virtue as an effort over instincts, as an enterprise on the inclinations we carry within us, as a fight with the original man. They own themselves that virtue is against nature, and going further on that opinion they cannot condemn an action of whatever kind, for what is common to it and virtue alike.

"I have made this digression, my son, to call your attention to the contemptible lightness of your reason. I should offend you by believing you still have any doubts of the innocence of the sensual intercourse men may have with Salamanders. Know then, now, that such marriages, far from being interdicted by religious law, are commanded by that law to the exclusion of all others. I will give you some conclusive evidence for it."

He stopped talking, took his snuff-box from his pocket, and filled his nose with a pinch.

The night was densely dark. The moon shed her limpid light over the river, and tremblingly enlaced with the reflections of the street lamps. The flying ephemerides enveloped us like a vaporous eddy. The shrill voice of insects rose into the world's silence. Such a sweetness fell slowly down from the sky that it seemed as if milk had been mixed with the sparkling of the stars.

M. d'Asterac spoke again:

"The Bible, my son, and especially the books of Moses, contains grand and useful verities. Such an opinion may appear absurd and unreasonable, in consequence of the treatment the theologians have inflicted on what they call the Scriptures, and of which they have made, by means of their commentaries, explications, and meditations, a manual of errors, a library of absurdities, a magazine of foolery, a cabinet of lies, a gallery of stupidities, a lyceum of ignorance, a museum of silliness, and a repository of human imbecility and wickedness. Know, my son, that at its origin it was a temple filled with celestial radiance.

"I have been fortunate enough to re-establish it in its primal splendour. Truth obliges me to acknowledge that Mosaïde has very much assisted me with his deep comprehension of the language and the alphabet of the Hebrews. But let us not lose sight of our principal subject. Be informed from the outset, my son, that the sense of the Bible is figurative, and that the capital error of the theologians was to take it literally, whereas it is to be understood as symbolical. Follow this truth in the whole course of my discourse.

"When Demiurge, who is commonly called Jehovah, and by many more names, as all terms expressing quality or quantity are generally applied to him, had, I do not want to say 'created' the world—for such would be an absurdity—but had laid out a small corner of the universe, as a dwelling place for Adam and Eve, there were some subtle creatures in space, which Jehovah had not formed, was not capable of forming. They were the work of several other demiurges, older and more skillful. His craft was not beyond that of a very clever potter, capable of kneading clay beings in the manner of pots, such as we men are now. What I say is not to slight him, because such work is still much beyond human power.

"But it became necessary to brand the inferior character of the work of the seven days. Jehovah worked, not in and with fire, which alone gives birth to the masterpieces of life, but with mud, out of which he could not produce other than the work of a clever ceramist. We are nothing, my son, but animated earthenware. Jehovah is not to be reproached for having illusions over the quality of his work. If he did find it well done in the first moment, and in the ardour of composition, he did not take long to recognise his error, the Bible·is full of expressions of his discontent, which often becomes ill-humour, sometimes actual rage.

"Never has artisan treated the objects of his industry with more disgust and aversion. He intended to destroy them, and, in fact, did drown the larger part. This deluge, the memory of which has been conserved by Jews, Greeks and Chinese alike, gave a last deception to the unhappy demiurges, who, aware of the uselessness and ridiculousness of such violence, became discouraged, and fell into an apathy, the progress of which has not been stopped from Noah's time to our present day, wherein it is extreme. But I see I have advanced too far. The inconvenience of these extensive subjects is the impossibility of remaining within their limits.

"Our mind thrown into them resembles yonder sons of the suns, who cross the whole of the universe in one single jump.

"Let us return to the earthly paradise, wherein the demiurge had placed the two vases formed by his hand, Adam and Eve. They did not live there alone, between the animals and plants. The spirits of the air, created by the demiurges of the fire, were flowing over and looking at them with a curiosity mixed with sympathy and pity. It was exactly as Jehovah had foreseen. Let us hasten to say, to his praise, he had relied on the genii of the fire, to whom we may now give their true names of Elves and Salamanders, to ameliorate and perfect his clay figures. In his prudence he may have said to himself: 'My Adam and my Eve, opaque and cemented in clay, are in want of air and light. I have failed to give them wings. But united to Elves and Salamanders, the creations of a demiurge more powerful and more subtle than myself, they will give birth to children, equally originated by light and clay, and who in their turn will have children still more luminous than themselves, till in the end their issue will be equal in beauty to the sons and daughters of air and fire.'

"It must be said he had neglected nothing to attract the eyes of Sylphs and Salamanders in forming Adam and Eve. He had modelled the woman in form of an amphora, with a harmony of curved lines quite sufficient to make him recognised as the prince of geometers, and he succeeded in amending the coarseness of the material by the magnificent charm of the form. For modelling Adam he made use of a less caressing, but more energetic, hand, forming his body with such order, and in such perfect proportions, that, applied later by the Greeks to their architecture, those same ordinances and measures made the beauty of the temples.

"You see, my son, that Jehovah applied his best means to render his creatures worthy of the aerial kisses he expected for them. I shall not insist on the care he took with a view of making these unions prolific. The harmony between the sexes is an ample proof of his wisdom in this regard. And surely at the outset he had reason to congratulate himself on his shrewdness and ability.

"I have said the Sylphs and Salamanders looked on Adam and Eve with that curiosity, sympathy and tenderness which are the first ingredients of love. They approached them, and fell into the clever traps Jehovah had disposed and spread intentionally in the body and on the belly of these two amphoræ.

"The first man and the first woman enjoyed during centuries the delicious embraces of the genii of the air, which conserved them in eternal youth.

"Such was their lot, and such could still be ours. Why was it that the parents of the human species, fatigued by celestial luxury, should try to find criminal enjoyments with one another?

"But what could you expect, my son? Kneaded of clay they had a taste for mud. Alas! they became acquainted with one another in the same way as they had known the genii.

"And that was what the demiurge had expressly forbidden them. Afraid, and with reason, that they would produce between them children as clumsy as themselves, terrestrial and heavy, he forbade them, under severest penalties, to approach each other. Such is the sense of Eve's words: 'But of the fruit of the tree which is in the midst of the garden, God hath said, Ye shall not eat of it, neither shall ye touch it lest ye die.' For you well understand, my son, that the apple which tempted wretched Eve was not the fruit of an apple-tree; that was an allegory the sense of which I have explained to you. Although imperfect, and sometimes violent and capricious, Jehovah was too intelligent a demiurge to be offended about an apple or a pomegranate. One has to be a bishop or a Capuchin to support such extravagant imaginations. And the proof that the apple was what I said, is that Eve was stricken by a punishment suitable to her fault. She had not been told 'You will digest laboriously,' but it was said to her 'You'll give birth in pain'; for logic sake what connection can be established, I beg of you, between an apple and difficult confinement? On the other hand, the suffering is correctly applied if the fault has been such as I showed you.

"That is, my son, the truthful explanation of original sin. It will teach you your duty, which is, to keep away from women. To follow this bent is fatal. All children born by those means are imbecile and miserable."

I was stupefied, and exclaimed:

"But, sir, could children be born in another way?"

"Happily, some are born in another way," was his reply; "a considerable number by the union of men with genii of the air. And such are intelligent and beautiful. By such means were born the giants of whom Hesiod and Moses speak. Thus also Pythagoras was born, to whose bodily formation his mother, a Salamander, had contributed a thigh of pure gold. Such also Alexander the Great, said to have been the son of Olympias and a serpent; Scipio Africanus, Aristomenes of Messina, Julius Cæsar, Porphyry, the Emperor Julian, who re-established the oath of fire abolished by Constantine the Apostate, Merlin the enchanter, child of a Sylph and a nun daughter of Charlemagne; Saint Thomas Aquinas, Paracelsus and, but recently, M. Van Helmont."

I promised M. d'Asterac, as such were the facts, that I would be willing to lend myself to the friendship of a Salamander, if one were to be found obliging enough to wish for me. He assured me that I should meet not one but a score or more, between whom I should have my free choice. And less by longing for the adventure than to give him pleasure, I asked the philosopher how it is possible to enter into communication with these aerial persons.

"Nothing easier," he replied. "All that's wanted is a glass ball, the use of which I'll explain to you. I have always at home a pretty good number of such balls, and in my study I'll very soon give you all necessary enlightenment. But, for to-day, my son, enough is said of it."

He rose, and walked in the direction of the ferry, where the ferryman waited for us, lying outstretched on his back and snoring at the moon. As soon as we had reached the opposite shore he quickly went on, and was soon lost in the darkness.

CHAPTER XIV

Visit to Mademoiselle Catherine—The Row in the Street and my
Dismissal

A CONFUSED sentiment as of a dream remained
with me after this long conversation, but the
thoughts of Catherine became keener. In despite of
the sublimities I had been listening to, I was overcome
by a powerful desire to see her, although I had not had any
supper. The ideas of philosophy had not sufficiently
penetrated me to cause anything like a disgust at that
pretty girl. I was resolved to follow my good fortune to
its end before becoming the prey of one of those beautiful
furies of the air, who do not want any human rival. My
only fear was that Catherine, at so late an hour, had become tired of waiting for me. So running along the river
bank, and passing the royal bridge at a gallop, I stormed
into the Rue du Bac. Within a single minute I had
reached the Rue de Grenelle, where I heard shouting
mixed up with the clashing of swords. The noise came
out of the very house Catherine had described to me.
In front of it, on the pavement, shadows and lanterns
were visible, and voices to be heard.

"Help, Jesus! I'm being murdered! . . . fall on the
Capuchin! Forward! Spike him! . . . Jesus, Mary, help
me! . . . Look on the pretty favourite lover! On him!
On him! Spike him, rascals, spike him hard!"

The windows of the adjoining houses were opened,
heads in night-caps appeared.

Suddenly all this noise and bustle passed before me
like a hunt in the forest, and I recognised Friar Ange

running away at such a speed that his sandals hammered on his behind, while three long devils of lackeys, armed like Swiss guards, followed him closely, larding him with the points of their javelins. Their master, a young gentleman, thick-set and ruddy-faced, continued to encourage them by voice and gesture, just as he would have done with dogs:

"Fall on! Fall on! Spike! The beast is tough!"

As he came close to me, I said:

"Oh! sir, have you no pity?"

"Sir," he replied, "it's easily seen that yonder Capuchin has not caressed your mistress, and you have not surprised madam, whom you see here, in the arms of this stinking beast. One cannot say anything about her financier, because one has manners. But a Capuchin cannot be borne. Burn the brazen-faced hussy!"

And he showed me Catherine under the doorway, clad in nothing but a chemise, her eyes glistening with tears, wringing her hands, more beautiful than ever, and murmuring in a dying voice, which cut deep into my soul:

"Don't kill him! It's Friar Ange, the little friar!"

The rascally lackeys returned, announcing that they had given up the pursuit at the appearance of the watch, but not without driving half a finger deep their pikes in the holy man's behind. The night-caps vanished from the windows, which were closed again, and whilst the young nobleman talked to his followers, I went up to Catherine, whose tears began to dry in the pretty folds of her smile. She said to me:

"The poor friar is safe, but I trembled for him. Men are terrible. When they love you they will not listen to anything."

"Catherine," I said, with no slight grudge, "did you make me come here for no other purpose than to listen to the quarrels of your friends? Alas! I have no right to take part in them."

"You would have had, M. Jacques," she said, "you should have had, if you had wanted."

"But," I continued, "you are the most courted lady in Paris. You never mentioned yonder young gentleman."

"I had no occasion to think of him. He came quite unexpectedly."

"And he surprised you with Friar Ange?"

"He fancied he saw things which did not occur. He is hot-headed and does not want to listen to any reason."

The half-opened chemise disclosed under transparent laces a breast swollen like a beautiful fruit and adorned like a budding rose. I took her in my arms and covered her bosom with kisses.

"Heavens!" she exclaimed, "in the street! Before M. d' Anquetil, who sees us."

"Who is M. d'Anquetil?"

"Pardi! he is the murderer of Friar Ange. Who else do you fancy he may be?"

"True, Catherine, no others are wanted. Your friends surround you in sufficient numbers."

"M. Jacques, do not insult me, if you please."

"I do not insult you, Catherine. I acknowledge your charms, to which I should like to render the same homage that others do."

"M. Jacques, what you have now said smells odiously of the cookshop, of that old codger who is your father."

"Not so very long ago, Mam'selle Catherine, you were mighty glad to smell its cooking-stove."

"Fie! the villain! the mean rascal! He outrages a woman!"

And now she began to squeak and squeal, and M

d'Anquetil left his servants, came up to us, and pushed
her into the house, calling her a cheat and a rake, went
into the passage behind her, and slammed the door in my
face.

CHAPTER XV

THE thought of Catherine occupied my mind all the
week following that vexatious adventure. Her
image glittered on the leaves of the folios over which I
bent in the library, close to my dear tutor; so much so that
Plotinus, Olympiodorus, Fabricius, Vossius spoke of
nothing else to me than a tiny damsel in a lace chemise.
These visions rendered me lazy. But, indulgent to others,
as to himself, M. Jérôme Coignard had a kind smile for
my trouble and distraction.

"Jacques Tournebroche," he said to me, one day,
"are you not struck by the variations in morals during
the course of the centuries? The books in this admirable
Asteracian collection witness to the uncertainties of mankind on this subject. If I reflect upon it, my son, it is
to put into your mind that solid and salutary idea that
no good morals are to be found outside religion, and that
the maxims of the philosophers, who pretend to institute
a natural morality, are nothing but whims and babblings
of foolish trash. The rationality of good morals is not
to be found in nature, which in itself is indifferent, ignorant of good or evil. It is in the divine word, which is
not to be trespassed against without after regret. The
laws of humanity are based on utility, and that can only
be an apparent and illusory utility, for nobody knows
naturally what is useful to mankind, nor what is really

103

appropriate to them. And we must not forget that our habits contain a good moiety of articles which are of prejudice alone. Upheld by the menace of chastisement, human laws may be eluded by cunning and dissimulation. Every man capable of reflection stands above them. Really they are nothing but booby traps.

"It is not the same thing, my boy, with laws divine. They are indefeasible, unavoidable and lasting. Their absurdity is in appearance only, and hides an inconceivable wisdom. If they wound our reason, it is because they are superior to it, and agree with the true issues of mankind, and not with the visible ends. It is useful to observe them when one has the good luck to know them. Yet I find no difficulty in confessing that the observance of those laws, contained in the Decalogue and in the commandments of the Church, is difficult at most times, even impossible without grace, and that sometimes has to be waited for, because it is a duty to hope. And therefore we are all miserable sinners.

"And that is where the dispositions of the Christian religion must be admired, which founds salvation principally on repentance. It must not be overlooked, my boy, that the greatest saints are penitents, and, as repentance is proportioned to the sin, it is in the greatest sinners that the material is found for the greatest saints. I could illustrate this doctrine with scores of admirable examples. But I have said enough to make you feel that the raw material of sanctity is concupiscence, incontinencies, all impurities of flesh and mind. After having collected the raw material nothing signifies but to fashion it according it theologic art and to model, so to say, a figure of penitence, which is a matter of a few years, a few days, sometimes of a single moment only, as is to be seen in the case of a perfect contrition. Jacques Tournebroche, if you listen well to my sayings, you will not consume yourself in miserable cares to become an honest man in a worldly sense, and you'll exclusively study to satisfy divine justice."

I could not help feeling the elevated wisdom enshrined in the maxims of my dear, good tutor; I was only afraid that these morals, should they be exercised without discrimination, would carry man to a disorderly life. I unfolded my doubts to M. Jérôme Coignard, who reassured me in the following terms:

"Jacobus Tournebroche, you do not take note of what I have just expressly told you, to wit, that what you call disorder is only such in the opinion of laymen and judges in law—ordinary and ecclesiastical—and in its bearing on human laws, which are arbitrary and transitory, and, in a word, to follow these laws is the act of a silly soul. A sensible man does not pride himself on acting according to the rules in force at the Châtelet and at the gaol.

"He is uneasy about his salvation, and does not think himself dishonoured by going to heaven by indirect ways as followed by the greatest saints. If the blessed Pélagie had not followed the same profession by which Jeannette, the hurdy-gurdy player you know, earned her living, under the portico of the Church of Saint Benoît ie Bétourné, that saint would not have been compelled to do full and copious penitence; and it is extremely probable that, after having lived in indifferent and banal chastity, she would not, at this very moment speak of her, be playing the psaltery before the tabernacle where the Holy of Holies reposes in his glory. Do you call disorder, so fine a regulation of a predestinated life? Certainly not! Leave such mean ways of speech to the Superintendent of Police, who after his death will hardly find the smallest place behind the unfortunates whom now he carries ignominiously to the spittel. Beyond the loss of the soul and eternal damnation there can be no other disorders, crimes or evils whatsoever in this perishable world, where one and all is to be ruled and adjusted with regard to a divine world. Confess, Tournebroche, my boy, that acts the most reprehensible in the opinion of men can lead to a good end, and do not try to reconcile the justice of men with the justice of God, which alone is just, not in our sense but with finality. And now, my boy, you'll greatly oblige me by looking into Vossius for the signification of five or six rather obscure words which the Panopolitan employs, and wherewith one has to do battle in the darkness of that insidious manner which astonished even the willing heart of Ajax, as reported by Homer, prince of poets and historians. These ancient alchemists had a tough style. Manilius, may it not displease M. d'Asterac, writes on the same subjects with more elegance."

Hardly had my tutor said these last words when a shadow arose between him and myself. It was that of M. d'Asterac, or rather it was M. d'Asterac himself, thin and black like a shadow.

It may be that he had not heard that talk, maybe he disdained it, for certainly he did not show any kind of resentment. On the contrary, he congratulated M. Jérôme Coignard on his zeal and knowledge, and further said that he relied on his enlightenment for the achievement of the greatest work that man had ever attempted. And turning to me he said:

"Be so good as to come for a moment to my study, where I intend to make known to you a secret of consequence."

I went with him to the same room where he had first received us, my tutor and myself, on the day we entered his service. I found there, exactly as on that occasion, ranged along the walls, the ancient Egyptians with golden faces. A glass globe of the size of a pumpkin stood on a table. M. d'Asterac sank on a sofa, and signed to me to take a seat near him, and having twice or thrice passed a hand covered with jewels and amulets across his forehead said:

"My son, I do not wish to injure you by believing that, after our conversation on the Isle of Swans, you still doubt of the existence of Sylphs and Salamanders, who are as real as men and perhaps more so, if one measures reality by the duration of the appearances by which it is displayed, their existence being very much longer than ours. Salamanders range from century to century in unalterable youth; some of them have seen Noah, Moses and Pythagoras. The wealth of their recollections and the freshness of their memory render their conversation attractive to the utmost. It has been pretended that they gain immortality in the arms of men, and that the hope of never dying led them into the beds of the philosophers. But those are fables unfit to seduce a reflecting mind. All union of sexes, far from ensuring immortality to lovers, is a sign of death, and we could not know love were we to live indefinitely. It could not be otherwise with the Salamanders, who look in the arms of the wise for nothing else but for one single kind of immortality— that is, of the race. It is also the only one which can be reasonably expected. And, much as I promise myself to prolong human life in a notable manner—that is, to extend it over at least five or six centuries—I have never flattered myself to assure it perpetuity. It would be in-·sane to want to go against the established rules of nature. Therefore, my son, reject as a vain fable the idea of immortality to be sucked in with a kiss. It is to the shame of more than one of the cabalists to have ever conceived such an idea. But for all that it is quite evident that Salamanders are inclined to man's love. You'll soon experience it yourself. I have sufficiently prepared you for a visit from them, and as, since the night of your initiation, you have not had any impure intercourse with a woman you will obtain the reward of your continency."

My natural candidness suffered by receiving praise which I had merited against my own will, and I wished to confess to M. d'Asterac my guilty thoughts. But he did not give me time to do so, and continued with vivacity:

"Nothing now remains for me, my son, but to give you the key which opens the empire of the genii. That is what I am going to do at once."

Rising he put a hand on the globe which covered one half of the table.

"This globe," he said, "is full of a solar powder which escapes being visible to you by its own purity. It is much too delicate to be seen by means of the coarse senses of men. So comes it, my son, that the finest parts of the universe are concealed from our sight and reveal themselves only to the learned, provided with apparatus proper for this discovery. The rivers and the aerial landscapes, for example, remain invisible, even as their aspect is a thousand times richer and more variegated than the most beautiful terrestrial landscape.

"Know, then, that in this bowl is a solar powder superlatively proper to exalt the fire we have within us. The effect of this exaltation is imminent. It consists of a subtlety of the senses allowing us to see and touch the aerial figures floating around us. As soon as you have broken the seal which locks the aperture of this globe, and inhaled the escaping solar powder, you will in this room discover one or more creatures resembling women by the system of curved outlines forming their bodies, but much more beautiful than was ever any woman, and who are in fact Salamanders. No doubt the one I saw last year in your father's cookshop will be the first one to appear here to you, as she has a liking for you, and I strongly counsel you to hasten to comply with her wishes. And now make yourself easy in that arm-chair, open the globe, and gently inhale the contents. Very soon you will see all I have announced to you realised, point by point. I leave you. Good-bye."

And he disappeared in a manner which was strangely sudden. I remained alone before that glass globe, hesitating to unlock it, afraid lest some stupefying exhalation should escape from it. I thought that perhaps M. d'Asterac had put in it, as an artifice, some of those vapours which benumb those who inhale them and make them dream of Salamanders. I was still not enough of a philosopher to be desirous of becoming happy by such means. Possibly, I said to myself, such vapours predispose to madness; and finally I became defiant enough to think of going to the library to ask advice of M. Jérôme Coignard. But I soon became aware that such would be a needless trouble; as soon as I began to speak to him of solar powder and aerial genii he would start: "Jacques Tournebroche, remember, my boy, that you must never put faith in absurdities, but bring home to your reason all matters except those of our holy religion. Stuff and nonsense all these globes and powders, with all the other follies of the cabala and the spagyric art."

I imagined I could hear him talk like that in the interval between two pinches of snuff, and I really did not know what to reply to such a Christian speech. On the other hand, I thought in advance how puzzled I should be to reply to M. d'Asterac when he inquired of me after news of the Salamander. What could I say? How was I to avow my reserve and my abstention without betraying my defiance and fear? And after all, without being aware of it, I was curious to try the adventure. I am not credulous. On the contrary I am marvellously inclined to doubt, and by this inclination to brave common-sense, as well as evidence and everything else. Of the strangest things that may be told me, I say to myself, "Why not?" This "Why not?" wronged my natural intelligence in sight of that globe. This "Why not?" pushed me towards credulity, and it may be interesting to remark, on this occasion, to believe in nothing means to believe in everything, and that the mind is not to be kept too free and too vacant, for fear that commodities of extravagant form and weight should enter by a loophole, commodities of a kind which could not find room in minds reasonably and tolerably well furnished with belief. And while, with my hand on the wax seal, I remembered what my mother had narrated to me of the magic bottle, my "Why not?" whispered to me that perhaps, after all, aerial fairies may be visible through the dust of the sun. But as soon as this idea, having entered into my mind, began to become easy therein, I found it to be odd, absurd and grotesque. Ideas, when they impose themselves, very soon become impudent. But few are apt to be better than pleasant passers-by; and, decidedly, this very one had somehow an air of madness. During the time I asked myself, "Shall I open it?" "Shall I not?" the seal, which I had held continuously between my pressing fingers, broke suddenly in my hand, and the flagon was open.

I waited, I observed, I saw nothing, I felt nothing. And I was disappointed, so much the hope of stepping out of nature is prone and ready to glide into our souls!

Nothing! Not even a vague or confused illusion, an uncertain image! What I had foreseen occurred. What a deception! I felt somewhat vexed. Reclined in my arm-chair I vowed to myself, before all the black-haired Egyptians surrounding me, to close my soul better in the future to the lies of the cabalists; and once more recognised my dear teacher's wisdom and resolved, like him, to be guided by reason in all matters not connected with faith, Christian and Catholic. Expecting the visit of a lady Salamander, what silliness! Is it possible that Salamanders exist? But what is known about it, and "Why not?"

Since noon the air was heavy, now it became stifling. Rendered torpid by long days of quietness and seclusion, I felt a weight on my forehead and eyes. The approach of a thunderstorm lay heavy on me. I let my arms hang down, and, with head thrown back, and eyes closed, I glided into a doze full of golden Egyptians and lustful shadows. In this uncertain state the sense of love alone was alive in my body, like a fire in the night. How long it had lasted I could not say, when I was awakened by a sound of light steps and the rustling of a dress. I opened my eyes and gave a great shout.

A marvellous creature stood before me, clad in black satin, a lace veil on her head—a dark woman with blue eyes, of resolute features in a juvenile and pure skin, round cheeks and the mouth animated as by an invisible kiss. The short skirt let little feet be seen, dancing, jolly, spirited feet. She held herself upright, but was round, somewhat thick-set, in her voluptuous perfection. Under the black velvet ribbon round her throat a little square of her bosom was visible, brown, but dazzling. She looked on me with an air of curiosity. I have said already how sleep had rendered me amorous. I rose quickly, and stepped forward.

"Excuse me," she said, "I am looking for M. d'Asterac."

I said to her:

"Madam, there is no M. d'Asterac. There is you and I. I expected you. You are a Salamander. I have opened the crystal flagon. You have come. You are mine."

I took her in my arms and covered with kisses all places my lips could find uncovered by her dress.

She tore herself away and said:

"You are mad."

"That is quite natural," I replied. "Who in my place could remain sane?"

She lowered her eyes, blushed, and smiled. I fell at her feet.

"As M. d'Asterac is not here," she said, "I had better retire."

"Remain!" I cried, and bolted the door.

"Do you know if he will soon be back?"

"No, madam! He will not return for a long time. He left me alone with the Salamanders. But I want one only, and that one is you."

I lifted her in my arms, carried her to the sofa, fell down on it with her, and smothered her with kisses. I was out of my senses. She screamed, I did not hear her; she pushed me back with outstretched hands; her finger-nails scratched me all over, and her vain defence only excited my frenzy. I pressed, enlaced her, she fell back worn out. Her mollified body gave way, she closed her eyes and soon, in my triumph, her beautiful arms, reconciled, pressed me on her bosom.

Released, alas! from that delicious embrace, we looked at one another with surprise. Occupied to get up again decently she put her dress in order and remained silent.

"I love you," I said. "What is your name?"

I did not think her to be a Salamander, and to say the truth never did think so.

"My name is Jahel," she said.

"What! you're the niece of Mosaïde?"

"Yes; but keep quiet. If he should know——"

"What would he do?"

"Oh! nothing to me—nothing. But to you the worst. He dislikes Christians."

"And you?"

"Oh! I? I dislike the Jews."

"Jahel, do you love me a little?"

"It seems to me, sir, that after what we have just now said to one another, your question is an offence."

"True, mademoiselle, but I try to obtain forgiveness for a vivacity, an ardour, which did not take the leisure to consult your sentiments."

"Oh! monsieur, do not make yourself out to be more guilty than you really are. All your violence, and all your passion, would not have served you at all, had I not found you lovable. When I saw you sleeping in that arm-chair, I liked your looks, waited for your awakening —the rest you know."

As reply I gave her a kiss, she gave it me back, what a kiss! I fancied fresh-gathered strawberries melting in my mouth. My desire revived and passionately I pressed her on my heart.

"This time," she said, "be less hasty, and do not think only of yourself. You must not be selfish in love. Young men do not sufficiently know that. But we teach them."

And we immersed ourselves in an unfathomable depth of deliciousness.

After that the divine Jahel asked of me:

"Have you a comb? I look like a witch."

"Jahel," I answered, "I have no comb. I had expected a Salamander. I adore you."

"Adore me, dearest, but remain secret. You do not know Mosaïde."

"What, Jahel. Is he still so terrible as that, at the age of one hundred and thirty years, of which he has lived sixty-five inside a pyramid?"

"I see, my friend, that stories of my uncle have been told you and that you were simple enough to believe them. Nobody knows his age; I myself am ignorant of it, but I have always known him as an old man. I know only that he is robust and of uncommon strength. He has been a banker at Lisbon, where he killed a Christian he surprised in the arms of my Aunt Myriam. He took to flight, and carried me with him. Since then he loves me with the tenderness of a mother. He tells me things that are told to little children only, and he cries when he sees me asleep."

"Do you live with him?"

"Yes, in the keeper's lodge, at the other end of the park."

"I know; you reach it by the lane where mandrakes are to be found. How is it that I did not meet you before? By what sinister destiny, living so near you, have I lived without seeing you? But what do I say, lived? Is it to live without knowing you? Are you shut up in yonder lodge?"

"It is true I am somewhat of a recluse, and cannot go for walks as I wish, to the shops, to theatres. Mosaïde's tenderness does not leave me any liberty. He guards me jealously, and, besides six small gold cups he brought with him from Lisbon, he loves but me on earth. As he is much more attached to me than he was to my Aunt

Myriam, he would kill you, dear, with a better heart than
he killed the Portuguese. I warn you so, to impress the
necessity of discretion on you, and because it is not a
consideration which could stop a brave gentleman. Are
you of a good family, my friend?"

"Alas! no; my father applies himself to a mechanic
art, and has a sort of trade."

"And he is not of any of the professions? Does not
belong to the banking world? No? It is a pity. Well,
you're to be loved for yourself. But speak the truth. Is
M. d'Asterac to be back shortly?"

At this name and question a terrible doubt came in my
mind. I suspected the enchanting Jahel to have been
sent by the cabalist to play the part of a Salamander with
me. I went so far as to excuse her in my mind of being
the nymph of that old fool. To obtain an immediate explanation I bluntly and coarsely asked her if she was in
the habit of acting the Salamander in the castle.

"I don't understand you," she replied, looking at me
with eyes full of innocent surprise. "You speak like M.
d'Asterac himself, and I could believe you to be attacked
by his mania also, if I had not proved that you do not
share the aversion to women that he has. He cannot
stand any female, and it is a real annoyance to me to see
and speak with him. Nevertheless I was looking for him
when I found you."

The pleasure of being reassured made me again
smother her with kisses.

She managed to let me see that she had black stockings
which, over the knees, were held up by garters ornamented
with diamond buckles and that sight brought back my
mind to ideas pleasant to her. Besides she entreated me
on the welcome subject with much ability and fervour, and
I was aware that she became excited over the game at

the very moment I began to get fatigued from it. However I did my best, and was fortunate enough to spare the beautiful girl a disgrace which she did not deserve in the least. It seemed to me that she was not discontented with me. She rose, very quietly, and said:

"Do you really not know if M. d'Asterac will soon be back? I confess to you that I came to ask him for a small amount of that pension he owes to my uncle, a trifle only. I very badly want it just now."

I took my purse out and handed her, with due excuses, the three crowns it contained. It was all that remained of the too rare liberalities of the cabalist who, professing to dislike money, unluckily forgot to pay me my salary.

I asked Mademoiselle Jahel if I should not have the pleasure of seeing her again.

"You will," she replied.

And we agreed that she should ascend at night-time to my room whenever she could escape from the lodge, where she was pretty nearly a prisoner.

"Take care to remember," I told her, "that my room is the fourth on the right of the corridor and Abbé Coignard's the fifth. The others give access to the lofts, where two or three scullions lodge, and hundreds of rats."

She assured me that she would be very careful not to make a mistake, and would scratch on my door and not on any other.

"Besides," she continued, "your Abbé Coignard seems to be a very good man, and I am pretty sure that we have in no way to be afraid of him. I looked at him, through a peephole, on the day he came with you to visit my uncle! I thought him amiable, though I could not hear what he said. Principally his nose I thought to be really ingenious and capable. A man with such a nose ought to be full of expedients and I very much wish to become acquainted with him. One can but better one's mind by having intercourse with people of high spirit. I am only sorry that my uncle was not pleased with his words and scoffing humour. Mosaïde hates him, and of his capacity for hate no Christian can form an idea."

"Mademoiselle," I replied, "Monsieur l'Abbé Jérôme Coignard is a very learned man, and he has in addition philosophy and kindness. He knows the world, and you are quite right in believing him to be a good counsellor. I regulate myself fully after his advice. But, tell me, did you see me also, on yonder day, at the lodge, through the peephole you spoke of?"

"I saw you," she said to me, "and I will not hide from you that I was pleased. But I must return to my uncle. Good-bye."

The same evening, after supper, M. d'Asterac did not fail to ask me for news of the Salamander. His curiosity troubled me somewhat. My answer was that the meeting had surpassed all my expectations, but that I thought it my duty to confine myself to a discretion due to such kind of adventures.

"That discretion, my son," he said, "is not of so much use in your case as you represent. Salamanders do not want their amours to be kept secret, they are not ashamed of them. One of those nymphs who loves me does not know of a sweeter pastime than to engrave my initials enlaced with hers on the bark of trees, as you can see for yourself by examining the stems of five or six Scotch firs, the exquisite tops of which you can see from yonder windows. But have you not, my son, learned that that kind of amour, truly sublime, far from leaving any fatigue behind, lends to the heart a new vigour? I am sure that after what passed to-day you'll employ your night in translating at least sixty pages of Zosimus the Pano-politan."

I confessed that on the contrary I felt very sleepy, which he explained by reason of the astonishment produced by such a first meeting. And so the great man remained convinced that I had had intercourse with a Salamander. I felt some scruples at deceiving him, but I was compelled to do it and, besides, he deceived himself to such a degree that it was hardly possible to add anything to his illusions. So I ascended peacefully to my room, went to bed, and blew the candle out at the end of the most glorious day of my life.

CHAPTER XVI

Jahel comes to my Room—What the Abbé saw on the Stairs—
His Encounter with Mosaïde

JAHEL kept her word. On the second day after, she
scratched at my door. We were a great deal more
comfortable in my room than we had been in M.
d'Asterac's study, and what had taken place at our first
meeting was but child's play in comparison to what love
inspired us at our second opportunity. She tore herself
out of my arms at the dawn with a thousand oaths to
join me again very soon, calling me her soul, her life,
her dearest sweetheart.

That day I rose very late. When I reached the library,
my master was already sitting over the papyrus of Zosimus, his pen in one hand, his magnifying-glass in the
other, and worthy of the admiration of anyone having
due consideration for good literature.

"Jacques Tournebroche," he said to me, "the principal
difficulty of this reading consists in not a few of the letters
being easily confounded with others, and it is important
for the success of the deciphering to make a list of the
characters lending themselves to similar mistakes, because by not taking such precautions we are running the
risk of employing the wrong terminations, to our eternal
shame and just vituperation. I have to-day already committed some ridiculous blunders. It must have been
because, since daybreak, my mind has been troubled by
what I saw last night, and of which I will give you an
account.

"I woke up in the morning twilight, and I felt a longing for a glass of that light white wine about which I made yesterday my compliments to M. d'Asterac, if you remember. For there exists, my son, between white wine and the crowing of the cock a sympathy, doubtless dating from Noah's time, and I am certain that if Saint Peter, in that sacred night he passed in the yard of the great high priest, had had just a mouthful of Moselle claret or only wine of Orleans, he never would have disowned Jesus Christ before the cock crowed a second time. But in no sense, my boy, have we to regret that bad action; it was of the utmost importance that the prophecies were fulfilled, and if Peter, or Cephas, had not committed on that very night the worst of infamies, he would not now be the greatest saint in heaven, and the corner-stone of our holy Church, to the confusion of honest men according to the world, who have to see the keys of their eternal bliss held by a dastardly knave. O salutary example, which, drawing man out of the fallacious inspirations of human honour, leads him on the road of salvation! O masterly disposition of religion! O divine wisdom, exalting the meek and wretched to the humiliation of the haughty! O marvel! O mystery! To the eternal shame of the Pharisees and lawyers, a common mariner of the Lake of Tiberias, who by his gross cowardice had become the laughing-stock of the kitchen wenches who warmed themselves with him in the courtyard of the high priest, a churl and a dastard, who denied his master and his faith before slatterns certainly not so pretty by far as the chamber-maid of the bailiff's wife at Séez, wears the triple crown, the pontifical ring on his finger and rules over princes and bishops, over kings and emperors, is invested with the right to bind and loose; the most respectable of men, the most honest dame, cannot enter heaven unless he gives them admission.

"But tell me, Tournebroche, my boy, at what part of
my narrative had I arrived when I got muddled over that
great Saint Peter, the prince of apostles? If I remember well I spoke to you of a glass of white wine I drank
at daybreak. I came down to the pantry in my shirt,
and took out of a certain cupboard, the key of which I
had prudently kept by me the day before, a bottle, the
contents of which I emptied with no little pleasure.
Afterwards reascending the stairs I met, between the
second and third flights, a tiny damsel clad as a pierrot,
who descended the steps. She seemed to be mightily
afraid, and fled into the farthest corner of the passage.
I followed her, caught her, took her in my arms, and
kissed her in a sudden and irresistible outbreak of sympathy. Don't blame me, my boy; in my place you would
have done as much, perhaps more. It was a pretty girl,
reminding me of the serving-maid of the bailiff's wife,
but with more vivacity in her looks. She did not dare to
scream. She whispered breathless in my ear: 'Leave me,
leave me; you're mad!' Look here, Tournebroche, I
still have the marks of her finger nails on my wrist. O
that I could keep as vivid on my lips the impression of
the kiss she gave me!"

"What, Monsieur Abbé," I exclaimed, "she gave you a
kiss?"

"Be sure, my boy, that in my place you would have had
one too—that is to say, if you, as I did, seized the opportunity. I believe I told you that I held the damsel in
close embrace. She tried to fly from me, she suppressed
her screams, she murmured groans. 'For heaven's sake,
leave me! It begins to be light, a moment more and I am
lost.' Her fears, her fright, her danger—who could be
barbarous enough not to be affected by them? I am not
inhuman. I gave her freedom at the price of a kiss,

which she gave me quickly. On my word, I never enjoyed a more delicious one."

At this part of his tale, my dear tutor, raising his nose
to sniff a pinch of snuff, became aware of my confusion
and pain, which he thought to be utter astonishment, and
continued to say:

"Jacques Tournebroche, all that remains for me to tell
will astonish you still more. To my regret I let the pretty
girl go, but curiosity tempted me to follow her. I went
down the stairs after her, saw her cross the lobby, go out
by a little door opening on the fields in the direction where
the park extends farthest, and run up the lane. I followed
swiftly. I was quite sure that she would not go far,
dressed as a pierrot and wearing a night-cap. She took
the path wherein the mandrakes dwell. My curiosity
doubled, and I followed her up to Mosaïde's lodge. At
this moment the hideous Jew appeared at a window in his
dressing-gown and monstrous headgear, like one of those
figures who show themselves at the stroke of noon, outside
those old clocks more Gothic and more ridiculous than the
churches wherein they are kept, for the enjoyment of the
yokels and the profit of the beadle.

"He discovered me, hidden as I was behind the foliage,
at the very moment when that pretty girl, fleet as Galatea,
slipped into the lodge. It looked as if I had followed
her up in the manner, way and habit of those satyrs of
which we have spoken of late when conferring on the
finest passages of Ovid. My dress could but add to such
resemblance—did I tell you, my boy, that I wore only a
shirt? Seeing me, Mosaïde's eyes vomited fire. Out of his
dirty yellow greatcoat he drew a neat little stiletto and
shook it through the window with an arm in no way
weighed down by age. He roared bilingual curses on
me. Yes, Tournebroche, my grammatical knowledge

authorises me to say that his curses were bilingual, that
Spanish, or rather Portuguese, was mixed in them with
Hebrew. I went into a rage at not being able to catch
their exact sense, as I do not know these languages,
although I can recognise them by certain sounds which
are frequent when they are spoken. It is very possible
that he accused me of wanting to corrupt that girl, whom
I believe to be his niece Jahel, whom, as you will remember, M. d'Asterac has repeatedly mentioned to us. As
such his invectives were rather flattering to me, as I have
become, my boy, by the progress of age and the fatigues
of an agitated life, so that I cannot aspire any longer to
the love of juvenile maidens. Alas! should I become a
bishop that is a dish of which I shall never taste. I am
sorry for it. But it is no good to be closely attached to the
perishable things of this world, and we are compelled to
leave what leaves us. Accordingly Mosaïde, brandishing
his stiletto, squalled out his hoarse sounds mingled with
sharp yelpings in such a manner that I felt insulted, as
well as vituperated, in a chant or song. And without
flattering myself, my dear boy, I can say that I have been
treated as a rake and a seducer in a tune solemn and
ceremonious. When yonder Mosaïde brought his imprecations to an end, I endeavoured to let him have my reply in
two languages also. I replied in a mixture of Latin and
French that he was a manslayer and a sacrilegist, who
murdered tiny babes and stabbed sacred hosts. The fresh
morning wind blowing between my naked legs reminded
me that I wore a shirt only. I felt somewhat embarrassed,
because it is evident, my boy, that a man without breeches
is in a state highly inconvenient to speak of sacred truth,
to confound error and to prevent crime. Withal I gave
him a prodigious sketch of his outrages, and I threatened
him with the terrors of justice both human and divine."

"What do you say, my good master?" I nearly screamed, "yonder Mosaïde, who has such a pretty niece, kills newborn babes and stabs hosts?"

"I don't know anything about him," M. Jérôme Coignard replied, "and besides cannot know it. But those crimes are his, they are of his race, and I can charge him with them without slandering him. I place on that miscreant's back a long array of flagitious ancestors. You cannot have remained ignorant of all that is said of the Jews and of their abominable rites. You may see in an ancient cosmography of Munster in Westphalia a drawing representing some Jews mutilating a child; they are recognisable by the wheel or round of cloth they wear on their clothes in sign of infamy. For all that I do not believe these misdeeds to be of their daily and domestic use. I also doubt that the majority of Israelites are inclined to outrage the holy wafers. To accuse them of doing so would be to believe that they are as deeply convinced of the divinity of our Lord Jesus Christ as we are ourselves. Sacrilege without faith is unbelievable, and the Jew who stabbed a host rendered by that very deed a sincere homage to the truth of transubstantiation. These are fables, my boy, to be left to the ignorant and, if I throw them in the face of that horrible Mosaïde, I do it less by the counsels of sound criticism than by the impressive suggestions of resentment and anger."

"Oh! sir," I said, "you might have contented yourself with reproaching him for the murder of the Portuguese he killed in the frenzy of his jealousy; that certainly was a murder."

"What!" broke out my good master. "Mosaïde has has killed a Christian? He is dangerous, my dear Tournebroche. You'll have to come to the same conclusion that I have arrived at myself about this adventure.

It is quite certain that his niece is the mistress of M.
d'Asterac, whose room she doubtless had just left when
I met her on the stairs.

"I am too religious a man not to be sorry that so
amiable a person comes of the Jewish race, who crucified
Jesus Christ. Alas! do not doubt, my dear boy, that
villain Mordecai is the uncle of an Esther who does not
need to macerate six months in myrrh to become worthy
of the bed of a king. That old spagyric raven is not the
man fit for such a beauty, and I am rather inclined to
take an interest in her myself.

"Mosaïde will have to hide her very secretly and
carefully; should she show herself once only at the
promenade or the theatre, she would have all the world
at her feet on the following morning. Don't you wish to
see her, Tournebroche?"

I replied that I wished it very much. And then both
of us drove deeper in our Greek.

CHAPTER XVII

Outside Mademoiselle Catherine's House—We are invited in by M. d'Anquetil—The Supper—The Visit of the Owner and the horrible Consequences

THAT evening my tutor and I happened to be in the Rue du Bac, and as it was rather warm M. Jérôme Coignard said to me:

"Jacques Tournebroche, my son, would it be agreeable to you to turn to the left, into the Rue de Grenelle, in quest of a tavern—that's to say, to some place where we could get a pot of wine for two sous? I am rather short of cash, my boy, and strongly suppose you to be no better off. M. d'Asterac, who possibly can make gold, does not give any to his secretaries and servants, as we well know, to our cost, you and I. He leaves us in a lamentable state. I have never a penny in my pocket, and it will become necessary to remedy that evil by industry and artifice. It is a fine thing to bear poverty with an even mind, like Epictetus of glorious memory. But it is an exercise I am tired of and which has become tedious by habit. I feel it is high time for a change of virtue, and to insinuate myself into the possession of wealth without being possessed by it, which certainly is the noblest state to be reached by the soul of a philosopher. I shall feel myself obliged, very soon, to earn profits of some kind to show that my sagacity has not failed me during my prosperity. I am in search of the means to reach such an issue; my mind is occupied by it, Tournebroche."

And as my dear tutor spoke with a noble distinction

of that matter, we came near the pretty dwelling wherein
M. de la Guéritude had lodged Mademoiselle Catherine.
"You'll recognise it, she had said to me, by the roses on
the balcony." There was not light enough to see the
roses, but I fancied I could smell them. Advancing a
few yards I saw her at the window watering flowers.
She recognised me, laughed, and threw me kisses with
her chubby little hand. Upon that a hand passing
through the open window slapped her cheek. In her surprise she let the water jug slip out of her hand, it fell
down into the street, at a hair's breadth from my tutor's
head. The slapped beauty disappeared from the window,
and the ear-boxer appeared; he leaned out and shouted:

"Thank God, sir, you are not the Capuchin. I cannot
stand seeing my mistress throw kisses to that stinking
beast, who continually prowls under this window. For
once I have not to blush at her choice. You look quite
an honest man, and I believe I have seen you before.
Do me the honour to come up. Within a supper is prepared. You'll do me a real favour to partake of it, as
well as the abbé, who has just had a pot of water thrown
over his head, and shakes himself like a wetted dog.
After supper we'll have a game of cards, and at daybreak
we'll go hence to cut one another's throats. But that will
be purely and simply an act of civility and only to do
you honour, sir, for, in truth, that girl is not worth the
thrust of a sword. She is a hussy. I'll never see her
any more."

I recognised in the speaker, the Monsieur d'Anquetil
whom I had seen a short time ago excite his followers so
vehemently to spike Friar Ange. Now he spoke with
courtesy and treated me as a gentleman. I understood
all the favour he conferred on me by his consent to cut
my throat. Nor was my dear tutor less sensible of so

much urbanity, and after having shaken himself he said
to me:

"Jacques Tournebroche, my son, we cannot say nay to
such a gracious invitation."

Already two lackeys had come down bearing torches.
They led us to a room where a collation had been prepared
on a table lit up by wax candles burning in two silver
candelabra. M. d'Anquetil invited us to be seated, and
my good master tied his napkin round his throat. He
already had a thrush on his fork when heart-rending
sobs were to be heard.

"Don't take any notice of yonder noise," said M.
d'Anquetil, "it's only Catherine, whom I have locked in
that room."

"Ah! sir; you must forgive her," said my kind-hearted
tutor, looking sadly on the gold-brown toasted little bird
on his fork. "The pleasantest meat tastes bitter when
seasoned with tears and moans. Could you have the
heart to let a woman cry? Reprieve this one, I beg of
you! Is she then so blamable for having thrown a kiss
to my young pupil, who was her neighbour and companion
in the days of their common mediocrity, at a time when
this pretty girl's charms were only famous under the
vine arbour of the *Little Bacchus*? It was but an innocent action, as much so as a human, and particularly a
woman's, action can ever be innocent, and altogether
free of the original stain. Allow me also to say, sir, that
jealousy is a Gothic sentiment, a sad reminder of barbaric
customs, which has no business to survive in a delicate,
well-born soul."

"Monsieur l'Abbé," inquired M. d'Anquetil, "on what
grounds do you presume me to be jealous? I am not!
But I cannot stand a woman mocking me."

"We are playthings of the winds," said my tutor, and

sighed. "Everything laughs at us, the sky, the stars, rain and shadow, zephyr and light and woman. Let Catherine sup with us. She is pretty and will enliven our table. Whatever she may have done, that kiss and the rest, do not render her the less pleasant to look at. The infidelities of women do not spoil their beauty. Nature, pleased to adorn them, is indifferent to their faults; follow her, and forgive Catherine."

I seconded my tutor's entreaties, and M. d'Anquetil consented to free the prisoner. He went to the door of the room from whence the cries came, unlocked it, and called Catherine, whose only reply was to redouble her wailing.

"Gentlemen," her lover said to us, "there she is lying flat on her belly, her head plunged in the pillows, and at every sob raising her rump ridiculously. Look at that. It is for such we take so much trouble and commit so many absurdities! Catherine, come to supper."

But Catherine did not move, and continued to cry. He pulled her by the arm, by the waist. She resisted. He became more pressing, and said caressingly:

"Come, darling, get up."

But she was stubborn, would not change place, and stuck there, holding to pillows and mattress.

At last her lover lost patience, swore, and shouted rudely:

"Get up, slut!"

At once she got up, and, smiling amid her tears, took his arm and came with him to the dining-room, looking the very picture of a happy victim.

She sat down between M. d'Anquetil and me, her head inclined on the shoulder of her lover the while her foot felt for mine under the table.

"Gentlemen," said our host, "forgive my vivacity, an

impulse I cannot regret, because it gives me the honour to entertain you at this place. To say the truth, I cannot endure all the whims of this pretty girl, and I have been very suspicious since I surprised her with her Capuchin."

"My dear friend," Catherine said, pressing at the same time her foot on mine, "your jealousy goes astray. You should know that my only liking is for M. Jacques."

"She jests," said M. d'Anquetil.

"Do not doubt of it," said I. "It is quite evident that she loves you, and you alone."

"Without flattering myself," he replied, "I have somehow attracted her attachment. But she is coquettish and fickle."

"Give me something to drink," said the abbé.

M. d'Anquetil passed him the demijohn and exclaimed:

"By gad! abbé, you who belong to the Church, you'll tell us why women love Capuchins."

M. Coignard wiped his lips and said:

"The reason is that Capuchins love humbly, and never refuse anything. Another reason is that neither reflection nor courtesy weakens their natural instincts. Sir, yours is a generous wine."

"You do me too much honour," replied M. d'Anquetil. "It is M. de la Guéritude's. I have taken his mistress. I may as well take his bottles."

"Nothing is more equitable," said my tutor. "I see, with pleasure, that you rise above prejudices."

"Do not praise me, abbé, more than I deserve. My birth renders easy to me what may be difficult for the vulgar. A commoner is compelled to have some restraint in all his doings. He is tied down to rigid probity; but a gentleman enjoys the honour of fighting for his king and his pleasure, and does not need to encumber

himself with foolish trifles. I have seen active service
under M. de Villars, and in the War of Succession, and
have also run the risk of being killed without any reason
in the battle of Parma. The least you can do is to leave
me free to lick my servants, to balk my creditors, and
take, if it please me, the wives of my friends—likewise
their mistresses."

"You speak nobly," said my good master, "and you
are careful to maintain the prerogatives of the nobility."

"I have not," replied M. d'Anquetil, "those scruples
which intimidate the crowd of ordinary men, and which
I consider good only to stop the timorous and restrain
the wretched."

"Well spoken!" said my tutor.

"I do not believe in virtue," replied the other.

"You're right," said my master again. "With his
quite peculiar shape, the human animal could not be
virtuous without being somewhat deformed. Look, for
an example, on this pretty girl supping with us; on her
beautiful bosom, her marvellously rounded form, and
the rest. In what part of her enchanting body could
she lodge a grain of virtue? There is no room for it;
everything is so firm, so juicy, solid, and plump! Virtue,
like the raven, nests in ruins. Her dwellings are the
cavities and wrinkles of the human body. I myself, sir,
who, since my childhood, have meditated over the austere
principles of religion and philosophy, could not insinuate
into myself a minimum of virtue otherwise than by means
of constitutional flaws produced by sufferings and age.
And ever more I absorbed less virtue than pride. In
doing so I got into the habit of addressing to the Divine
Creator of this world the following prayer: 'My Lord,
preserve me from virtue if it is to lead me from godliness.'

Ah! godliness; this it is possible and necessary to attain. That is our decent ending. May we reach it some day! In the meantime, give me something to drink."

"I'll confess," said M. d'Anquetil, "that I do not believe in a God."

"Now, for once, sir, I must blame you," said the abbé "One must believe in God, and all the truths of our holy religion."

M. d'Anquetil protested.

"You make game of us, abbé, and take us to be worse ninnies than we really are. As I have said, I do not believe either in God or devil, and I never go to Mass— the king's Mass alone excepted. The sermons of the priests are stories for old women, bearable, perhaps, in such times as when my grandmother saw the Abbé de Choisy, dressed as a woman, distribute the holy bread at the Church of Saint Jacques du Haut Pas. In those times there may have been religion; to-day there is none, thank God!"

"By all the Saints and all the devils, don't speak like that, my friend," exclaimed Catherine. "As sure as that pie stands on this table God exists! And if you want a proof of it, let me say, that when, last year, on a certain day, I was in direful distress and penury, I went, on the advice of Friar Ange, to burn a wax candle in the Church of the Capuchins, and on the following I met M. de la Guéritude at the promenade, who gave me this house, with all the furniture it contains, the cellar full of wine, some of which we enjoy to-night, and sufficient money to live honestly."

"Fie! fie!" said M. d'Anquetil, "the idiot makes God Almighty interfere in dirty affairs. This shocks and wounds one's feelings, even if one is an atheist."

"My dear sir," said my good tutor, "it is a great deal

better to compromise God in dirty business, as does that simple-minded girl, than, as you do, to chase Him out of the world He has created. If He has not expressly sent that burly contractor to Catherine, His creature, He at least suffered her to meet him. We are ignorant of His ways, and what this simpleton says contains more truth, maybe mixed and alloyed with blasphemy, than all the vain words a reprobate draws out of the emptiness of his heart. Nothing is more despicable than the libertinism of mind that the youth of our days make a show of. Your words make me shiver. Am I to reply to them by proofs out of the Holy Scriptures and the writings of the fathers? Shall I make you hear God speaking to the patriarchs and to the prophets: *Si locutus est Abraham et semini ejus in sæcula?* Shall I spread out before you the traditions of the Church? Invoke against you the authority of both Testaments? Blind you with Christ's miracles, and His words as miraculous as His deeds? No! I will not arm myself with those holy weapons. I fear too much to pollute them in such a fight, which is not at all solemn. In her prudence the Church warns us not to risk turning edification into a scandal. Therefore I will not speak, sir, of that wherewith I have been fed on the steps of sanctuaries. But, without violating the chaste modesty of my soul, and without exposing to profanation the sacred mysteries, I'll show you God overawing human reason, I'll show you it by the philosophy of pagans, and by the tittle-tattle of ungodly persons. Yes, sir, I'll make you avow that you recognise Him, against your own free will. Much as you want to pretend He does not exist you cannot but agree that, if a certain order prevails in this world, such order is divine—flows out of the spring and fountain of all order."

"I agree," replied M. d'Anquetil, reclining in his arm-chair and fondling his finely shaped calves.

"Therefore, take care," said my good tutor. "When you say that God does not exist what else are you doing but linking thought, directing reason, and manifesting in your innermost soul, the principle of all thought, and all reason, which is God? Is it possible only to attempt to establish that He is not, without illuminating, by the most paltry reasoning, which still is reasoning, some remains of the harmony He has established in the universe?"

"Abbé," replied M. d'Anquetil, "you are a humorous sophist. It is well known in our days that this world is the work of chance, and it is superfluous to speak of a providence, since natural philosophers have discovered, by means of their telescopes, that winged frogs are living on the moon."

"Well, sir," replied my good master, "I am in no way angry that winged frogs are living on the moon; such kind of marsh-birds are very worthy inhabitants of a world which has not been sanctified by the blood of our Lord Jesus Christ. True, we only know the minor part of the universe, and it is quite possible, as M. d'Asterac says—who is a bit of a fool—that this earth is no more than a spot of mud in the infinity of worlds. Maybe the astronomer Copernicus was not altogether dreaming when he taught that, mathematically, the earth is not the centre of creation. I have also read that an Italian of the name of Galileo, who died miserably, shared Copernicus' opinion, and in our days we see little M. de Fontenelle entertaining the same ideas. But all this is but a vain imagination, fit only to unhinge weak minds. What does it matter if the physical world is larger or smaller, of one shape or another? It is quite sufficient that it can be duly considered only by intelligence and reason for God to be manifest therein.

"If a wise man's meditations could be of some use to you, sir, I will inform you how such proof of God's existence, better than the proof of St Anselm, and quite independent of that resulting from Revelation, appeared to me suddenly in unclouded limpidity. It was at Séez, five and twenty years ago when I was the bishop's librarian. The gallery windows opened on a courtyard where, every morning, I saw a kitchen wench clean the saucepans. She was young, tall, sturdy. A slight down, shadowlike, over her lips lent irritating and proud gracefulness to her countenance. Her entangled hair, meagre bosom, and long, naked arms were worthy of an Adonis or a Diana. She was of a boyish beauty. I loved her for it, loved her strong, red hands. All in all that girl evoked in me a longing as rude and brutal as herself. You know how imperious such longings are. I made her understand by sign and word. Without the slightest hesitation she quickly let me know that my longings were not stronger than hers, and appointed the very next night for a meeting, to take place in the loft, where she slept on the hay, by gracious permission of the bishop, whose saucepans she cleaned. Impatiently I waited for the night. When at last her shadow covered the earth I climbed, by means of a ladder, to the loft, where the girl expected me. My first thought was to embrace her, my second to admire the links which brought me into her arms. For, sir, a young ecclesiastic—a kitchen wench—a ladder—a bundle of hay. What a train! What regulation! What a concourse of pre-established harmonies! What a concatenation of cause and effect! What a proof of God's existence! I was strangely struck by it, and mightily glad I am to

be able to add this profane demonstration to the reasons
furnished by theology, which are, however, amply
sufficient."

"Abbé," said Catherine, "the only weak point in your
story is that the girl had a meagre bosom. A woman
without breasts is like a bed without pillows. But don't
you know, d'Anquetil, what we might do?"

"Yes," said he, "play a game of ombre, which is
played by three."

"If you will," she said. "But, dear, have the pipes
brought in. Nothing is pleasanter than to smoke a pipe
of tobacco when drinking wine."

A lackey brought the cards and pipes, which we lit.
Soon the room was full of dense smoke, wherein our
host and the Abbé Coignard played gravely at piquet.

Luck followed my dear tutor up to the moment when
M. d'Anquetil, fancying he saw him for the third time
score fifty-five when he had only made forty points, called
him a Greek, a villainous trickster, a Knight of Transyl-
vania, and threw a bottle at his head, which broke on
the table, flooding it with wine.

"Well, sir," said the abbé, "you'll have to take the
trouble to open another bottle: we are thirsty."

"With pleasure," replied M. d'Anquetil. "But, abbé,
know that a gentleman does not mark points he has not
made, and does not cheat at cards except at the king's
card-table, round which all sorts of people are assembled,
to whom one owes nothing. On any other table it is a
vile action. Abbé, say, do you want to be looked on as
an adventurer?"

"It is remarkable," said my good tutor, "that you
blame at cards or dice a practice so much commended in
the art of war, politics and trade; in each of these people
glorify themselves by correcting the injuries of fortune.

It is not that I do not pique myself on honesty when playing at cards. Thank God, I always play straight, and you must have been dreaming, sir, when you fancied I had marked points I did not make. Had it been otherwise, I would appeal to the example given by the blessed Bishop of Geneva, who did not scruple to cheat at cards. But I cannot defend myself against the reflec-tion that at play men are much more sensitive than in serious business, and that they employ the whole of their probity at the backgammon board, where it incommodes them but indifferently, whereas they put it entirely in the background in a battle or a treaty of peace, where it would be troublesome. Polyænus, sir, has written, in the Greek language a book on Stratagems, wherein is shown to what excess deceit is pushed by the great leaders."

"Abbé," said M. d'Anquetil, "I have not read your Polyænus, and do not think I ever shall read him. But, like every true gentleman, I have been to the wars. I have served the king for eighteen months. It is the noblest of all professions. I'll tell you exactly what war is. I may tell the secret of it, as nobody is present to listen but yourself, some bottles, yonder gentleman whom I intend to kill very shortly, and that girl, who begins to undress herself."

"Yes," said Catherine, "I undress, and will keep only my chemise on, because I feel too hot."

"Well then," M. d'Anquetil continued, "whatever may be printed of it in the gazettes, war consists, above all things, of stealing the pigs and chickens of peasants. Soldiers in the fields have no other occupation."

"You are right," said M. Coignard, "and in days of yore it was the saying in Gaul that the soldier's best friend was Madame Marauding. But I beg of you not to kill my pupil, Jacques Tournebroche."

"Ouf!" exclaimed Catherine, arranging the lace of her chemise on her bosom. "Now I feel easier."

"Abbé," replied M. d'Anquetil, "honour compels me to do it."

But my kind-hearted tutor went on:

"Sir, Jacques Tournebroche is very useful to me for the translation, I have undertaken, of Zosimus the Panopolitan. I would give you many thanks not to fight him before the finishing touch has been given to that grand work."

"To the deuce with your Zosimus," said M. d'Anquetil. "To the deuce with him! Do you hear, abbé! I'll send him to the deuce, as a king would do with his first mistress."

And he sang:

> "Pour dresser un jeune courrier
> Et l'affermir sur l'étrier
> Il lui fallait une routière
> Laire lan laire."

"What's that Zosimus?"

"Zosimus, sir, Zosimus of Panopolis, was a learned Greek, who flourished at Alexandria in the third century of the Christian era, and wrote treatises on the spagyric art."

"Do you fancy it matters to me? Why do you translate it?

> "Battons le fer quand il est chaud
> Dit-elle, en faisant sonner haut
> Le nom de sultan première
> Laire lan laire."

"Sir," said my dear tutor, "I quite agree with you; there is no practical utility in it, and by it the course of the world will not be changed in the slightest. But

making clearer by annotations and comments this treatise,
which that Greek compiled for his sister Theosebia——"

Catherine interrupted him by singing in a high-pitched
voice:

> "Je veux en dépit des jaloux
> Qu'on fasse duc mon epoux
> Lasse de le voir secrétaire
> Laire lan laire."

And my tutor continued:

"——I contribute to the treasure of knowledge gathered
by erudite men, and bring forward one stone of my own
for a monument to true history, which is a better one
than the chronicles of war and treaties; for, sir, the
nobility of man——"

Catherine continued to sing:

> "Je sais bien qu'on murmurera
> Que Paris nous chansonnera
> Mais tant pis pour le sot vulgaire
> Laire lan laire."

And my dear tutor went on:

"——is thought. And concerning that, it is not indifferent to know what idea the Egyptians had formed of the
nature of metals and the qualities of the primitive
substance."

The Abbé Jérôme Coignard, having come to the end
of his discourse, emptied a big glass of wine, while
Catherine sang:

> "Par l'épée ou par le fourreau
> Devenir duc est toujours beau
> Il n'importe le maniére
> Laire lan laire."

"Abbé," said M. d'Anquetil, "you do not drink, and
in spite of such abstinence you lose your reason. In Italy,

during the War of Succession, I was under the orders of a brigadier who translated Polybius. But he was an idiot. Why translate Zosimus?"

"If you want my true reason," replied the abbé, "because I find some sensuality in it."

"That's something like!" protested M. d'Anquetil. "But in what can M. Tournebroche, who at this moment is caressing my mistress, assist you?"

"With the knowledge of Greek I have given him."

M. d'Anquetil turned round to me and said:

"What, sir, you know Greek! You are not then a gentleman?"

"No, sir," I replied, "I am not. My father is the banner-bearer of the Guild of Parisian Cooks."

"Well, under such conditions it is impossible for me to kill you. Kindly accept my excuses. But, abbé, you don't drink. You imposed upon me. I believed you to be a real good tippler, and wished you to become my chaplain as soon as I could set up my own establishment."

However, M. Coignard did drink all that the bottle contained, and Catherine, inclining to me, whispered in my ear:

"Jacques, I feel that I shall never love anyone but you."

These words, spoken by a really fine woman clad in no other wrapper than a chemise, troubled me to the extreme. Catherine ended by fuddling me entirely, by making me drink out of her own glass, an action passing unobserved in the confusion of a supper which had overheated the heads of us all.

M. d'Anquetil knocked off the neck of a bottle on the corner of the table and filled our bumpers; from this moment on, I cannot give a reliable account of what was said and done around me. One incident I remember: Catherine treacherously emptying her glass into her lover's

neck, between the nape and the collar of his coat; and
M. d'Anquetil retorting by pouring the contents of two
or three bottles over the girl. Wearing nothing beyond
her chemise, it changed Catherine into a kind of mytho-
logical figure of a humid species like nymphs and
naiads. She cried herself into a rage and twisted in
convulsions.

At that very moment, in the silence of the night, we
heard knocks at the house door. We became suddenly
motionless and dumb, like people bewitched.

The knocks soon redoubled in strength and frequency.
M. d'Anquetil was the first to break the silence by questioning himself aloud, swearing horribly the while, who
the deuce the pesterers could be. My good tutor, to whom
the most ordinary circumstances often inspired admirable
maxims, rose and said with unction and gravity:

"What does it matter whose hand knocks so violently
at closed doors for a vulgar, perhaps ridiculous, reason?
Do not let us seek to know, and consider them as knocking
on the door of our hardened and corrupted souls. At
each knock let us say to ourselves: This one is to give
us notice to amend and think on the salvation we neglect
in the turmoil of our pleasures, that other one is to remind
us of eternity. In that way we shall draw the utmost
profit out of an incident which, after all, is as paltry as
it is frivolous."

"You're humorous, abbé," said M. d'Anquetil; "to
judge by the sturdiness of their knocks, they'll burst the
door open."

And as a fact the knocker resounded like thunder.

"They are robbers," exclaimed the soaked girl. "Jesus!
We shall be massacred; it is our chastisement for having
sent away the little friar. Many times I have told you.

M. d'Anquetil, that misfortune comes to houses from which a Capuchin has been driven."

"Hear the stupid!" replied M. d'Anquetil. "That damned monk makes her believe any imbecility he chooses to dish her up. Thieves would be more polite, or at least more discreet. I rather think it is the watch."

"The watch! Worse and worse," said Catherine.

"Bah!" M. d'Anquetil exclaimed, "we'll lick them."

My dear tutor took the precaution to put one bottle in one of his pockets, and as an equipoise another bottle in the other pocket. The house shook all over from the furious knocks. M. d'Anquetil, whose military qualities were aroused by the knocker's onslaught, after reconnoitring, exclaimed:

"Ah! Ah! Ah! Do you know who knocks? It is M. de la Guéritude with his full-bottomed periwig and two big flunkeys carrying lighted torches."

"That's not possible," said Catherine, "at this very moment he is in bed with his old woman."

"Then it is his ghost," said M. d'Anquetil. "And the ghost also wears his periwig, which is so ridiculous that any self-respecting spectre would refuse to copy it."

"Do you speak the truth, and not jeer at me?" asked Catherine. "Is it really M. de la Guéritude?"

"It's himself, Catherine, if I may believe my own eyes."

"Then I am lost!" exclaimed the poor girl. "Women are indeed unhappy! They are never left in peace. What will become of me? Would you not hide, gentlemen, in some of the cupboards?"

"That could be done," said M. Jérôme Coignard, "as far as we are concerned, but how are we to hide all those empty bottles, mostly smashed, or at least broken necked; the remains of that demijohn M. d'Anquetil threw at me; that tablecloth; those plates, candelabra and mademoi-

selle's chemise, which in its soaked state is nothing but a
transparent veil encircling her beauty?"

"It is true," said Catherine, " yonder idiot has drenched
my chemise, and I am catching cold. But listen. Perhaps M. d'Anquetil could hide in the top room, and I
would make the abbé my uncle and Jacques my brother."

"No good at all," said M. d'Anquetil. "I'll go myself
and kindly ask M. de la Guéritude to have supper with us."

We urged him, all of us—my tutor, Catherine and I—
to keep quiet; we entreated him, hung on his neck. It
was useless. He got hold of a candelabra and descended
the stairs. Trembling we followed him. He unlocked
the door. M. de la Guéritude was there, exactly as M.
d'Anquetil had described him, with his periwig, between
two flunkeys bearing torches. M. d'Anquetil saluted with
the utmost correctness and said:

"Accord us the favour to come in, sir. You'll find some
persons as amiable as singular. Tournebroche, to whom
Mam'selle Catherine throws kisses from the window, and
a priest who believes in God."

Wherewith he bowed respectfully.

M. de la Guéritude was of the dry sort, very tall, and
little inclined to the enjoyment of a joke. That of M.
d'Anquetil provoked him strongly, and his anger rose
when he saw my good tutor, one bottle in hand and two
peeping out of his pockets, and by the look of Catherine
with her wet chemise sticking to her body.

"Young man," he said in an icy fit of passion to
M. d'Anquetil, "I have the honour to know your father,
of whom I will inquire, not later than to-morrow, the
name of the town to which the king shall send you to
meditate over the shame of your behaviour and impertinence. That worthy nobleman, to whom I have lent some
money I do not reclaim, can refuse me nothing. And our

well-beloved Prince, who is in precisely the same position as your father, has always a kindness for me. Consider it a matter done. I have settled, thank God, others more difficult. Now as to that lady yonder, of whom neither repentance nor improvement can be expected. I'll say to-morrow before noon, two words to the Lieutenant of Police, whom I know to be well disposed, to send her to the spittel. I have nothing else to say to you. This house is my property, I have paid for it and I intend to enter when I like." Then, turning to his flunkeys, and pointing out my tutor and myself with his walking stick, he said:

"Throw these two drunkards out."

M. Jérôme Coignard was commonly of an exemplary forbearance, and he used to say that he owed his gentleness to the vicissitudes of life; chance having treated him as the sea treats the pebbles—that is, polishing them by means of the rolling of flood and ebb. He could easily stand insults, as much by Christian spirit as by philosophy. But what helped him best thereto was his deeprooted contempt of mankind, not excepting himself. However, for once he lost all measure and forgot all prudence.

"Hold your tongue, vile publican," he shouted and brandished a bottle like a crowbar. "If yonder rascals dare to approach me I'll smash their heads, to teach them respect for my cloth, which proves in an ample way my sacred calling."

In the faint glimmer of the torches, shiny from sweat, his eyes starting out of their sockets, his coat unbuttoned, and his big belly half out of his breeches, he looked a fellow not easy to be got rid of. The lackeys hesitated.

"Out with him, out with him," shouted M. de la Guéritude; "out with this bag of wine! Can't you see that all you have to do is to push him in the gutter, where he'll remain till the scavengers throw him into the dustcart? I would throw him out myself were I not afraid to pollute my clothes."

My good tutor flew into a passion, and shouted in a voice worthy to sound in a church:

"You odious money-monger, infamous partisan, barbarous evildoer, you pretend this house to be yours? So that everyone may know it belongs to you, inscribe on the door the gospel word *Aceldema,* which in our language means Bloodmoney. And then we'll let the master enter his dwelling. Thief, robber, murderer, write with the piece of charcoal I throw in your face, write with your own filthy hand, on the floor, your title deed. Bloodmoney of the widow and orphans, bloodmoney of the just. *Aceldema.* If not, out with you, man of quantities! We'll remain."

M. de la Guéritude had never in his life heard anything of this sort, and thought he had to deal with a madman, as one might easily suppose, and, more for defence than attack, he raised his big stick. My good tutor, out of his senses, threw a bottle at the head of the contractor, who fell headlong on the floor, howling, "He has killed me!" And as he was swimming in red wine he really looked as though murdered. Both the flunkeys wanted to throw themselves on the murderer, and one of them, a burly fellow, tried to grasp him, when M. Coignard gave the fellow such a butt that he rolled in the stream beside the financier.

Unluckily he rose quickly, and, arming himself with a still burning torch, jumped into the passage, where bad luck awaited him. My good master was no longer there; he had taken to his heels. But M. d'Anquetil was still there with Catherine, and he it was who received the burning torch on his forehead, an outrage he could not stand. He drew his sword, and drove it to the hilt in the unlucky knave's stomach, teaching him, at his own expense, how fatal it may be to attack a gentleman. Now M. Coignard had not got twenty yards away from the house when the other lackey, a tall fellow, with the limbs of a daddy-longlegs, ran after him, shouting for the guard.

"Stop him! Stop him!" The footman ran faster than the abbé, and we could see him, at the corner of the Rue Saint Guillaume, extending his arms to catch M. Coignard by the collar of his gown. But my dear tutor, who had more than one trick, veering abruptly, got behind the fellow, tripped him up, and sent him on to a stone post, where he got his head broken. It was done before M. d'Anquetil and I, running to the abbé's assistance, could reach him. We could not leave M. Coignard in this pressing danger.

"Abbé," said M. d'Anquetil, "give me your hand. You're a gallant man."

"I really cannot help thinking," my good master replied, "that I have been somewhat murderously inclined; but I am not cruel enough to be proud of it. I am quite satisfied so long as I am not reproached too vehemently. Such violence does not lie in my habits, and as you can see, sir, I am better fitted to lecture from the chair of a college on belles-lettres than I am to fight with lackeys at the corner of a street."

"Oh!" replied M. d'Anquetil, "that's not the worst of the whole business. I fully believe you have knocked the Farmer-general on the head."

"Is it true?" questioned the abbé.

"As true as that I have perforated with my sword yonder scoundrel's tripes."

"Under such circumstances we ought to ask pardon of God, to whom alone we are responsible for the blood shed by us, and secondly to hasten to the nearest fountain, there to wash ourselves, because I perceive that my nose is bleeding."

"Right you are, abbé," said M. d'Anquetil; "for the blackguard now dying in the gutter has cut my forehead. What an impertinence!"

"Forgive him," said the abbé, "as you wish to be forgiven yourself."

At the place where the Rue de Bac loses itself in the fields, we fortunately found along the wall of a hospital a little bronze Triton, shooting a spirt of water into a stone tub. We stopped to wash and drink, for our throats were dry.

"What have we done," said my master, "and how could I have lost my temper, usually so peaceable? True men must not be judged by their deeds, which depend on circumstances, but rather, on the example of God our Father, by their secret thoughts and their deepest intentions."

"And Catherine," I asked, "what has become of her through this horrible adventure?"

"I left her," was M. d'Anquetil's answer, "breathing into the mouth of her financier, to revive him. But she had better save her breath. I know La Guéritude. He is pitiless. He'll send her to the spittel, perhaps to America. I am sorry for her. She was a fine girl. I did not love her, but she was mad after me. And, an extraordinary state of things, I am now without a mistress."

"Don't bother," said my good tutor. "You'll soon find another, not different, or hardly differing in essentials, from her. What you look for in a woman, as it appears to me, is common to all females."

"It is clear," said M. d'Anquetil, "that we are in danger: I of being sent to the Bastille, you, abbé, together with your pupil, Tournebroche, who certainly has not killed anybody, of being hanged."

"That's but too true," said my good master. "We have to look out for safety. Perhaps it will be necessary to leave Paris, where, no doubt, we shall be wanted; and even to fly to Holland. Alas! I foresee that there I shall write lampoons for ballet girls with that same hand which has been employed to annotate right amply the alchemistic treatises of Zosimus the Panopolitan."

"Listen to me, abbé," said M. d'Anquetil, "I have a friend who will hide us at his country seat for any length of time. He lives within four miles of Lyons, in a country horrid and wild, where nothing is to be seen but poplars, grass and woods. There we must go. There we'll wait till the storm is over. We'll pass the time hunting and shooting. But we must at once find a post-chaise or, better still, a travelling coach."

"I know where to get that," said the abbé. "At the *Red Horse* hotel, at the Circus of the Bergères, you can have good horses, as well as all sorts of vehicles. I made the acquaintance of the landlord at the time I was secretary to Madame de Saint Ernest. He liked to oblige people of quality. I am not quite sure if he is still alive, but he ought to have a son like himself. Have you money?"

"I have with me a rather large sum," replied M. d'Anquetil, "and I am glad of it, as I cannot dream of going home, where the constables will not fail to be on the lookout to arrest and conduct me to the Châtelet. I forgot my servants, whom I left in Catherine's house, and I do not know what has become of them. I thrashed them, and never paid their wages, and withal I am not sure of their fidelity. In whom can you have confidence? Let's be off at once for the Circus of the Bergères."

"Sir," said the abbé, "I'll make you a proposal, hoping it may be agreeable to you. We are living, Tournebroche and I, in an alchemistic and ramshackle castle at the Cross of the Sablons, where we can easily stay for a dozen hours without being seen by anyone. There we will take you and wait quietly till our carriage is ready. The advantage is that the Sablons is very near the Circus of the Bergères."

M. d'Anquetil had nothing against the abbé's proposal, and so we resolved in front of the Triton, who blew the water out of his fat cheeks, to go first to the Cross of the Sablons, and to hire, later on, at the *Red Horse* hotel, a travelling coach for our journey to Lyons.

"I want to inform you, gentlemen," said my dear tutor, "that of the three bottles I took care to carry with me, one was broken on the head of M. de la Guéritude, another one was smashed in my pocket during my flight. They are both regretted. The third, against all hope, has been preserved. Here it is!"

Pulling it out of his pocket, he placed it on the edge of the fountain.

"That's well," said M. d'Anquetil. "You have some wine, I have dice and cards in my pocket. We can play."

"It is true," said my good master, "that is a pleasant pastime. A pack of cards is a book of adventure, of the kind called romances. It is so far superior to other books of a similar kind that it can be made and read at the same time, and that it is not necessary to have brains to make it, nor knowledge of reading to read it. It is a marvellous work, also, in that it offers a regular and new sense every time its pages are shuffled. It is a contrivance never to be too much admired, because out of mathematical principles it extracts thousands on thousands of curious combinations, and so many singular affinities that it is believed, contrary to all truth, that in it are discoverable the secrets of hearts, the mystery of destinies and the arcanum of the future. What I have said is particularly applicable to the tarot of the Bohemians, which is the finest of all games, piquet not excepted. The invention of cards must be ascribed to the ancients, and as far as I am concerned—I have, to speak candidly, no kind of documentary evidence for my assertion—I believe them to be of Chaldean origin. But in their present appearance the piquet cards cannot be traced further back than to King Charles VII., if what is said in a learned essay, that I remember to have read at Séez, is true, that the queen of hearts is an emblematical likeness of the beautiful Agnes Sorel, and that the queen of spades is, under the name of Pallas, no other than that Jeanne Dulys, better known as Joan of Arc, who by her bravery re-established the business of the French monarchy and was afterwards boiled to death by the English, in a cauldron, shown for two farthings at Rouen, where I have seen it in passing through that city. Certain historians pretend that she was burnt alive at the stake. It is to be read in the works of Nicole Gilles and in Pasquier that St Catherine and St Margaret appeared to her. Certainly it was not God who sent these saints to her, because there is no person of any learning and solid piety who does not know that Margaret and Catherine were invented by Byzantine monks, whose abundant and barbarous imaginations have altogether muddled up the martyrology. It is a ridiculous impiety to pretend that God made two saints who never existed appear to Jeanne Dulys. However, the ancient chroniclers were not afraid to publish it. Why have they not said that God sent to the Maid of Orleans the fair Yseult, Mélusine, Berthe the Bigfooted, and all the other heroines of the romances of chivalry the existence of whom is not more fabulous that that of the two virgins, Catherine and Margaret? M. de Valois, in the last century, rose with full reason against these clumsy fables, as much opposed to religion as error is to truth. It is desirable that an ecclesiastic learned in history undertook to show the distinction between real saints and saints such as Margaret, Luce or Lucie, Eustache, and perhaps Saint George, about whom I have my doubts.

"If on a future day I should be able to retire to some beautiful abbey, possessing a rich library, I will devote to this task the remainder of a life, half worn out in frightful tempests and frequent shipwrecks. I am longing for a harbour of refuge, and I have the desire and the taste for a chaste repose suitable to my age and profession."

While M. Coignard was holding this memorable discourse, M. d'Anquetil, without listening to the abbé's words, was seated on the edge of the fountain, shuffling the cards and swearing like a trooper, because it was too dark to play a game of piquet.

"You are right," said my good master; "it is a bad light, and I am somewhat displeased over it, less because I cannot play cards than because I have a desire to read a few pages of the 'Consolations' of Boethius, of which I always carry a small edition, so as to have it handy when something unfortunate overcomes me, as has been the case this day. It is a cruel disgrace, sir, for a man of my calling to be a homicide, and liable at any moment to be locked up in one of the ecclesiastical prisons. I feel that a single page of that admirable book would strengthen my heart, crushed by the very idea of the officer."

Having spoken, he let himself gently slide over the edge of the basin, so deep that the best part of his body went into the water. But not taking the slightest notice, and hardly feeling it, he took the Boethius out of his pocket—it was really there—and putting his spectacles on, wherein one glass only remained, and that one cracked in three places, he looked in the little book for the page most appropriate for his present situation. He doubtless would have found it, and extracted from it new strength, if the rotten state of his barnacles, the tears that came into his eyes, and the feeble light which came from the sky, had permitted him to search for it. Very soon he had to confess that he was unable to see a wink, and became angry with the moon, who showed her pointed sickle on the edge of a cloud. He reproached her and heaped bitter invectives on her. He shouted:

"Luminary obscene, mischievous and libidinous, you never tire of illuminating men's wickedness, and you deny a ray of your light to him who searches for virtuous maxims!"

"The more so, abbé, as this bitch of a moon gives just light enough to find our way along the streets, and not sufficient to play a game of piquet. Let's go at once to the castle you spoke of, where I have to slip in without being seen."

That was good advice, and after we had drunk the wine to the last drop we took the road, all three of us, to the Cross of the Sablons. I walked with M. d'Anquetil. My good tutor, hindered by the water his breeches had soaked in, followed us, crying, moaning and disgusted.

CHAPTER XVIII

THE morning light already pricked our jaded eyes when we reached the green door to the park. We had not to use the knocker, as some time ago the porter had given us the keys of his domain. It was agreed that my good tutor, with d'Anquetil, should cautiously advance in the shadow of the lane, and that I should remain behind on the lookout for the faithful Criton, and the kitchen boys who might perhaps see us coming along. This arrangement, which was nothing but reasonable, was to turn out rather badly for me. My two companions had gone up without being discovered, and reached my room, where we had decided to hide M. d'Anquetil until the moment of escape in the post-chaise, but as I was climbing the second flight of steps I met M. d'Asterac, in a red damask gown, carrying a silver candlestick. He put, as he habitually did, his hand on my shoulder.

"Hello! my son," he said, "are you not very happy, having broken off all intercourse with women, and by that escaped all dangers of bad company? With the august maidens of the air you need not be in fear of quarrels, scuffles, injurious and violent rows which usually occur with creatures following a loose life. In your solitude, which delights the fairies, you enjoy a delicious peace."

I thought at first that he mocked me. But I soon found out that nothing was further from his thoughts.

"I am pleased to have met you, my son," he continued, "and will thank you to come with me to my studio for a moment."

I followed him. He unlocked, with a key nearly an ell long, that confounded room where I had seen the glare of infernal fires. When we were inside the laboratory he asked me to kindly make up the smouldering fire. I threw some short logs into the furnace, where I don't know what was steaming, exhaling a suffocating odour. While he was occupied with his black cookery, cupellating and matrassing, I remained seated on a settle, and, against my will, closed my eyes. He made me reopen them to admire a green earthenware vessel, with a glass top, which he had in his hand.

"You ought to know, my son," he said, "that this subliming pot is called aludel. It contains a liquid to be looked at with the greatest attention, as it is nothing less than the mercury of the philosophers. Do not suppose that it is to keep its present dark colour for ever. Soon it will change to white and in that state will change all metals into silver. Hereafter, by my art and industry, it will turn red, and acquire the virtue of transmuting silver into gold. It certainly would be of advantage to you that, shut in this laboratory, you should not leave it before these sublime operations have fully taken place, a process which cannot require more than two or three months. But as to ask you to do so would perhaps be imposing too hard a restriction on your youth, be satisfied, for this time, to observe the preludes of the work, while putting, if you please, as much wood on the fire as possible."

Having said that he returned to his phials and retorts,

and I could not help thinking of the sad position wherein ill-luck and imprudence had placed me.

"Alas!" I said to myself, and threw logs into the fire, "at this very moment the constables are searching for my good tutor and myself; perhaps we shall have to go to prison, certainly we have to leave this castle. I have in default of money, at least board and an honourable position. I shall never again dare to stand before M. d'Asterac, who believes me to have passed the night in the silent voluptuousness of magic, which perhaps would have been better for me. Alas! I'll never more see Mosaïde's niece, Mademoiselle Jahel, who at night-time woke me in my room in such a charming way. No doubt she will forget me. Perhaps she'll love someone else, and bestow on him the same caresses as she gave to me." The idea of such an infidelity became unbearable. But as the world goes, one has to be ready for anything.

"My son," M. d'Asterac began to say again, "you do not sufficiently feed the athanor. I see that you are still not fully convinced of the excellency of fire, which is capable of ripening this mercury and transforming it into the wonderful fruit I expect to gather very soon. More wood! The fire, my son, is the superior element; I have told you enough, and now I'll show you an example. On a very cold day last winter, visiting Mosaïde in his lodge, I found him sitting, his feet on a warming pan. I observed that the subtle particles of fire escaping from the pan had power enough to inflate and lift up the folds of his gown, wherefrom I inferred, that had the fire been hotter, it would have raised Mosaïde himself into the air, of which he is certainly worthy, and that, if it should be possible to close into some kind of a vessel a very large quantity of such fire particles, it would be possible to sail on the clouds as easily as we sail on the sea, and to visit the Salamanders in their aerial abodes, a problem I shall keep in mind. I do not despair of constructing such a fireship. But let us go back to our work of putting wood on the fire."

He kept me for some time in the glow of the laboratory whence I wanted to escape as quickly as possible, to join Jahel, whom I was anxious to inform of my misfortune. At last he left me, and I thought myself free, a hope shortly to be disappointed by his return.

"It is rather mild this morning," he said, "but the sky is somewhat cloudy. Would it please you to go for a walk in the park with me before returning to the translation of Zosimus the Panopolitan, which will be a great honour to you and your tutor if you finish it as you have begun?"

With much regret I followed him into the park, where he said to me:

"I am not sorry, my son, to be alone with you, to warn you, as it is high time to do, against a great danger by which you may be threatened one day; I reproach myself not to have thought of warning you before, as what I shall communicate to you is of the utmost consequence."

And speaking in this way, he led me through the grand avenue which leads down to the marshes of the Seine, whence Rueil is to be seen and Mont Valérien with its calvary. It was his usual walk. The alley was practicable in spite of some dead trees which had fallen across it.

"It is important for you to know to what you expose yourself by betraying your Salamander. I do not want to interrogate you as to what intercourse you have had with that superhuman person I have been fortunate enough to make you acquainted with. I dare say you feel somewhat reluctant to discuss it. Possibly you deserve praise for that. If the Salamanders have not, in what concerns the discretion of their lovers, the same ideas that court ladies and tradeswomen have, it is not less true that it is the special quality of beautiful amours to be unutterable, and that it would profane a grand sentiment to spread it abroad.

"But your Salamander (of which I could easily find the name if I had any idle curiosity) has perhaps omitted to give you information about one of the most violent passions—jealousy; this character is common to them. Know well, my son, Salamanders are not to be betrayed without punishment awaiting you. Their vengeance on the perjurer is of the cruelest. The divine Paracelsus gives one example, which will suffice to inspire in you a salutary fear.

"There was in the German town of Staufen a spagyric philosopher who had, like yourself, connection with a Salamander. He was depraved enough to deceive her with a woman, certainly pretty, but not more beautiful than a woman can be. One evening, having supper with his new mistress in company with some friends, they saw a thigh of marvellous beauty shining over their heads. The Salamander exposed it to impress on them all, that she did not deserve the wrong inflicted by her lover; after that the outraged celestial struck down the unfaithful lover with apoplexy. The vulgar, who are made to be deceived, believed his to be a natural death; the initiated knew by whose hand he was slain. I owed you this advice, my son, and this example."

They were less useful to me than M. d'Asterac thought. Listening to them I mused on other subjects of alarm. Without doubt my face must have betrayed the state of anxiety I was in; because the great cabalist, having looked at me, asked me if I was not afraid that an engagement, guarded by conditions so severe, would be troublesome to my youth.

"I am able to reassure you," he added. "The jealousy of a Salamander is awakened only by rivalry with women, and to speak truly it is more resentment, indignation, disgust, than real jealousy. The souls of the Salamanders are too noble, their intelligence too subtle, to envy one another, and to give way to a sentiment pertaining to the barbarity wherein humanity is still half plunged. On the contrary they delight to share with their playmates the joys they taste beside a sage, and are pleased to bring to their lovers the most beautiful of their sisters. Very soon you'll experience that, as a fact, they push politeness to the point I mentioned, and not a year, nay not six months, will pass before your room will be the trysting place of five or six daughters of the light, who will untie before you their sparkling girdles. Do not be afraid, my son, to answer their caresses. Your own fairy love will not take umbrage. How could she be offended, wise as she is? And on your side, do not get irritated if your Salamander leaves you for a moment to visit another philosopher. Consider that the proud jealousy men bring into the union of the sexes is but a savage sentiment, founded on the most ridiculous of illusions. It rests on the idea that a woman belongs to you because she has given herself to you, which is nothing but a play on words."

While making this speech, M. d'Asterac had turned into the lane of the mandrakes, where we could see Mosaïde's cottage, half hidden by foliage, when suddenly an appalling voice burst upon us and made my heart beat faster—hoarse sounds, accompanied by a sharp gnashing, and on getting nearer the sounds seemed to be modulated, and each phrase ended in a sort of very feeble melody, which could not be listened to without shuddering.

Advancing a few paces we could, by listening closely, understand the sense of the strange words. The voice said:

"Hear the malediction with which Elisha cursed the insolent and mirthful children. Listen to the anathema Barak flung on Meros.

"I curse thee in the name of Archithuriel, who is also called the lord of battles, and holds the flaming sword. I doom thee to perdition in the name of Sardaliphonos, who presents to his master the flowers and garlands of merit offered by the children of Israel.

"Be cursed, hound! Anathema, swine!"

Looking from whence the voice came, we could see Mosaïde on the threshold of his house, standing erect, his arms raised, his hands in the form of fangs, with nails crooked, appearing inflamed by the fiery light of the sun. His head was covered with his dirty tiara, and he was enveloped in his gorgeous gown, showing when flying open his meagre bow-legs in ragged breeches. He looked like some begging magician, immortal, and very old. His eyes glared, and he said:

"Be cursed in the name of all globes, be cursed in the name of all wheels, be cursed in the name of the mysterious beasts Ezekiel saw."

Out he stretched his long arms, ending in claws, and continued:

"In the name of the globes, in the name of the wheels, in the name of the mysterious beasts, descend among those who are no more."

We advanced a few paces between the half-grown trees to see the object over which Mosaïde extended his arms and his anger, and discovered, to our great surprise, M. Jérôme Coignard, hanging by a lapel of his gown on an evergreen thorn bush. The night's disorder was visible all over his body; his collar and his shoes torn, his stockings smeared with mud, his shirt open, all reminded me of our common misadventures, and, worse than all, the swelling of his nose spoilt entirely the noble and smiling expression which never left his features.

I ran up to him and unhooked him so luckily off the thorns that only a small piece of his breeches stuck to them. Mosaïde, having had his say, re-entered the cottage. As he wore only slippers I could observe that his legs fitted right into the middle of his feet, so that the heel stuck out behind pretty nearly as much as the forefoot in front, a singular deformation, rendering his walking uncouth, which otherwise would have been noble and full of dignity.

"Jacques Tournebroche! my dear boy," said my tutor, with a sigh, "that Jew must be Isaac Laquedem in person, so to blaspheme in all languages. He vowed me to a death near and violent with an enormous abundance of metaphors, and he called me a pig in fourteen distinct languages, if I counted them correctly. I could believe him to be the Antichrist, and he does not want some of the signs by which that enemy of God is to be recognised. Under any circumstances he is a dirty Jew, and never has the wheel as a brand of infamy been exposed on the vestments of a worse or more rabid miscreant. As for himself, he not only deserves the wheel formerly attached to the garments of Jews, but also that other wheel on which scoundrels have their bones broken."

And my good master, mightily angry in his turn, shook his fist in the direction where Mosaïde had disappeared, and accused him of crucifying children and devouring the flesh of new-born babes.

M. d'Asterac went up to him and touched his breast with the ruby he used to wear on his finger.

"It is useful," said the great cabalist, "to know the peculiar qualities of precious stones. Rubies soothe resentments, and you'll soon see the Abbé Coignard regain his natural suavity."

My dear tutor smiled already, less by virtue of the stone than by the influence of a philosophy which raised this admirable man above all human passions, for I feel it my duty to say, at the very moment my narrative becomes clouded and sad, that M. Jérôme Coignard has given me examples of wisdom under circumstances in which it is but rarely met with.

We inquired the cause of the quarrel, but easily understood by the vagueness of his embarrassed replies that he did not intend to satisfy our curiosity. I surmised at once that Jahel was mixed up with it in some way, when I heard with the gnashing of Mosaïde's voice the grating of locks and bolts, and later on the noise, in the lodge, of a violent dispute between uncle and niece. When we tried again to bring my tutor to some explanation, he said:

"Hate for Christians is deeply rooted in every Jew's heart, and yonder Mosaïde is an execrable example of it. I fancy I discovered in his horrible yelpings some parts of the imprecations the Amsterdam synagogue vomited in the last century on a little Dutch Jew called Baruch or Benedict, but better known under the name of Spinoza, for having framed a philosophy which has been perfectly refuted, as soon as it was brought to public knowledge, by excellent theologians. But this old Mordecai has added to it, so it seems to me, many and much more horrible imprecations, and I confess to having somewhat resented them. For a moment I thought of escaping by flight this torrent of abuse, when to my dismay I found myself entangled in yonder thorn, and sticking to it by different parts of my clothes and skin so fast that I really expected to have to leave the one or the other behind me. I should still be there, in smarting agony, if Tournebroche, my dear pupil, had not freed me."

"The thorns count for nothing," said M. d'Asterac, "but I'm afraid, Monsieur l'Abbé, that you have trodden on a mandrake."

"Mandrakes," replied the abbé, "are certainly the least of my cares."

"You're wrong," said M. d'Asterac. "It suffices to tread on a mandrake to become involved in a love crime, and perish by it miserably."

"Ah! sir," my dear tutor replied, "here are all sorts of dangers, and I become aware that it was necessary to be closely shut in between the eloquent walls of the 'Asteracian,' which is the queen of libraries. For having left it for a moment only, I get the beasts of Ezekiel thrown at my head, not to speak of anything else."

"Would you kindly give me news of Zosimus the Panopolitan?" inquired M. d'Asterac.

"He goes on," replied my master; "goes on nicely, though slowly at the moment."

"Do not forget, abbé," said the cabalist, "that possession of the greatest secrets is attached to the knowledge of those ancient texts."

"I think of it, sir, with solicitude," said the abbé.

M. d'Asterac, after this assurance, left us standing at the statue of the faun, who continued to play the flute without taking any notice of his head, fallen into the grass. He disappeared rapidly between the trees, looking for Salamanders.

My tutor linked his arm in mine with the air of one who can at last speak freely.

"Jacques Tournebroche, my son, I must not conceal from you that this very morning, in the attics of the castle, a rather peculiar chance meeting has taken place, while you were kept in the room of yonder mad fire-blower. I plainly heard him ask you to assist him for a moment in his cooking, which is a great deal less savoury and Christian than that of Master Léonard your father. Alas! when shall I be lucky enough to see again the cookshop of the *Queen Pédauque* and the bookshop of M. Blaizot, with the sign of *Saint Catherine,* where I enjoyed myself so heartily thumbing the books newly arrived from The Hague and Amsterdam!"

"Alas!" I exclaimed, the tears coming into my eyes, "when shall I return to it again? When shall I return to the Rue St Jacques again, where I was born, and see my dear parents, who'll feel burning shame when they hear of our misfortunes? But do be so good, my dear tutor, as to explain that strange encounter you said you had this very morning, and also the events of the day."

M. Jérôme Coignard willingly consented to give me all the enlightenment I wished for. He did it in the following words:

"Know then, my dear boy, that I reached the upper storey of the castle without hindrance in company with M. d'Anquetil, whom I like well enough, although rude and uncultured. His mind is possessed neither of fine knowledge nor deep curiosity. But youth's vivacity sparkleth pleasantly with him, and the ardour of his blood results in amusing sallies. He knows the world as well as he knows women, because he is above them, and without any kind of philosophy. It's a great frankness on his part to call himself an atheist. His ungodliness is without malice, and will disappear with the exuberance of his sensuality. In his soul God has no other enemies than horses, cards and women. In the mind of a real libertine, like M. Bayle for example, truth has to meet more formidable and malicious adversaries. But, my dear boy, I give you a character sketch instead of the plain narrative you wish to have of me.

"I'll satisfy you. Let's see. Having arrived at the top storey of the castle in company with M. d'Anquetil, I made the young gentleman enter your room, and wished him, in accordance with the promise we made him at the Triton fountain, to use the room as his own. He did so willingly, undressed, and, keeping nothing on but his boots, went into your bed, the curtains of which he closed so as not to be incommoded by the bright morning light, and was not long before he was sound asleep.

"As to myself, my dear boy, having reached my room, tired as I was, I did not want to go to rest before I had looked up in my Boethius one or two sentences appropriate to my state of mind. I could not find the very one fit for it. It must not be forgotten that this great thinker had not had occasion to meditate on the disgrace of having broken the head of a Farmer-general with a bottle out of his own cellar. But I was able to pick up here and there, in his admirable treatise, some maxims applicable to present conjunctures. Having done so, I drew the night-cap over my eyes, recommended my soul to God, and quietly went to sleep. After what seemed to me, without being able to measure it, a very short space of time—be mindful, my son, that our actions are the only measure for time, which, if I may say so, is suspended for us by sleep—I felt my arm pulled, and heard a voice shouting in my ear: 'Eh! Abbé! Eh! Abbé, wake up!' Half dozing as I was, I believed it was a constable wanting to conduct me to the officer, and I deliberated with myself the easiest way in which I could break his head, and rapidly came to the conclusion that the candle-stick would be the handiest weapon. It is unhappily, too true, my dear boy, that having once stepped aside from the road of kindness and equity, where the wise man walks with a firm and prudent step, one becomes compelled to sustain violence by violence and cruelty by cruelty, thereby proving that a first fault leads invariably to other faults—evil always follows evil done. One has to be reminded of this if one wants to fully understand the lives of the Roman emperors, of whom M. Crevier has given such an exact account. Those princes were not born more evilly disposed than other men. Caius, surnamed Caligula, was wanting neither in natural spirit nor in judgment, and was quite capable of friendship. Nero had an inborn liking for virtue, and his temperament disposed him towards all that is grand and sublime. Both of them were led by a first fault on the nefarious, villainous road whereon they walked to their miserable end. Their history is cleverly treated in M. Crevier's book. I knew that remarkable writer when he was a teacher of literature and history at the College of Beauvais, as I might be teaching to-day, had my life not been crossed by a thousand impediments, and if the natural easiness of my spirit had not drawn me into the manifold snares laid in my way. M. Crevier, my boy, led a pure life; his morals were severe, and I have myself heard him say that a woman who had broken her conjugal vows was capable of the crimes of murder and incendiarism. I repeat this saying of his, to impress you with the saintly austerity of that model priest.

"But, once more, I digress, and I must hasten to return to my narrative. Well, as I have said, I thought a constable had come to arrest me, and I could see myself in one of the archbishop's dungeons, when I opened my eyes and recognised the features and voice of M. d'Anquetil. 'Abbé,' said that young gentleman to me, 'I have just had a singular adventure in Tournebroche's room. During my sleep a woman entered my room, glided into my bed, and awoke me with a shower of caresses, tender epithets, sweet murmurings, and passionate kisses. I pushed the curtains back to see the features of my good luck. She was dark and had ardent eyes, one of the finest women I have ever held in my arms. But all at once she screamed and jumped out, violently angry, but not quick enough to prevent me catching her in the passage and pressing her closely in my arms. She began by striking me and scratching my face. After having lacerated it sufficiently to satisfy her outraged womanly honour, we began to explain ourselves. She was well pleased to learn that I am a gentleman, and none of the poorest, and sooner than I might have expected I ceased to be odious to her, and she began to be tender with me, when a scullion appeared in the passage; his appearance put her to flight at once.

" 'I am quite aware,' said M. d'Anquetil, 'that that admirable girl had come for another than myself; she must have entered the wrong room, and the surprise frightened her. I did my best to reassure her, and should doubtless have won her amity had not that sot of a scullion come between us.'

" I confirmed him in that supposition. We put our heads together to get an idea of the man for whom that beautiful woman had ventured on such an early morning visit, and were easily agreed that it could be no other but that old fool d'Asterac—you know, Tournebroche, I suspected him before—who awaits her intimacy in an adjoining room, if not, and without your knowledge, in your own. Are you not of the same opinion?"

"Nothing is more credible," I replied.

"No doubt it is so. That sorcerer amuses himself when he talks to us of his Salamanders. The truth is, he caresses that amazingly pretty girl. He's an impostor."

I asked my tutor to favour me with the continuance of his narrative. He willingly complied and said:

"Well, my dear boy, I'll briefly report the remainder of M. d'Anquetil's discourse. I know very well that it's rather commonplace, almost vulgar, to lay much stress on trifling circumstances. It is, on the contrary, some sort of duty to express them in the fewest possible words, to condense them carefully and reserve the tempting abundance of word-flow to moral instruction and exhortation, which may be hurled as the avalanches are hurled from the mountains. On this principle I shall have mentioned enough of M. d'Anquetil's sayings when I have told you that he impressed on me that yonder young girl's beauty, charms, and accomplishments are quite extraordinary. In the end he inquired of me if I knew her name and position. And I replied to him that, from his description of her, I was pretty sure that she was Rabbi Mosaïde's niece Jahel, whom by a lucky accident I had embraced one night on that very same staircase, with this difference only, that my luck occurred between the first and second flights of steps. 'I hope and trust,' said M. d'Anquetil, 'that there may be other differences too, for, as far as I am concerned, I embraced her very closely. I am also sorry that, as you say, she is a Jewess, as, without believing in God, I feel that I should have liked better for her to be a Christian. But can anyone be sure of his own family? Who knows if she has not been kidnapped as a child? Jews and gypsies steal children daily. And we do not, as a rule, remember sufficiently that the Holy Virgin was born a Jewess. But let her be Jewess or not, she pleases me; I want her and shall have her!' Such were that reckless youngster's words. But allow me, my boy, to sit down on yonder moss-covered stone; last night's work, my fights, my flight, too, have nearly broken my legs."

He sat down, took his snuff-box out of his pocket, and looked quite disconsolate when he found it void of tobacco.

I took a seat at his side, agitated, crestfallen. Coignard's discourse caused me acute pain. I cursed Fate for having given my place to a brute at the very moment when my beloved mistress had come to bring me her most passionate tenderness, expecting to find me in my bed, the while I had to throw logs of wood on the fire in the alchemist's furnace. The but too probable inconstancy of Jahel tore my heart to pieces, and I could have wished that my dear tutor had been more discreet with my rival. So I took the liberty to reproach him mildly for his disclosure of Jahel's name.

"Sir," I said, "was it not somewhat imprudent to furnish such indications to a gentleman so luxurious and violent as M. d'Anquetil?"

M. Coignard seemed not to hear what I said, and continued his speech:

"My snuff-box has unfortunately opened itself in my pocket during the fight at Catherine's house, and the tobacco it contained, mixed with the wine of the broken bottle, has formed a quite disgusting paste. I do not dare ask Criton to grind down a few leaves for me; the hard and cold features of that servant and judge inspire me with awe. I suffer from the want of snuff, as my nose is irksome in consequence of the shock I had last night, and I am quite disconcerted by my failure to satisfy the never-tiring wants of that nose of mine. I shall have to bear the misfortune quietly, till M. d'Anquetil may, perhaps, let me have a few grains out of his box. Now to return to that young gentleman, he said expressly to me: 'I love that girl. Know, abbé, that I am resolved to take her with us in the post-chaise should I be compelled to stay here a week, a month, six months or longer; I will not go away without her.' I represented all the dangers to him, which might occur through any delay in our departure. He said he did not care a rap for those dangers, less so as they were smaller for him than for us. 'You, abbé, you and Tournebroche are both in danger of being hanged; my risk is the Bastille only, where I can get cards and girls, and whence my family could, and would, soon deliver me, as my father would interest some duchess or some ballet dancer in my doom, and my mother, devotee as she has become, could and would still get the assistance of one or other of the royal princes. It is irrevocably fixed; I take Jahel with me or I remain here. You and Tournebroche are at liberty to hire a post-chaise of your own."

"The cruel boy knows but too well that we have not the means to do it. I tried to make him change his mind. I became pressing, unctuous, parental. It was no use, and I wasted on him an eloquence which, employed in the pulpit of a parish church, would have brought me a full reward in honour and coin. Alas! my dear boy, it seems to be written that none of my actions will ever produce any kind of savoury fruit, and for me ought to have been written the following words from Ecclesiastes:—*'Quid habet am plius homo de universe labore suo, quo laborat sub sole?'* Far from bringing him to reason, my discourses strengthened the young nobleman's obstinacy, and I cannot deny that he actually counted on me for the success of his desires, and pressed me to go to Jahel and induce her to fly with him, promising her the gift of a trousseau of Dutch linen, of plate, jewels and a handsome annuity."

"Oh, sir!" I exclaimed, "this M. d'Anquetil is very

insolent. What do you think will be Jahel's reply to
his propositions when she knows of them?"

"My boy, she knows by now, and I think she will
accept them."

"If such is the case," I said, "then Mosaïde must be
warned."

"That he is already," replied my tutor. "You have
just assisted at the outbreak of his rage."

"What, sir?" said I, with much warmth, "you have
informed yonder Jew of the disgrace awaiting his family!
That's nice of you! Allow me to embrace you. But,
if so, Mosaïde's wrath threatened M. d'Anquetil, and
not yourself?"

The abbé replied with an air of nobility and honesty,
with a natural indulgence for human weaknesses, an
obliging sweetness, and the imprudent kindness of an
easy heart—by all of which men are often induced to do
inconsiderate things and expose themselves to the severity
of the futile judgments of mankind:

"I will not keep it a secret from you, my dear
Tournebroche, that, giving way to the pressing solicita-
tions of that young gentleman, I obligingly promised to
go on his errand to Jahel and to neglect nothing to induce
her to elope with him."

"Alas!" I exclaimed, "you did, sir. I cannot fully
tell how deeply your action wounds and affects me."

"Tournebroche," replied he sternly, "you speak like
a Pharisee. One of the fathers, as amiable as he was
austere, has said: 'Turn your eyes on yourself and take
care not to judge the doings of others. Judging others
is an idle labour; usually one is erring, often sinning,
by so doing, but by examining and judging oneself your
labour will always be fruit-bearing.' It is written, 'Thou
shalt not be afraid of the judgment of men,' and the

Apostle Paul said that he did not trouble himself about being judged by men. If I refer to some of the finest texts in morals it is to enlighten you, Tournebroche, to make you return to the humble and sweet modesty which suits you, and not to defend my innocence, when the multitude of my iniquities weighs on me and bears me down. It is difficult not to glide into sin, and proper not to fall into despondency at every step one takes on this earth, whereon everything participates, at one and the same time, in the original curse, and the redemption effected by the blood of the Son of God. I do not want to colour my faults, and I freely confess that the embassy I undertook at the request of M. d'Anquetil is an outcome of Eve's downfall, and it was, to say it bluntly, one of the numberless consequences, on the wrong side, of the humble and painful sentiment which I now feel, and is drawn out of the desire and hope of my eternal welfare. You have to represent to yourself mankind balancing between damnation and redemption to understand me truly when I say that at the present hour I am sitting on the good end of the seesaw after having been this very morning on the wrong end. I freely avow that in passing through the mandrake lane, from whence Mosaïde's cottage is to be seen, I hid behind an ivy-thorn bush, waiting for Jahel to appear at her window. Very soon she came. I showed myself, and beckoned her to come down. She came as soon as she was able to escape her uncle's vigilance. I gave her a brief report of the events of the night, of which she had not known. I informed her of M. d'Anquetil's impetuous plans, and represented to her how important it was for her own interest, and for my and your safety, to make our escape sure by coming with us. I made the young nobleman's promises glitter before her eyes and said to her: 'If you consent to go with him to-night you'll have a solid annuity, inscribed at the Hôtel de Ville, and an outfit richer than any ballet dancer or Abbess of Panthémont may get, and a cupboard full of the finest silver.' 'He thinks me to be one of those creatures,' she said; 'he is an impudent fellow.' 'He loves you,' I replied; 'you could not expect to be venerated?' 'I must have an olio pot,' she said, 'an olio pot, and the heaviest one. Did he mention the olio pot? Go, Monsieur Abbé, and tell him.' 'What shall I tell him?' 'That I am an honest girl.' 'And what else?' 'That he is very audacious!' 'Is that all, Jahel? Think on our safety!' 'Tell him that I shall not depart before he has given me his legally worded written promise for everything.' 'He'll do it, consider it as done.' 'Oh, monsieur, I will not consent to anything if he does not consent to have lessons given me by M. Couperin; I want to study music.'

"We had just reached this item of our negotiations when, unhappily, Mosaïde surprised us, and without having overheard our conversation got the scent of its meaning.

"He called me at once a suborner, and heaped outrageous insults on me. Jahel went and hid herself in her own room, and I remained alone exposed to the fury of that God-killer, in the state you found me, and out of which you helped me, you dear boy! As a fact, I may say that the business had been concluded, the elopement assented to, our flight assured. The wheels and Ezekiel's beasts are of no value against a heavy silver olio pot. I am only afraid that yonder old Mordecai has imprisoned his niece too securely."

"I must avow," I replied, without disguising my satisfaction, "that I heard a loud noise of keys and bolts at the very moment I freed you from the midst of the thorns. But is it really true, that Jahel agreed so quickly to your propositions, which have not been quite decorous, and which, for certain, you did not make with an easy heart? I am abashed; and, say, my good master, did she not speak of me, not mention my name, with a sigh or otherwise?"

"No, my boy, she did not pronounce your name, at least not in an audible way. Neither did I hear her mention the name of M. d'Asterac her lover, which ought to have been nearer to her feelings than yours. But do not be surprised by her forgetting the alchemist. It is not sufficient to possess a woman to impress on her soul a profound and durable mark. Souls are almost impenetrable, a fact showing the cruel emptiness of love. The wise man ought to say to himself, I am nothing in the nothingness which that creature is. To hope that you could leave a remembrance in a woman's heart is equivalent to trying to impress a seal on running water. And therefore let us never nurse the wish to establish ourselves in what is fleeting, and let us attach ourselves to that which never dies."

"After all," I said, "Jahel is locked and bolted up, and one may rely on the vigilance of her guardian."

"My son, this very evening she has to join us at the *Red Horse.* Twilight is favourable to evasions, abductions, stealthy movements and underhand actions. We have to trust to the cunning of that girl. As to you, be sure to attend at the Circus of the Bergères in the dusk. You know M. d'Anquetil is not patient, and it quite the man to start without you."

When he gave me this counsel, the luncheon bell sounded.

"Have you by chance," he said to me, "a needle and thread? My garments are torn at more than one place, and I should like to repair them as much as possible before going to luncheon. Especially my breeches do not leave me

without some apprehension. They are so much torn that,
should I not promptly mend them, I run the risk of losing
them altogether."

CHAPTER XIX

I TOOK my accustomed place that day at the dining-table of the cabalist, oppressed by the idea that I sat down at it for the last time. Jahel's treachery had saddened my soul. Alas! thought I, my most fervent wish had been to fly with her, a wish which looked like being granted, and was now fulfilled in a very cruel manner. Again and again I admired my beloved tutor's wisdom who, on a day when I desired too vivaciously the success of some affair, answered with the following citation: *"Et tribuit eis petitionem eorum."* My sorrows and anxieties spoilt my appetite, and I partook sparingly of the dishes served. However, my dear tutor had preserved the unalterable gracefulness of his soul.

He abounded in amiable discourse, and one might have said that he was one of those sages which Telemachus shows us conversing in the shades of the Elysian Fields, and not a man pursued as a murderer and reduced to a roving and miserable life. M. d'Asterac, believing that I had passed the night at the cookshop, kindly inquired after my parents, and, as he could not abstract himself for a single moment from his visions, said:

"When I speak of that cook as being your father it is

175

quite understood that I express myself in a worldly sense, and not according to nature. Nothing proves, my son, that you have not been begot by a Sylph. It is the very thing I prefer to believe, in so far as your spirit, still delicate, shall grow in strength and beauty."

"Oh, sir! don't speak like that," replied my tutor, and smiled. "You oblige him to hide his spirit so as not to damage his mother's good name. But if you knew her better you could not but think with me that she never had any intercourse with a Sylph; she is a good Christian who has never accomplished the work of the flesh with any other man than her husband, and who carries her virtue written distinctly on her features, very different from the mistress of that other cookshop, Madame Quonion, about whom they talked so much in Paris, as well as in the provinces, in the days of my youth. Have you never heard of her, sir? Her lover was M. Mariette, who later on became secretary to M. d'Angervilliers. He was a stout man, who left a jewel every time he visited his beloved; one day a Cross of Lorraine or a Holy Ghost; another day a watch or a chatelaine, or perhaps a handkerchief, a fan, a box. For her sake he rifled the jewellers and seamstresses of the fair of St Germain. He gave her so much that, finding his shop decorated like a shrine, the mastercook became suspicious that all that wealth could not have been honestly acquired. He watched her, and very soon surprised her with her lover. It must be said that the husband was but a jealous fellow. He flew into a temper, and gained nothing by it, but very much the reverse. For the amorous couple, plagued by his wrangling, swore to get rid of him. M. Mariette had no little influence. He got a *lettre de cachet* in the name of that unhappy Quonion. On a certain day the perfidious woman said to her husband:

" 'Take me, I beg of you, on Sunday next out to dinner somewhere in the country. I promise myself uncommon pleasure from such an excursion.'

"She became caressing and pressing, and the husband, flattered, agreed to all her demands. On the Sunday, he got with her into a paltry hackney coach to go to Porcherons. But they had hardly got to Roule when a posse of constables placed in readiness by Mariette arrested him, and took him to Bicêtre, from whence he was sent to the Mississippi, where he still remains. Someone composed a song which finished thus:

> 'Un mari sage et commode
> N'ouvre les yeux qu'à demi
> Il vaut mieux être à la mode,
> Que de voir Mississippi.'

And such is, doubtless, the most solid lesson to be derived from the example given by Quonion the cook.

"As to the story itself, it only needs to be narrated by a Petronius or by an Apuleius to equal the best Milesian fables. The moderns are inferior to the ancients in epic poetry and tragedy. But if we do not surpass the Greeks and Latins in story-telling it is not the fault of the ladies of Paris, who never cease enriching the material for tales by their ingenious and graceful inventions. You certainly know, sir, the stories of Boccaccio. I am sure that had that Florentine lived in our days in France he would make of Quonion's misfortune one of his pleasantest tales. As far as I am myself concerned I have been reminded of it at this table for the sole purpose, and by the effect of contrast, to make the virtue of Madame Léonard Tournebroche shine. She is the honour of cookshops, of which Madame Quonion is the disgrace. Madame Tournebroche, I dare affirm it, has never abandoned those ordinary commonplace virtues the practice of which is recommended in marriage, which is the only contemptible one of the seven sacraments."

"I do not deny it," said M. d'Asterac. "But Mistress Tournebroche would be still more estimable if she should have had intercourse with a Sylph, as Semiramis had and Olympias and the mother of that grand pope Sylvester II."

"Ah, sir," said the Abbé Coignard, "you are always talking to us of Sylphs and Salamanders. Now, in simple good faith, have you ever seen any of them?"

"As clearly as I see you this very moment," replied M. d'Asterac, "and certainly closer, at least as far as Salamanders are concerned."

"That is not sufficient, my dear sir, to make me believe in their existence, which is against the teachings of the Church. For one may be seduced by illusions. The eyes, and all our senses, are messengers of error and couriers of lies. They delude us more than they teach us, and bring us but uncertain and fugitive images. Truth escapes them, because truth is eternal, and invisible like eternity."

"Ah!" said M. d'Asterac, "I did not know you were so philosophical, nor of so subtle a mind."

"That's true," replied my good master. "There are days on which my soul is heavier, and with preference attached to bed and table. But last night I broke a bottle on the head of an extortioner, and my mind is very much exalted over it. I feel myself capable of dissipating the phantoms which are haunting you, and to blow off all that mist. For after all, sir, these Sylphs are but vapours of your brain."

M. d'Asterac stopped him with a kind gesture and said:

"I beg your pardon, abbé; do you believe in demons?"

"Without difficulty I can reply," said my good master, "that I believe of demons all that is reported of them in the Scriptures, and that I reject as error and superstition all and every belief in spells, charms and exorcism. Saint Augustine teaches that when the Scriptures exhort us to resist the demons, it requires us to resist our passions and intemperate appetites. Nothing is more detestable than the deviltries wherewith the Capuchins frighten old women."

"I see," said M. d'Asterac, "you do your best to think as an honest man. You hate as much as I do myself the coarse superstitions of the monks. But, after all, you do believe in demons, and I have not had much trouble to make you avow it. Know, then, that they are no other than Sylphs and Salamanders, ignorance and fear have disfigured them in timid imaginations. But, as a fact, they are beautiful and virtuous. I will not lead you in the ways of the Salamanders, as I am not quite sure of the purity of your morals; but I can see no impediment, abbé, to a frequentation of the Sylphs, who inhabit the fields of air, and voluntarily approach man in a spirit of friendliness and affection, so that they have been rightly named helping genii. Far from driving us to perdition, as the theologians believe, who change them into devils, they protect and safeguard their terrestrial friends. I could make you acquainted with numberless examples of the help they give. But to be short I'll repeat to you one single case which was told to me by Madame la Maréchale de Grancey herself. She was middle-aged, and a widow for several years, when, one night, in her bed, she received the visit of a Sylph, who said to her: 'Madame, have search made in the wardrobe of your deceased husband. In the pocket of a pair of his breeches a letter will be found, which, if it became known, would ruin M. des

Roches, my good friend and yours. Find that letter and burn it.'

"The maréchale promised not to neglect this recommendation and inquired after news of the defunct maréchal from the Sylph, who, however, disappeared without giving any reply. On waking she summoned her women, and bade them look if some of the late maréchal's garments remained in his wardrobe. The attendants reported that nothing was left, and that the lackeys had sold them all to old clothes dealers. Madame de Grancey insisted on her women trying to find at least one pair of breeches.

"Having searched in every corner they finally discovered a very old-fashioned pair of black satin, embroidered with carnations, and handed them to their mistress, who found a letter in one of the pockets, which contained more than would have been needed to incarcerate M. des Roches in one of the state prisons. She burned the letter at once and so that gentleman was saved by his good friends the Sylph and the maréchale.

"Are such, I ask you, abbé, the manners of demons? But let me give you another startling hit on the matter which will impress you more, and will I am sure go to the heart of a learned man such as yourself. It is doubtless known to you that the Academy of Dijon is rich in wits. One of them, whose name cannot be unknown to you, living in the last century, prepared with great labour an edition of Pindar. One night, worrying over five verses the sense of which he could not disentangle, so much was the text corrupt, he dozed off, quite despairing, at cockcrow. During his sleep, a Sylph, who wished him well, transported his spirit to Stockholm into the palace of Queen Christina, conducted him to the library, and took from one of the shelves a manuscript of Pindar showing him the difficult passage. The five verses were there, as well as two or three annotations which rendered them perfectly intelligible.

"In the violence of his contentment, our savant woke up, struck a light, and pencilled down the verses as they appeared to him in his sleep. After that he went to sleep again profoundly. On the following morning, thinking over his night's adventure, he at once resolved to try to get a confirmation. M. Descartes happened at that very time to be in Sweden, reading to the queen on philosophy. Our Pindarist knew him, but was on still closer terms with M. Chanut, the Swedish ambassador in France. He wrote requesting him to forward a letter to M. Descartes, in which he asked him to be informed if there really was in the queen's library at Stockholm a manuscript of Pindar containing the version he mentioned. M. Descartes, an extremely courteous man, replied to the academician of Dijon that, as a fact, her Majesty possessed a manuscript of Pindar, and that he had himself read there the verses, with the various readings contained in the letter."

M. d'Asterac, who had been peeling an apple during his narration, looked at M. Coignard to enjoy the success of his discourse.

My dear tutor smiled and said:

"Ah, sir! I clearly see that I flattered myself with an idle hope, and that one cannot make you give up your vain imaginations. I confess with a good grace that you have shown us an ingenious Sylph, and that I actually wish for such an obliging secretary. His assistance would be particularly useful to me on two or three passages in Zosimus the Panopolitan which are very obscure. Could you not be so good as to give me the means to evoke, if necessary, some Sylph librarian as expert as that of Dijon?"

M. d'Asterac replied gravely:

"That's a secret, abbé, that I will willingly unveil to you. But be warned that you would be a lost man should you communicate it to a profane person."

"Don't be uneasy," said the abbé. "I have a strong desire to know so fine a secret, but I will not conceal from you that I do not expect any effect from it, as I do not believe in Sylphs. Instruct me, if you please."

"You request me?" replied the cabalist. "Well, then, know that whenever you want the assistance of a Sylph, you have but to pronounce the simple word *Agla,* and the sons of the air will at once come to you. But understand, M. Abbé, that the word must be spoken by the heart as well as by the lips, and that faith alone gives it its virtue. Without faith it is nothing but a useless murmur. Pronounce it as I do at this moment, putting in it neither soul nor wish, it has, even in my own mouth, but a very slight power, and at the utmost some of the children of light, if they have heard it, glide into this room, the light shadows of light. I've divined rather than seen them on yonder curtain, and they have vanished when hardly visible. Neither you nor your pupil has suspected their presence. But had I pronounced that magic word with real fervour you would have seen them appear in all their splendour. They are of a charming beauty. Now, sir, I have entrusted you with a grand and useful secret. Let me say again, do not divulge it imprudently. And do not sneer at the example of the Abbé de Villars who, for having revealed their secrets, was murdered by the Sylphs, on the road to Lyons."

"On the Lyons road?" said my good tutor. "How strange!"

M. d'Asterac left us suddenly.

"I will now for the last time," said the abbé, "visit that noble library where I have enjoyed such austere pleasures and which I shall never see again. Do not fail, Tournebroche, to be at nightfall at the Bergères Circus."

I promised to be there; it was my intention to lock myself in my room for the purpose of writing to M. d'Asterac, and my dear parents, asking them to kindly excuse me for not taking personal leave of them, as I had to fly after an adventure wherein I was more unlucky than guilty.

When I reached the door of my room, I heard heavy snoring from within. Peeping in I saw M. d'Anquetil in my bed, sleeping, his sword at the bedside, playing cards strewn all over the quilt. For a moment I felt tempted to run him through with his own sword, but the temptation did not last, and I left him sleeping. Notwithstanding my grief I could not help laughing when I thought that Jahel, being locked and bolted in by Mosaïde, could not rejoin him.

So I went to my tutor's room, to write my letters, where I disturbed five or six rats, who had begun to make a meal off his Boethius, which had remained on the night table. I wrote to my mother and to M. d'Asterac, and I composed the most touching epistle to Jahel. My tears fell on this when I read it over for a second time. "Perhaps," I said to myself, "the faithless girl will cry too, and her tears will mix with mine."

Then, overwhelmed as I was by fatigue and sorrow, I threw myself on my tutor's bed, and soon went off into a kind of semi-sleep, troubled by dreams, erotic and sinister. I was awakened by the taciturn Criton, who had entered the room and presented to me, on a silver salver, a sort of curling paper, whereon a few badly written words were scribbled in pencil. Someone expected me at once outside the castle. The note was signed "Friar

Ange, unworthy Capuchin." I went as quickly as I could, and found the little friar seated on the bank of a ditch in a state of pitiable dejection. Wanting strength to get up, he looked at me with his big dog's eyes, nearly human and full of tears; his sighs moved his beard and chest. In a tone which really pained me he said:

"Alas! Monsieur Jacques, the hour of trial has come to Babylon, as it is said in the prophets. At the request of M. de la Guéritude, the Lieutenant of Police had Mam'selle Catherine taken by the constables to the spittel, from whence she'll be sent to America by the next convoy. I was informed of it by Jeannette the hurdy-gurdy player, who saw Catherine brought in a cart to the spittel, as she left it herself after having been cured of an evil ailment by the surgeon's art—at least I hope so, please God! And Catherine is to be transported, and no reprieve to be expected."

And Friar Ange at this point in his discourse groaned and shed tears abundantly. After doing my best to console him I asked if he had nothing else to tell me.

"Alas! M. Jacques," he replied. "I have intimated the essential, and the remainder floats in my head like the Spirit of God on the waters, without comparison if you please. The matter is dark altogether. Catherine's misfortune has taken away my senses. It needed the necessity of giving you important news to bring me to the threshold of this cursed house, where you live in company with all sorts of devils, and it was with dismay, and after having recited the prayer of Saint Francis, that I ventured to knock at the door for the purpose of handing to a lackey the note I wrote to you. I do not know if you have been able to read it, as I have but little practice in forming letters, and the paper was not of the best to write on, but you see it is the honour of our holy order not to give way to the vanities of our century! Ah! Catherine at the spittel! Catherine in America! Is it not enough to break the hardest heart? Jeannette herself wept abundantly, and did so in spite of her jealousy of Catherine, who prevails over her in youth and beauty just as Saint Francis surpasses in holiness all the other blessed ones. Ah, M. Jacques! Catherine in America! Such are the strange ways of Providence. Alas! our holy religion is true, and King David was right in saying that we are like the grass of the field—is not Catherine at the spittel? The stones on which I am sitting are happier than I, notwithstanding that I wear the signs of a Christian and a monk. Catherine at the spittel!"

He sobbed again. I waited till the torrent of his sorrow had passed away, and then asked him if he had any news of my parents.

"M. Jacques," he replied, " 'tis they who have sent me to you, bearer of a pressing message. I must tell you that they are not very happy, through the fault of Master Léonard, your father, who passes in drinking and gambling all the days God has given him. And savoury fumes of roasting geese and fowls do not now arise to the signboard of *Queen Pédauque* swinging sadly in the damp wind which rusts it. Where are the times when the smell of your father's cookshop perfumed the Rue Saint Jacques, from the *Little Bacchus* to the *Three Maids*? Since yonder sorcerer visited it, everything wastes away, beasts and men, in consequence of the spell he has thrown on it. And vengeance divine is manifest there since that fat Abbé Coignard made his entry, and I was cast out. It was the beginning of the evil, inaugurated by M. Coignard, who prides himself on the depths of his knowledge, and the distinction of his manners. Pride is the spring of all evil. Your pious mother was very wrong, M. Jacques,

not to have been satisfied with such teaching as I charitably
gave you, and which would have made you fit to superin-
tend the cooking, to manage the larding, and to carry the
banner of the guild after the demise, the funeral service
and the obsequies of your worthy father, which cannot
be very far off, as all life is transitory and he drinks to
excess."

It may be easily understood how sorely I was afflicted
by this news. My tears and those of Friar Ange mixed
freely together. However, I inquired after my mother.

Friar Ange replied:

"God, who afflicted Rachel in Rama, has sent to your
mother, Monsieur Jacques, sundry tribulations for her
good, and to chastise Master Léonard for the sin he committed by maliciously expelling, in my humble person, our
Lord Jesus Christ from his cookshop. He has transferred
most of the purchasers of poultry and pies to the daughter
of Madame Quonion, who turns the spit at the other end
of the Rue Saint Jacques. Your mother sees with sorrow
that the other house is blessed at the cost of her own, and
that her shop is now deserted to such a degree that, figura-
tively speaking, moss covers its threshold. She is sus-
tained in her trials, firstly, by her devotion to Saint
Francis; secondly, by the consideration of the progress
of your worldly position, which enables you to wear a
sword like a man of condition.

"But this second consolation has been much shaken by
the constables calling this very morning at the cookshop
to take you into custody, and carry you to the Bicêtre
Prison, to break stones for a year or two. It was Catherine who denounced you to M. de la Guéritude, but you
must not blame her for it; she did her duty as a Christian by confessing the truth. She accused you and the
Abbé Coignard of being M. d'Anquetil's accomplices, and

gave a faithful account of all the murder and bloodshed perpetrated in the course of that terrible night. Alas! her truthfulness was of no use; she was carried to the spittel. It's downright horrible to think of it."

At this point of his story, the little friar covered his face with his hands and sobbed and cried anew.

Night had come, and I was afraid to fail in my appointment. Pulling the little friar out of the ditch, I put him on his feet, and wished him to keep me company on my walk along the Saint Germain road to the Circus of the Bergères. He obeyed me willingly. Sadly walking by my side, he asked my assistance in disentangling the mixed-up threads of his thoughts. I put him back to where the constables came to search for me at the cookshop.

"As they could not find you," he continued, "they wanted to take your father. Master Léonard pretended he did not know where you were hidden. Your mother said the same, and took her sacred oath on it. May God forgive her, Monsieur Jacques, as evidently she perjured herself. The constables began to get cross. Your father reasoned well with them, and took them to have a drink with him, after which they parted quite friendly. Meanwhile your mother went after me to the *Three Maids,* where I was soliciting alms according to the holy rules of my order. She sent me to you to warn you that immediate flight is your only safety, as the Lieutenant of Police would soon discover your retreat."

Listening to this sad news, I walked with a quicker step, and we passed the bridge of Neuilly.

On the rather steep hill leading to the circus, the elms of which soon became visible, the little friar said with a dying voice:

"Your mother particularly asked me to warn you of the

danger you are in, and handed to me a little bag she had secreted under her dress. I cannot find it," he added, after having felt all over his body. "How do you expect me to find anything after losing Catherine? She was devoted to Saint Francis, and lavish of alms, and now they have treated her like a harlot, and will shave her head; it's heartbreaking to think that she will look like a milliner's doll, and be shipped in that state to America, where she runs the risk of dying by fever and being eaten by cannibal savages."

When he ended this discourse with a sigh we had reached the circus. To the left, the inn of the *Red Horse* showed its roof over a double row of elms, its dormer windows with their pulleys, while under the foliage the gateway was to be seen wide open.

I slackened my walk, and the little friar sat down on the roots of a tree.

"Friar Ange," I said to him, "you mentioned a satchel my dear mother handed you for me."

"Quite right; she wished me so to do," replied the little Capuchin, "and I have put it somewhere so safely that I cannot remember where, and you ought to know, Monsieur Jacques, that I could not have lost it for any other reason but from too much carefulness."

I rather sharply said that I did not believe he had lost the satchel, and should he not find it at once I would search for it myself.

He understood and, sighing deeply, brought out from under his frock a little bag made of coloured calico, and handed it to me. It contained a crown piece and a medal with the effigy of the Black Virgin of Chartres, which I kissed fervently, shedding tears of tenderness and repentance. The little friar took out of his large pockets a parcel of coloured prints and prayers, badly illuminated, made a rapid selection, and gave me two or three of them, those he considered the most useful to pilgrims, travellers, and all wandering people, saying:

"They are blessed and of good effect against danger of death and sickness. You have only to recite the text printed on them, or to lay them on the skin of your body. I give them to you, M. Jacques, for the love of God. Do not forget to give me an alms. Keep in mind that I beg in the name of Saint Francis. He'll protect you, without fail, if you assist the most unworthy of his sons, and that is precisely myself."

Listening to his speech, I saw in the doubtful twilight a post-chaise and four come out of the gateway of the *Red Horse* inn, heard the whips cracking and the horses pawing the ground when the driver stopped on the highroad, close to the tree on the roots of which Friar Ange was sitting. It was not an ordinary post-chaise, but a very large, clumsy vehicle, having room to seat four, and a small *coupé* in front. I looked at it for a minute or two, when up the hill came M. d'Anquetil, with Jahel, carrying several parcels under her cloak and wearing a mob-cap. M. Coignard followed them, loaded with five or six books wrapped up in an old thesis. When they reached the carriage the post boys lowered the carriage steps, and my beautiful mistress, raising her skirt like a balloon, ascended into the carriage, pushed from behind by M. d'Anquetil.

I ran towards them and shouted:

"Stop, Jahel! Stop, sir!"

But the seducer only pushed the perfidious girl the more, and her charming rounded figure quickly disappeared. Preparing himself to climb after her, one foot on the steps, he looked at me with surprise.

"Oh! Monsieur Tournebroche! You would then take

from me all my mistresses! Jahel after Catherine. Do
you do it for a wager?"

But I did not hear what he said, and continued to call
Jahel, the while Friar Ange, having risen from his seat
under the elm-tree, came up to the carriage door, and
offered to M. d'Anquetil pictures of Saint Roch, a prayer
to be recited during the shoeing of a horse, another
against fever, and asked him for charity with a mournful
voice.

I should have stopped there the whole of the night,
calling Jahel, if my good tutor had not got hold of me and
pushed me inside the large compartment of the carriage,
which he entered after me.

"Let them have the *coupé* by themselves," he said to me,
"and let us travel in the large compartment. I have been
looking for you, Tournebroche, and, not to withhold anything from you, had quite made up my mind to depart
without you when, happily, I discovered you in company
with the Capuchin under yonder elm-tree. We could
not delay any longer, as M. de la Guéritude has given
sharp orders to look everywhere for us. He has a long
arm, having lent money to the king."

The carriage was moving on, but Friar Ange clung to
the door, with hand outstretched, begging pitifully.

I sank into the cushions.

"Alas, sir," I exclaimed, "did you not tell me that
Jahel was locked in threefold?"

"My son," replied my good master, "not too much confidence may be placed in women, who always play their
tricks on the jealous and their locks. If the door is closed,
they jump out of the window. You have no idea, my dear
Tournebroche, of the cunning of women. The ancients
have reported admirable examples of it, and many a one
you'll find in Apuleius, where they are sprinkled like salt

in the 'Metamorphoses.' But the best example is given
in an Arabian tale recently brought to Europe by M.
Galand, and which I will tell you.

"Schariar, Sultan of Tartary, and his brother,
Schahzenan, walked one day on the seashore, when they
saw rise suddenly above the waves a black column, moving
towards the shore. They recognised it as a genie of the
most ferocious kind, in the form of an immensely tall
giant, carrying on his head a glass case locked with four
iron locks. Both were seized with dismay, so much so
that they hid themselves in the fork of a tree standing near.
The genie however came on shore, and brought the glass
case to the tree where the two princes were hiding. Then
he lay down and soon went to sleep. His outstretched
legs reached the sea, and his breathing shook earth and
heaven. During his terrifying repose the cover of the
glass case rose by itself, and out of it came a woman
with a majestic body and of the most perfect beauty.
She raised her head——"

Here I interrupted his narrative, which I had hardly
listened to, and exclaimed:

"Ah! sir, what do you think Jahel and M. d'Anquetil
are saying at this moment, all by themselves in the *coupé?*"

"I don't know," replied my dear tutor: "it's their
business, not ours. But let me finish the Arabian tale,
which is full of sense. You've interrupted me inconsiderately, Tournebroche, at the very moment when the
damsel, looking up, discovered the two princes in the tree.
She made them a sign to come down; but desirous as they
were to respond to the appeal of a person of so much
beauty, they were afraid to approach so terrible a giant.
Seeing that they hesitated she said to them in an undertone:
'Come down at once, or I wake up the genie.' Her
resolute and resolved countenance made them understand

that it was not a vain threat, and that the safest, as also the most pleasant, thing to do was to go down without delay, which they did as quietly as possible, so as not to wake the giant. The lady, taking their hands, led them somewhat farther away under the trees, and gave them to understand very clearly that she was ready at once to give herself to both. Gracefully they accepted the beauty's offer, and as they were men of courage, fear did not spoil their enjoyment. Having obtained from both what she had wished for, and seeing that each of the two princes wore a ring, she asked them for their rings. Returning to the glass case where she lived, she took out of it a chaplet of rings, and showed it to the princes.

" 'Do you know what is the meaning of this chaplet of rings? They are those of all the men for whom I have had the same kindness as for you. Their number, all told, is ninety-eight. I keep them as souvenirs, for that same reason, and to complete the century I have asked for yours. And now to-day I have had a full hundred lovers, in spite of the vigilance and care of yonder giant, who never leaves me. He may lock me in the glass case as much as he likes, and hide me in the depths of the sea. I deceive him as often as I please.'

"That ingenious apologue," added my good tutor, "shows you that the women of the Orient, who are shut up and cloistered, are as cunning as their sisters of the Occident, who are free of their movements. Whenever a woman wants something there is no husband, lover, father, uncle, or tutor able to prevent her carrying out her will. And therefore, my dear boy, you ought not to be surprised that to deceive that old Mordecai was but child's play for Jahel, whose perverse spirit is made up of all the cuteness of our she-geldings and the perfidy of the Orient. I guess her to be as ardent in sensual pleasure, as greedy after gold and silver; altogether a worthy descendant of the race of Aholah and Aholibah.

"She is of an acid and mordant beauty, and I do not deny that somehow she excites me, although age, sublime meditations, and the miseries of an agitated life have sufficiently mortified in me the lust of the flesh. You're suffering over the success of M. d'Anquetil's adventure with her, wherefore I reckon that you feel much more than I do the sharp tooth of desire, and that jealousy is tearing you. And that's the reason you blame an action, irregular certainly, contrary to vulgar propriety, but withal indifferent in character, or at least not adding much to the universal evil. Inwardly you condemn me for having had a part in it, and you fancy you defend the principle of chaste living when you do nothing except from the prompting of your passions. Such is the way, my dear boy, that we colour for the use of our own eyes our worst instincts. Human morals have no other origin. Confess, however, that it would have been a pity to leave such a fine girl for a single day longer with that old lunatic. Acknowledge that M. d'Anquetil, young and handsome, is a better mate for such a delicious creature, and resign yourself to accept what cannot be altered. Such wisdom is difficult to practise; but it would have been more difficult still, had your own mistress been taken from you. In such a case you'd feel the iron teeth torture your flesh, filling your soul with images odious and precise. This consideration, my boy, ought to ease your present sufferings. Besides, life is full of labour and pain. It is this which evokes in us the just hope of an eternal beatitude "

Thus spoke my good tutor, while the elms of the king's highway passed quickly before our eyes. I did not let him know that he irritated my griefs in trying to soothe them, and that he, without being aware of it, had laid his finger on my wound.

Our first stoppage was at Juvisy, where we arrived in the rain early in the morning. Entering the post inn I found Jahel in the corner of the fireplace, where five or six fowls were roasting on a spit. She was warming her feet, and showed part of a silken stocking, which was a great trouble to me, because it brought her leg to my mind. I seemed to see all the beauty of her satin skin, the down, and all other striking circumstances. M. d'Anquetil was leaning on the back of the chair whereon she was sitting, holding her cheeks with his hands. He called her his soul and his life, asked her if she was hungry, and on her saying yes, he went out to give the necessary orders.

Remaining alone with the unfaithful one I looked in her eyes, which reflected the flames of the fire.

"Ah! Jahel," I exclaimed, "I am very unhappy; you have betrayed me, and you no longer love me."

"Who says that I do not love you any more?" she asked, and looked at me with her velvety eyes of flame.

"Alas! mademoiselle, your conduct shows it sufficiently."

"But, Jacques, could you envy the trousseau of Dutch linen and the godroon plate that the gentleman is to present me with! I only ask for your forbearance till he has fulfilled his promises, and after that you'll see that I am still to you as I was at the Croix-des-Sablons."

"And in the meantime, Jahel? Alas! he will enjoy your favours."

"I feel," she replied, "that that will be a trifle, and that nothing will efface the strength of the feeling you have inspired me with. Do not torment yourself with such mere nothings; they are only of value by your idea of them."

"Oh!" I exclaimed, "my idea of them is horrible, and

I am really afraid that I shall not be able to survive your treachery."

She looked at me with a somewhat mocking sympathy, and said with a smile:

"Believe me, my friend, neither of us will die of it. Think, Jacques, that I am in want of plate and linen. Be prudent, do not show the feelings that agitate you, and I promise to reward you for your discretion, later on."

This hope softened somewhat my poignant grief. The innkeeper's wife laid on the table the lavender-scented cloth, the pewter plates, goblets and pitchers. I was very hungry, and when M. d'Anquetil, in company with the abbé, re-entered the dining-hall, inviting us to eat a morsel with him, I willingly sat down between Jahel and my dear old tutor. We were afraid of being followed, so after having put away three omelets and a couple of spring chickens we resumed our journey. We resolved, seeing the danger of pursuit, to pass every halting place without stopping as far as Sens, where we decided to stay the night.

My imagination went horribly to that night at Sens, thinking that there Jahel's treachery would be completed. And so much was I troubled by those but too legitimate apprehensions that I listened with but half an ear to the discourse of my good master, to whom every trifling incident of our journey suggested the most admirable reflections.

My jealous fears were not groundless. We alighted at the best inn at Sens, that paltry hostelry of *The Armed Man.* Supper hardly over, M. d'Anquetil took Jahel with him to his room, which was next to mine. You may believe that I could not enjoy a wink of sleep. Jumping out of bed at daybreak, I left my chamber of torture. I seated myself under the waggoner's porch, where the

postboys drank white wine and played the deuce with
the servants. I remained there two or three hours con-
templating my misery. The horses were already harnessed
when Jahel appeared under the porch, shivering all over,
under her black cloak. I could not bear the sight of her,
and turned my moistened eyes away. She came to me,
sat close to me on the stone, and told me sweetly not to be
disconsolate, as what I thought monstrous was but a trifle;
that one has to be reasonable; that I was too much a man
of spirit to want a woman for myself alone; that if one
wished for that one had to take a housekeeper without
brains or beauty, and even then it was a big risk to run.

"And now, Jacques," she added somewhat hurriedly,
"I must leave you, and quickly; I can hear the steps of
M. d'Anquetil descending the stairs."

She pressed a hasty kiss on my burning lips, giving
and prolonging it with the violent voluptuousness of fear,
as the spurred boots of her sweetheart made the wooden
steps of the stairs creak, and the intriguer was in fear of
losing her Dutch linen trousseau and her godroon silver pot.

The postboy lowered the steps of the *coupé*, but M.
d'Anquetil asked Jahel if it would not be more pleasant
to travel all four together in the large compartment, and I
recognised that that was the first effect of his intimacy
with Jahel, and that the full satisfaction of his desires
had left it less agreeable to be alone with her. My good
old tutor had taken care to provide himself with five or
six bottles of white wine from the cellar of *The Armed
Man,* which he laid under the cushions, and which we
drank to overcome the monotony of the journey.

At midday we arrived at Joigny, a neat and pretty
town. Foreseeing that my ready money would be all used
before we could arrive at the end of our journey, and
finding the idea intolerable of letting M. d'Anquetil pay

my part in the travelling expenses unless I was compelled
to do so by the most unavoidable necessity, I resolved
to sell a ring and a medallion, gifts from my mother,
and went about the town in quest of a jeweller ready to
buy them. I discovered one in the square opposite the
church, who sold crosses and chains in a shop under the
sign of *The Good Faith*. What was my astonishment
to find in this very shop, before the counter, my good
master, showing to the jeweller five or six little diamonds,
and asking the shopman what price he would offer for
those stones. I recognised them immediately as those
which M. d'Asterac had shown us.

The jeweller examined the stones, and looking at the
abbé from under his spectacles said:

"Sir, these stones would be of great value if they were
genuine. But they are not, and no touchstone is needed
to find that out. These are nothing but glass beads,
good only for children to play with, or to be used in the
crown of a village Holy Virgin, where they would have
a charming effect."

Having listened to that reply, M. Coignard picked up
his diamonds and turned his back on the jeweller. In
so doing he became aware of my presence, and looked
rather confused over it. I brought my business to an
end promptly, and meeting my dear old tutor at the shop
door I mildly reproached him with the wrong he had
done to himself, as well as to his companions, by taking
these stones, which for his greater guilt might have
been real.

"My son," he replied, "God, to keep me innocent of
crime, willed these stones to be false and a mere sham.
I avow to you that I did wrong to take them. You seem
sorry about it; it's a leaf of my life's book I should like
to tear out, like some others not so neat and immaculate

as they ought to be. I understand deeply all that is
reprehensible in my conduct. But no man has a right to
be entirely cast down when he is faulty, and just now,
and in this special case, I think I ought to say of myself,
in the words of an illustrious learned man: 'Consider
your great frailty, of which you make but too often a show;
and withal it is for your salvation that such things should
rise up in the road of your life. Not everything is lost
for you if oftentimes you find yourself afflicted and
rudely tempted; and if you succumb to temptation you're
a man, not a god; you're flesh and blood, not an angel.
How could you expect to remain always in a state of virtue
when the angels in heaven and the first man in Eden
could not remain faithful to virtue?' Such are, my dear
Tournebroche, the only conversations adapted to the
present state of my soul. But, after this unhappy
occurrence, which I do not wish to dwell on longer, is it
not time to return to the inn, there to drink, in company
with the postboys, who are simpleminded and of easy
intercourse, one or more bottles of country wine?"

I quite agreed, and we soon reached the hostelry, where
we found M. d'Anquetil, who, returning like ourselves
from the town, had brought some playing cards. He
played a game of piquet with my tutor, and when we
resumed our journey they continued to play in the carriage.
That rage for play which occupied my rival gave me
occasion for an undisturbed conversation with Jahel, who
liked very much to chat with me, since she was left to
herself. Her talk had a kind of bitter sweetness for me.
Reproaching her for her perfidy and unfaithfulness, I
gave vent to my grief in feeble or violent complaints.

"Alas! Jahel!" I said, "the memory and the image
of your tenderness, which made but lately my dearest
delight, have become a cruel torture to me when I think

that to-day you belong to another person, whereas formerly you were mine."

She replied:

"A woman does not behave equally to all men."

And when I prolonged my lamentations and reproaches to excess she said:

"I am quite aware that I have caused you some pain. But that is no reason for you to plague me a hundred times a day with your useless moans."

M. d'Anquetil when he lost was in a bad temper and molested Jahel, while she, anything but patient, threatened to write to her Uncle Mosaïde to come and fetch her back. These quarrels were at first rather pleasant to me, and gave me no small hopes; but after a repeated renewal of them I became rather anxious, as they were always followed by impetuous reconciliations, which exploded suddenly into kisses and lascivious whisperings. M. d'Anquetil could hardly bear my presence. He had on the other hand a vivid tenderness for my good tutor, which he well deserved for his always joyful humour and the incomparable elegance of his mind. They played and drank together with a daily growing sympathy. Knee to knee, so as to steady the table whereon they played cards, they laughed, bantered, chaffed each other, and if occasionally they became angry, and threw the cards in one another's face, and swore at each other with such oaths as would have made the boxers of Port Saint Nicolas or the bargemen of the Mail blush, M. d'Anquetil swore by God Almighty, the Holy Virgin and all the saints, that in all his life he had never met with a worse thief than the Abbé Coignard. Notwithstanding it remained clearly evident that he liked my good tutor; and it was a real pleasure, as soon as one of these quarrels had termi-nated, to listen to his laughter as he said:

"Abbé, you'll be my almoner and play piquet with me. You'll also have to hunt with us. In the remotest corner of the Perche we will look out for a horse strong enough to carry your weight, and you'll get hunting clothes like the ones I saw worn by the Bishop of Uzès. It is, besides, high time you had a new suit of clothes; your breeches, abbé, hardly keep on your behind."

Jahel also inclined towards the irresistible charm with which my dear tutor influenced all mankind. She made up her mind to repair, if possible, all the disorders of his dress. First she tore up one of her gowns and used the pieces to patch up the coat and breeches of my venerable friend; she also made him a present of a laced handkerchief to use as a band. My good tutor accepted these little presents with a dignity full of graciousness. More than once I had occasion to observe that he was a gallant when talking to women. He took a lively interest in them without ever showing the slightest indiscretion. He praised them with the science of a connoisseur, giving them counsels out of his long experience, diffusing over them the unlimited indulgence of a heart always ready to forgive any kind of human weakness, and withal, never omitted any occasion to make them understand the great and useful truths.

We arrived on the fourth day of our journey at Montbard, and alighted on a hill, from which we could overlook the whole town, which appeared in a small space as if it had been painted on canvas by a clever limner anxious to reproduce every detail.

"Look," my dear old tutor said, "on these steeples, towers, roofs, which rise up out of the green. It is a town, and without actually searching for its history and name, it is well to contemplate it as the worthiest subject of meditation we may encounter on the surface of the world. As a fact any town furnishes material for speculations of the spirit. The postboys tell us that yonder is Montbard, a place utterly unknown to me. Nevertheless I am not afraid to affirm, by analogy, that the people living therein resemble ourselves, are egotistic cowards, perfidious gluttons, dissolute. Otherwise they could not be human beings and descendants of Adam, at once miserable and venerable, and in whom all our instincts, down to the most ignoble, have their august origin. The only possible doubtful matter with yonder people, is to know if they are more inclined to food or to procreation. But a doubt is hardly permissible; a philosopher will soundly opine that hunger is for these unhappy ones a more pressing necessity than love. In the greenness of my youth I believed that the human animal is before all things inclined to sexual intercourse. But that was a wanton error, as it is quite clear that human beings are more interested in conserving their own life than in giving life to others. Hunger is the axis of humanity; but after all, as it seems to be useless to discuss the matter any further, I'll say, with your permission, that the life of mortals has two poles—hunger and love. And here it is that one has to open ears and soul! These hideous creatures who are born only to devour or to embrace furiously, one the other, live together under the sway of laws which precisely interdict their satisfying that double and fundamental concupiscence. These ingenious animals, having become citizens, voluntarily impose on themselves all sorts of privations; they respect the property of their neighbours, which is prodigious, if you take their avaricious nature into consideration; they observe the rules of modesty, which is an enormous hypocrisy, but generally consists in but seldom speaking of that of which they think without ceasing. Then, let's be true and honest, gentlemen, when we look on a woman, we do not attach our thoughts to the beauties of her soul or the pleasantness of her spirit; when we approach her we have in view principally her natural form. And the amiable creatures know it so well that they have their dresses made by the fashionable dressmakers and take good care not only not to veil their charms, but to exaggerate them by all sorts of artifices. And Mademoiselle Jahel, who certainly is not a savage, would be distressed if, on her, art had gained the advantage over nature to such a degree as to prevent the fulness of her bosom and the roundness of her thighs being seen. And so it is that, since Adam's fall, we see mankind hungry and incontinent. Why do they, when assembled in towns, impose on themselves privations of all kinds, and submit to a rule of life contrary to their own corrupted nature? It is said that they find it advantageous, and that they feel that their individual security depends on such restriction. But that would be to suppose them to have too much reasoning power, and, what's more, a false reasoning, because it is absurd to save one's life at the expense of all that makes it reasonable and valuable. It is further said that fear keeps them obedient, and it is true that prison, gallows and wheels are excellent assurers of submission to existing laws. But it is also certain that prejudice conspires with the laws, and it is not easy to see how compulsion could have been universally established. Laws are said to be the necessary conformity of things; but we have become aware that that conformity is contradictory to nature, and far from being necessary. Therefore, gentlemen, I'll look for the source and origin of the laws not in man, but outside man, and I should think that, being strangers to mankind, they derive from God, who not only formed with His own mysterious hands earth and water, plants and animals, but the people also,

and human society. I'm inclined to believe that the laws
come direct from Him, from His first decalogue, and that
they are inhuman because they are divine. It must be
well understood that I here consider the codes in their
principles and in their essence, without taking note of
their ridiculous diversities and their pitiable complications.
The details of customs and prescriptions, the written as
well as the oral, are man's work, and to be despised.
But do not let us be afraid to recognise that the town is
a divine institution. As a result, every government ought
to be theocratic. One priest, famous for the part he
took in the declaration of 1682, M. Bossuet, was not in
error, when he wanted to form the rules of polity after
the maxims of the Scriptures; and if he has pitiably
failed in this endeavour, you have to accuse the weakness
of his genius alone, which was too narrowly attached to examples taken from the books of Judges and Kings, without
seeing that God, when He works on this world, proportions
Himself to time and space, and knows the difference
between Frenchmen and Israelites. The city established
under His true and sole legitimate authority will not be
the town of Joshua, Saul and David; it will rather be the
town of the gospels, the town of the poor, where working-
man and prostitute will not be humiliated by the Pharisee.
Oh, sirs, how excellent it would be to extract from the
Scriptures a polity more beautiful and more saintly than
that which was extracted therefrom by that rocky and
sterile M. Bossuet! What a city, more harmonious than
that erected by the sounds of the lyre of Orpheus, could be
built on the maxims of Jesus Christ, on the day when
His priests, no more sold to emperors and kings, manifest
themselves as the true princes of the people!"

While, standing round my good master, we listened to
his discourse, we were, without noticing it, surrounded

by a troop of beggars, who, limping, shivering, spitting, frightening the sparrows, shook their swellings and deformities, spreading evil smells and suffocating us with their blessings. They struggled passionately for some small silver pieces M. d'Anquetil threw among them, fell to the ground, and rolled in the dust.

"It's painful to look on these people," said Jahel with a sigh.

" 'That pity," said M. Coignard, "suits you like a jewel, Mademoiselle Jahel; your sighs ornament your bosom heaving under them like a breath each of us would like to respire from your lips. But allow me to say that such tenderness, which is not less touching from being an interested one, troubles you inwardly by a comparison of yonder miserable beings with yourself, and by the instinctive idea that your young body touches, so to say, this hideous, ulcerated and mutilated flesh, as in truth it is bound and attached to them in as far as members of Our Lord Jesus Christ. In consequence you cannot look on such corruption of a human body without seeing it at the same time as a possibility of your own body. And these wretches have shown themselves to you like prophets, announcing that sickness and death are the lot of the family of Adam in this world. For this very reason you sighed, mademoiselle.

"As a fact, there is not the slightest reason to believe yonder ulcerated and verminous beggars less happy than kings and queens. It must not be said that they are poorer, if, as it appears, that farthing picked up by that crippled woman, and which she presses on her heart in frantic joy, seems to her more precious than a pearl collar is to the mistress of a prince-bishop of Cologne and Salzburg. To really understand our spiritual and true interests we should rather envy the life of that cripple who crawls towards us on his hands than that of the King of France or the Emperor of Germany. Being equal before God, they perhaps have peace in their hearts, which the other has not, and the invaluable treasure of innocence. But hold up your petticoats, mademoiselle, for fear that you introduce the vermin with which I see they are covered."

Such was my good tutor's speech, and we all listened willingly.

At the distance of three leagues from Montbard, one of the harnesses broke, and, the postboys having failed to bring rope with them, we were detained on the road, as the place of the accident was far from any human dwelling. My good master and M. d'Anquetil whiled away the time by playing and sympathetic quarrels, of which they had made a habit. While the young nobleman was surprised to see his opponent turn up the king oftener than seemed possible by the laws of chance, Jahel, full of emotion, asked me in a whisper if I could not see behind us a carriage in one of the turnings of the road. Looking back to the place she indicated, I could actually see a kind of Gothic vehicle of a ridiculous and strange form.

"Yonder carriage," said Jahel, "stopped at the same moment as ours. That means that we are followed. I am curious to discover the features of the people travelling in that vehicle. I feel very uneasy about it. Does not one of the travellers wear a very narrow and high headgear? The carriage very much resembles the one in which my uncle brought me, when a child, to Paris after he had killed the Portuguese. It remained, I believe, in one of the coach-houses at the Castle of Sablons. It really seems to be the same, of horrible memory, because I remember my uncle in it, fuming with rage. You cannot conceive, Jacques, how violent his hate is. I myself had

to bear his rage the day I came away. He locked me
in my room and vomited the most horrible curses on the
Abbé Coignard. I shiver when I think what his rage
must have been when he found my room empty and the
sheets still attached to the window by which I left to fly
with you."

"You ought to say with M. d'Anquetil."

"How punctilious you are! Did we not depart together?
Yonder carriage torments me, it is so much like my
uncle's."

"Be sure, Jahel, that it's the carriage of some honest
Burgundian, who goes about his business and does not
think of us."

"You don't know," said Jahel. "I'm afraid."

"You cannot fear, however, that your uncle could run
after you in his state of decrepitude. He does not
occupy himself with anything but cabala and Hebraic
dreams."

"You don't know him," she replied, and sighed. "He
is occupied with naught but myself. He loves me as
much as he hates the rest of the universe. He loves me
in a manner——"

"In a manner?"

"—In all the manners—in short he loves me."

"Jahel, I shudder to hear you. Good heavens: that
Mosaïde loves you without that disinterestedness which is
so admirable in an old man, and so well suited for an
uncle? Tell me all, Jahel—all!"

"Oh! you can tell it better than I, Jacques."

"I remain stupid. At his age, is it possible?"

"My dear friend, your skin is white, and your soul
also. Everything astonishes you. That candour is your
most striking charm. You're deceived by anyone who
wants to deceive you. They make you believe that

Mosaïde is a hundred and thirty years old; but he is hardly older than sixty. They told you that for years he lived in the Great Pyramid, but as a fact he has been a banker at Lisbon. And it depended only on me to pass in your eyes as a Salamander."

"What, Jahel, do you tell me the truth? Your uncle——"

"Yes, and that is the secret of his jealousy. He believes the Abbé Coignard to be his rival. He disliked him instinctively, at first sight. But it is a great deal worse since he overheard a few words of the conversation I had with that good abbé in the thorn bush, and I'm sure he hates him now as the cause of my flight and my elopement. For, after all, I've been abducted, my friend; a fact that ought to enhance my worth in your eyes. I was certainly very ungrateful to leave so good an uncle. But I could not endure any longer the slavery he kept me in. And I also had an ardent wish to become rich, and it is very natural, is it not, to wish for all the good things when one is young and pretty? We have but one life, and that is short enough. No one has taught me all the fine lies about the immortality of the soul."

"Alas! Jahel," I exclaimed, in an ardour of love, provoked by her own coolness. "Alas! I did not want anything else with you at the Château des Sablons. What was wanting for your happiness?"

She made me a sign to show that M. d'Anquetil was observing us. The harness had been repaired and our carriage rolled on again along the road bordered on both sides by vineyards.

We stopped at Nuits to sup and to sleep. My dear tutor drank half-a-dozen bottles of Burgundy, which warmed up his eloquence marvellously. M. d'Anquetil kept him company, glass in hand, but to hold his own in conversation also was a thing of which this nobleman was not quite capable.

The meat was good, the beds were bad. M. Coignard slept in the lower chamber, under the stairs, in the same feather bed with the host and his wife, and all three thought they would be suffocated. M. d'Anquetil with Jahel took the upstairs room, where the bacon and the onions were suspended on hooks driven into the ceiling. I myself climbed by means of a ladder to a loft and stretched out on a bundle of straw. Being awakened by the moonlight, a ray of which fell into my eyes, I suddenly saw Jahel in her night-cap coming through the trap door. At a cry that I gave she put her finger to her lips.

"Hush!" she said to me, "Maurice is as drunk as a stevedore and a marquis. He sleeps the sleep of Noah."

"Who is Maurice?" I inquired, rubbing my eyes.

"It's Anquetil. Who did you think it was?"

"Nobody, but I did not know that his name was Maurice."

"It's not long that I knew it myself, but never mind."

"You are right, Jahel, it's of no importance."

She was in her chemise, and the moonlight fell like drops of milk on her naked shoulders. She slipped down at my side, called me by the sweetest of names and by the most horrid of coarse names, in whispers sounding out of her lips like heavenly murmurs. And then she became dumb, and kissed me with the kisses she alone was able to give, and in comparison with which the caresses of any other woman were but an insipidity.

The constraint and the silence enhanced the furious tension of my nerves. Surprise, the joy of revenge, and, perhaps, a somewhat perverse jealousy inflamed my desires. The elastic firmness of her flesh and the supple violence of the movements wherewith she enveloped me demanded, promised, and deserved the most ardent caresses. We became aware, during that wonderful night, of voluptuousness the abyss of which borders on suffering.

When I came down to the innyard in the morning I met M. d'Anquetil, who, now that I had deceived him, appeared to me less odious than formerly. On his part he felt better inclined to me than he had yet done since we started on our travels. He talked familiarly to me, with sympathy and confidence; his only reproach was that I did not show to Jahel all the regard and attention she deserved, and did not give her the care an honest man ought to bestow on every woman.

"She complains," he said, "of your want of civility. Take care, my dear Tournebroche; I should be sorry for a difference to arise between her and yourself. She's a pretty girl, and loves me immensely."

The carriage had rolled on for more than an hour when Jahel put her head out of the coach window and said to me:

"The other carriage has reappeared. I should like to discover the features of the two men who occupy it, but I cannot."

I replied that at such a distance, and in the morning mist, it would be impossible to discern them.

"But," she exclaimed, "those are not faces."

"What else do you want them to be?" I questioned, and burst out laughing.

Now, in her turn, she inquired of me what silly idea had sprung into my brain to laugh so stupidly and said:

"They are not faces, they are masks. Yonder two men follow us and are masked."

I informed M. d'Anquetil that seemingly an ugly carriage followed us. But he asked me to let him alone.

"If all the hundred thousand devils were on our track," he exclaimed, "I should not care a rap for it as I have enough to do to look after that obese old abbé who plays his tricks with the cards in the most artful way, and who robs me of my money. I almost suspect, Tournebroche, you call my attention to yonder coach for the purpose of aiding and abetting that old sharper. Cannot a carriage be on the same road as ours without causing you anxiety?"

Jahel whispered to me:

"I predict, Jacques, that yonder carriage brings trouble for us. I have a presentiment of it, and my presentiments have never failed to come true."

"Do you want to make me believe that you have the gift of prophecy?"

Gravely, she replied:

"Yes; I have."

"What, you are a prophetess!" I cried, smiling. "Here is something strange!"

"You sneer and you doubt because you have never seen a prophetess so near at hand. How did you wish them to look?"

"I thought that they must be virgins."

"That's not necessary," she replied, with assurance.

The threatening carriage had disappeared at a turning of the road. But Jahel's uneasiness had, without his acknowledging it, impressed M. d'Anquetil, who ordered the postboys to hurry their horses, promising them extra good tips. And by an excess of care he passed to each of them a bottle of the wine that the abbé had placed in reserve in the bottom of the carriage.

The postillions made their horses feel the stimulus that the wine gave to them.

"You can calm yourself, Jahel," said he; "at the speed we are going that antique coach, drawn by the horses of the Apocalypse, will never catch us."

"We run like cats on hot bricks," said the abbé.

"If only it would last!" said Jahel.

We saw the vineyards on our right disappear rapidly. On the left the River Saône ran slowly. Like a hurricane we passed the bridge of Tournus. The town itself rose on the other side of the river on a hill crowned by the walls of an abbey, proud as a fortress.

"That," said the abbé, "is one of the numberless Benedictine abbeys which are strewn like so many gems on the robe of ecclesiastical Gaul. If it had pleased God that my destiny should match my character I should have lived an obscure life, gay and sweet, in one of these abodes. There is no other religious order I hold in such high esteem, for their doctrines as well as for their morals, as the Benedictines. They have admirable libraries. Happy he who wears their habit and follows their holy rules! It may be from the inconvenience I feel at this moment in being shaken to pieces in this carriage, which no doubt will very soon be upset by sinking into one of the many holes of this confounded road, or it may perhaps be the effect of age, which is the time for retreat and grave thinking; whatever be the cause I wish more ardently than ever to seat myself at a table in one of those venerable galleries, where books plenty and choice are assembled in quiet and silence. I prefer their entertainment to that of men, and my dearest wish is to wait, in the work of the spirit, for the hour in which it will please God to call me from this earth. I shall write history, and by preference that of the Romans at the decline of the Republic, because it is full of great actions and examples. I'll divide my zeal between Cicero, Saint John Chrysostom and Boethius and my modest and fruitful life would resemble the garden of the old man of Tarentum.

"I have experienced different manners of living, and I think the best is to give oneself to study, to look on peace-

fully at the vicissitudes of men, and to prolong, by the
spectacle of centuries and empires, the brevity of our days.
But order and continuity are needed. And that's the
very thing that has always been wanting in my existence.
If, as I hope, I am able to disentangle myself from the bad
position I'm in just now, I'll do my best to find an
honourable and safe asylum in some learned abbey
where *bonnes lettres* are held in honour and respect. I
can see myself there already, enjoying the illustrious peace
of science. Could I obtain the good offices of the Sylph
assistants of whom that old fool d'Asterac speaks, and who
appear, it is said, when they are invoked by the cabalistic
name of AGLA——"

At the very moment my dear tutor spoke these words
a violent shock brought down a rain of glass on our
heads, in such confusion that I felt myself blinded, as
well as suffocated under Jahel's petticoats, while the abbé
complained in a smothered voice that M. d'Anquetil's
sword had broken the remainder of his teeth, and over
my head Jahel screamed fit to tear to pieces all the air of
the Burgundian valleys. M. d'Anquetil, in rough, bar-
rack-room style, promised to get the postboys hanged.
When at last I was able to rise, he had already jumped
out through a broken window. We followed him, my dear
tutor and I, by the same exit, and then all three of us
pulled Jahel out of the overturned vehicle. No harm
had been done to her, and her first thought was to adjust
her head-dress.

"Thank God!" said my tutor, "I have not suffered any
other damage than the loss of a tooth, and that was neither
whole nor white. Time had already effected its decay."

M. d'Anquetil, legs astride and arms akimbo, examined
the carriage.

"The rascals," he said, "have put it in a nice state.

If the horses are got up they will break it all to pieces. Abbé, that carriage is no good for anything else but to play spillikins with."

The horses had fallen topsy-turvy, one on the other, and were kicking furiously. In a heap of croups and legs and steaming bellies, one of the postboys was buried, his boots in the air. The other was spitting blood in the ditch, where he had been thrown. M. d'Anquetil shouted to them:

"Idiots! I really don't know why I do not spit you on my sword."

"Sir," said Abbé Coignard, "would it not be better to get that poor fellow out of the midst of these horses wherein he is entangled?"

We all went to work with a will, and when the horses were freed and raised we were able to discover the extent of the damage done. One of the springs was broken, one of the wheels also, and one of the horses lame.

"Fetch a smith," ordered M. d'Anquetil.

"There is no smith in the neighbourhood," was the postboy's reply.

"A mechanic of some kind."

"There is none."

"A saddler."

"There is no saddler."

We looked round. To the west the vineyards extended to the horizon their long peaceful lines. On the hill smoke came out of a chimney near a steeple. On the other side, the Saône, veiled by a light mist, lost itself slowly in the calm running of her flowing waters. The shadows of the poplars elongated themselves on the banks. The shrill cry of a bird pierced the deep silence.

"Where are we?" asked M. d'Anquetil.

"At two full leagues from Tournus," replied the post-

illion, spitting blood, "and at least four leagues from
Mâcon."

And, extending his arm towards the smoking chimney:
"Up there, that village ought to be Vallars, but it's not
up to much."

"Blast you!" roared M. d'Anquetil.

While the horses struggled we went near the carriage,
which was lying sadly on its side.

The little postboy who had been taken out from the
midst of the horses said:

"As to the spring, that could be mended by a strong
piece of wood. It will only make the carriage shake you
more. But there is the broken wheel! And, worst of all,
my hat is under it, smashed to pieces."

"Damn your hat!" said M. d'Anquetil.

"Your lordship may not be aware that it was quite
new," was the postboy's meek reply.

"And the window glasses are broken!" sighed Jahel,
seated on a portmanteau, at the side of the road.

"If it were but the glasses," said M. Coignard, "a remedy could soon be found by lowering the blinds, but the
bottles cannot be in the same state as the windows. I
must look to it as soon as the coach can be raised. I
am also in fear for my Boethius, which I had placed
under the cushions with some other good books."

"It does not matter," said M. d'Anquetil. "I have
the cards in my waistcoat pocket. But shall we not get
any supper?"

"I had thought of it," said the abbé. "It is not in
vain that God has given to the use of men the animals
who crowd the earth, the sky and the water. I am
an excellent angler; the care necessary to allure
the fish particularly suits my meditative mind, and
the River Orne has seen me managing my line while

meditating on the eternal verities. Do not trouble over your supper. If Mademoiselle Jahel will be good enough to give me one of the pins which keep her garments together I'll soon make a hook of it, to enable me to fish in yonder river, and I flatter myself I shall return before nightfall laden with two or three carp, that we will grill over a brushwood fire."

"I am quite aware," said Jahel, "that we are reduced to somewhat of a savage state. But I could not give you a pin, abbé, without your giving me something in exchange for it; otherwise our friendship would be jeopardised. And that I do not want in any case."

"Then I will make an advantageous exchange, mademoiselle: I'll pay for your pin with a kiss."

And, taking the pin out of Jahel's hand, he kissed her on both cheeks with inconceivable courtesy, gracefulness and decency.

After having lost plenty of time, a reasonable step was at last taken. The big postillion, who no longer spat blood, was sent to Tournus on one of the horses to bring back with him a blacksmith; the other boy was ordered to light a fire, as the air became fresh, and a sharp wind was rising.

We discovered on the road, a hundred paces from the place of our breakdown, a cliff of soft stone, the foot of which was quarried in several places. We resolved to wait in one of those caves, warming ourselves until the return of the boy sent to Tournus. The second boy tied the three remaining horses to the trunk of a tree, near our cavern. The abbé, who had made a fishing rod with the branch of a willow-tree, some string, a cork and a pin, went a-fishing as much for his philosophical and meditative inclination as for the sake of bringing us back fish. M. d'Anquetil, remaining with Jahel and me in the grotto, proposed a game of *l'ombre,* which is played by three, and which he said, being a Spanish game, was the very one for persons as adventurous as ourselves. And true it is that, in that quarry, in a deserted road, our little company would not have been unworthy to figure in some of the adventures of Don Quixote in which menials take such a strong interest. And so we played *l'ombre.* I committed a great many errors, and my impetuous partner got cross, when the noble and laughing face of my good tutor became visible at the light of our fire. He untied his handkerchief, and took out of it some four or five small fish, which he opened with his knife, decorated with the image of the late king, dressed as a Roman emperor, standing on a triumphal column; and cleaned them with dexterity, as if he had never lived anywhere else than in the midst of the fishwomen at the market. He excelled as much in trifles as in matters of the greatest importance. Arranging the fish on the embers, he said:

"I will tell you, in all confidence, that following the river in search of a favourable place for fishing, I perceived the apocalyptic coach which frightens Mademoiselle Jahel. It stopped somewhat behind our carriage. You ought to have seen it pass by while I was fishing, and mademoiselle's soul ought to have been comforted by it."

"We have not seen it," replied Jahel.

"Then it may have moved on only after the night had become dark. But at least you heard it rumbling?"

"We have not," said Jahel.

"It is then that this night is blind as well as deaf. It is not to be supposed that yonder coach, which had not a wheel broken, not a horse lamed, would have remained standing still on the road. What for?"

"Yes, what for?" said Jahel.

"Our supper," said my good tutor, "reminds me of the

simplicity of the repasts described in the Bible, where the pious traveller divided with an angel, on the bank of the river, the fishes of the Tigris. But we are in want of bread, salt and wine. I'll try to take out of our coach the provisions put there, and look if by a fortunate chance some bottles have remained intact. There are occasions when glass remains whole but steel is broken. Tourne-broche, my son, give me your steel; and you, mademoiselle, do not fail to turn the grilling fish. I'll be back in a moment."

He left. His somewhat heavy tread sounded in a *de crescendo,* and soon we could hear him no more.

"This very night," said M. d'Anquetil, "reminds me of the night before the battle of Parma. You may be aware that I have served under Villars and been in the War of Succession. I was with the scouts. We could not see anything. That's one of the best ruses of war. Men are sent out to reconnoitre the enemy who return without having reconnoitred anything. But reports are drawn up, after the battle, and then it is that the tacticians are triumphant. Thus, at nine o'clock at night, I was sent out scouting with twelve men——"

And he gave us a narrative of the War of Succession and of his amours in Italy; his story had lasted for well-nigh a quarter of an hour when he exclaimed:

"That rascal of an abbé does not come back. I bet he drinks all the wine which remained in the coach."

Thinking that my dear tutor might possibly be embarrassed, I rose and went to help him. It was a moonless night, and if the sky was resplendent in the light of thousands of stars, the earth was clad in a darkness which my eyes, dazzled by the light of the flames, could not pierce.

Having walked about fifty steps on the black road,

I heard a terrible cry, which did not sound as if coming from a human breast, a cry altogether unlike all cries I had heard before, a horrible cry. I ran in the direction from whence came this clamour of fatal distress. But fear and darkness checked my steps. Arrived at last at the place where our coach lay on the road, shapeless and enlarged by the night, I found my dear tutor seated on the side of the ditch, bent double. Trembling I asked him:

"What's the matter? Why did you shout?"

"Yes; why did I shout?" he said, in a new and altered voice. "I did not know I had cried out. Tournebroche, did you not see a man? He struck me in the dark, very fiercely; he gave me a blow with his fist."

"Come," I said to him, "get up, my dear master."

Having risen he fell back heavily on the ground.

I tried to raise him, and my hands became moist when I touched his breast.

"You're bleeding!"

"Bleeding? I'm a dead man. He has killed me. I thought that it was but a blow with the fist. But it's a wound, and I feel that I shall never recover from it."

"Who struck you, my dear tutor?"

"It was the Jew. I did not see him, but I know it was he. How can I know that it was the Jew, when I did not see him? Yes; how is it? What strange things! It's not to be believed, is it, Tournebroche? I have the taste of death in my mouth, which cannot be defined. It was to be, my God! But why rather here than somewhere else? That's the mystery! *Adjutorium nostrum in nomine Domini—Domine exaudi orationem meam——*'"

For a short time he prayed in a low voice, then:

"Tournebroche, my son," he said to me, "take the two bottles I found in the coach and have placed here beside me. I can do no more. Tournebroche, where do you think the wound is? It's in the back I suffer most, and it seems to me that life runs out by the legs. My spirits are going."

Murmuring these words he fainted softly in my arms. I tried to carry him, but I had only strength enough to lay him lengthwise on the ground. Opening his shirt, I discovered the wound; it was in the breast; very small, and bleeding little. I tore my wristbands to pieces and laid them on the wound; I called out, shouted for help. Soon I thought I heard help coming from the side of Tournus, and I recognised M. d'Asterac. Unexpected as the meeting was, I did not actually feel surprised; too deeply was I the prey of the immense sorrow I felt holding in my arms, dying, that best of all masters.

"What's the matter, my son?" asked the alchemist.

"Help me, sir," I replied, "the Abbé Coignard is dying. Mosaïde has killed him."

"It is true," said M. d'Asterac, "that Mosaïde has come here in an old chariot in pursuit of his niece, and that I have accompanied him to exhort you, my son, to return to your employment with me. Since yesterday we came near your coach, which we saw break down just now in a rut. At that very moment Mosaïde alighted from the carriage, and it may be that he wanted to take a walk, or perhaps he made himself invisible, as he can do. I have not seen him again. It is possible that he has already found his niece to curse her; such is the intention. But he has not killed M. Coignard. It is the Elves, my son, who have killed your master, to punish him for the disclosure of their secrets. Nothing is surer than that."

"Ah! sir," I exclaimed, "what does it matter, if it was the Jew or the Elves who killed him; we must assist him."

"On the contrary, my son," replied M. d'Asterac, "it is of the greatest importance. For should he have been stricken by a human hand it would be easy for me to cure him by magic operation; but having provoked the Elves he could never escape their infallible vengeance."

As he spoke, M. d'Anquetil and Jahel, having heard my shouts, approached, with the postboy, who carried a lantern.

"What," said Jahel, "is M. Coignard unwell?"

And kneeling close to my good tutor, she raised his head and made him inhale the smell of her salts.

"Mademoiselle," I said to her, "you're the cause of his death, which is the vengeance for your abduction. Mosaïde has killed him."

From my dying master she lifted up her face pale with horror and shining with tears.

"And you too," she said, "believe that it's easy to be a pretty girl without causing mischief?"

"Alas!" I replied, "what you say is but too true. But we have lost the best of men."

At this moment Abbé Coignard sighed deeply, opened his eyes, called for his book of Boethius, and fainted again into unconsciousness.

The postboy thought it would be best to carry the wounded man to the village of Vallars, which was only half-a-league distant.

"I'll go," he said, "to fetch the steadiest of the horses which remain. We'll tie the poor fellow securely on it, and lead it slowly ahead. I think him very ill. He looks exactly like the courier who was murdered at Saint Michel on the same road, at four stages from here, near Senecy, where my sweetheart lives. That poor devil moved his eyelids and turned up the whites of his eyes like a bad woman, saving your presence, gentlemen. And your abbé did the same when mam'selle tickled his nose with her bottle. It's a bad sign with a wounded man; girls don't die of it when they turn their eyes up in that

fashion. Your lordships know it well. And there is
some distance, thank God! between the little death and
the great. But it's the same turning up of the eyes. . . .
Remain, gentlemen, I'll go and fetch the horse."

"This rustic is amusing," said M. d'Anquetil, "with
his turned-up eyes and his bad women. I've seen in
Italy soldiers who died on the battlefield with a fixed
look and eyes starting out of their head. There are no
rules for dying of a wound, actually not even in the
military service, where exactitude is pushed to the extreme.
But will you, Tournebroche, in default of a better qualified
person, present me to yonder gentleman in black, who
wears diamond studs, and whom I reckon to be M.
d'Asterac?"

"Ah! sir," I replied, "consider the presentation to be
made. I have no other feelings but to assist my dear
tutor."

"Be it so!" said M. d'Anquetil.

And approaching M. d'Asterac:

"Sir, I have taken your mistress away: I'm ready to
answer for my deed."

"Sir," replied M. d'Asterac. "Grace be to heaven!
I have no connection with any woman, and do not
understand what you mean."

At this very moment the postboy returned with a horse.
My dear tutor had slightly recovered. We lifted him up,
all four of us, and put him with the greatest difficulty
on the horse, where we tied him as securely as possible.
And we went off. I held him on one side, M. d'Anquetil
on the other. The postboy led the horse and carried the
lantern. M. d'Asterac had returned to his carriage. All
went well as long as we kept on the highroad; but when
it became necessary to climb the small lanes of the vineyards, my dear master, slipping at every movement of the

horse, lost the rest of his little strength, and fainted away again. We thought it best to take him off the horse and carry him in our arms. The postboy held him under the arms and I by the legs. The ascent was very rough, and I expected to fall at least four times with my living cross, on the stones of the path. At last the hill became easier. We entered a small lane bordered by bushes, and soon discovered on our left the first roofs of Vallars. We laid our burden softly on the turf, and for a moment took breath. Lifting up the abbé again, we carried him into the village.

A pink light appeared eastwards on the horizon. The morning star, in the pale sky, shone as white and peaceful as the moon, the light crescent of which paled away in the west. The birds began to chirp; my master sighed heavily.

Jahel ran before us, knocking at the doors, in quest of a bed and a surgeon. Carrying baskets and panniers the vine-growers went grape-gathering. One of them said to Jahel that Gaulard on the market place lodges man and beast.

"As to the surgeon, Coquebert, you'll see him yonder under the shaving plate which serves as his trade sign. He leaves his house to go to his vineyard."

He was a very polite little man. He told us that he had a bed free in his house, as a short time ago his daughter had got married.

By his order, his wife, a stout dame wearing a white cap covered by a felt hat, put sheets on the bed in the lower chamber. She helped us to undress the Abbé Coignard and to put him to bed. And then she went out to fetch the vicar.

In the meanwhile M. Coquebert examined the wound "You see," I said, "it's small, and bleeds but little."

"That's not good at all," he replied, "and I do not

like it, my dear young gentleman. I like a large wound which bleeds freely."

"I see," said M. d'Anquetil, "that for a leech and a village squirt your test is not a bad one. Nothing is worse than those little but deep wounds which look a mere nothing. Tell me of a nice cut across the face. It's pleasant to look on, and heals in no time. But know, my good sir, that this wounded man is my chaplain, and plays piquet with me. Are you the man to put him on his legs again, notwithstanding your looks, which are rather those of a vet?"

"At your service," replied the barber-surgeon, bowing profoundly. "But I also set broken bones and treat wounds. I'll examine this one."

"Make haste, sir," I said.

"Patience!" he replied. "First of all the wound must be washed, and I must wait till the water gets warm."

My good tutor, a little restored, said slowly, but with a fairly strong voice:

"Lamp in hand, he'll visit the corners of Jerusalem, and what is hidden in darkness will be brought to light."

"What do you mean, dear master?"

"Don't, my son," he replied; "I'm entertaining the sentiments fit for my state."

"The water is hot," the barber said to me. "Hold the basin close to the bed. I'll wash the wound."

And while he pressed on my tutor's breast a sponge soaked in hot water, the vicar entered the room with Madame Coquebert. He had a basket and a pair of vine shears in his hand.

"Here is then the poor man," said he. "I was going to my vineyard, but that of Jesus Christ has to be attended to first; my son," he said as he approached the stricken abbé, "offer your wound to our Lord. Perhaps it's not

so serious as it's thought to be. And for the rest, we must
obey God's will."

Turning to the barber, he asked:

"Is it very urgent, M. Coquebert, or could I go to my
vineyard? The white ones can wait; it's not bad if they
do get a little overripe, and a little rain would only
produce more and better wine. But the red must be
gathered at once."

"You speak the truth, Monsieur le Curé," M. Coquebert
replied. "I've in my vineyard some grapes which cover
themselves with a certain moisture, and which escape the
sun only to perish by the rain."

"Alas!" said the vicar, "humidity and drought are
the two enemies of the vine-grower."

"Nothing is truer," said the barber, "but I'll inspect
the wound."

Having said so he pushed one of his fingers into the
wound.

"Ah! Torturer!" exclaimed the patient.

"Remember," said the vicar, "that our Lord forgave
His torturers."

"They were not barbarous," said the abbé.

"That's a wicked word," said the vicar.

"You must not torment a dying man for his jokes,"
said my good master. "But I suffer horribly; that man
assassinates me and I die twofold. The first time was
by the hands of a Jew."

"What does he mean?" asked the vicar.

"It is best, reverend sir," said the barber, "not to
trouble yourself about it. You must never want to hear
the talk of a patient. They are only dreams."

"Coquebert," said the vicar, "you don't speak well.
Patients' confessions must be listened to, and some
Christians who never in all their lives said a good word

may, at the end, pronounce words which open Paradise
to them."

"I spoke temporally only," said the barber.

"Monsieur le Curé," I said, "the Abbé Coignard, my
good master, does not wander in his mind, and it is but
too true that he has been murdered by a Jew of the name
of Mosaïde."

"In that case," replied the vicar, "he has to see a special
favour of God, who willed that he perishes by the hand
of a nephew of those who crucified His Son. The behaviour of Providence is always admirable. M. Coquebert,
can I go to my vineyard?"

"You can, sir," replied the barber. "The wound is not
a good one, but yet not of the kind by which one dies at
once. It's one of those wounds which play with the
wounded like a cat with a mouse, and with such play
time may be gained."

"That's well," said the vicar. "Let's thank God, my
son, that He lets you live, but life is precarious and
transitory. One must always be ready to quit it."

My good tutor replied earnestly:

"To be on the earth without being of it, to possess without being in possession, for the fashion of this world
passes away."

Picking up his shears and his basket, the vicar said:

"Better than by your cloak and shoes, which I see on
yonder cupboard, I recognise by your speech that you
belong to the Church and lead a holy life. Have you
been ordained?"

"He is a priest," I said, "a doctor of divinity and a
professor of eloquence."

"Of which diocese?" queried the vicar.

"Of Séez in Normandy, a suffragan of Rouen."

"An important ecclesiastical province," said the vicar,

"but less important by antiquity and fame than the diocese of Reims, of which I am a priest."

And he went away. M. Jérôme Coignard passed the day easily. Jahel wanted to remain the night with him. At about eleven o'clock I left the house of M. Coquebert and went in search of a bed at the inn of M. Gaulard. I found M. d'Asterac in the market place. His shadow in the moonlight covered nearly all the surface. He laid his hands on my shoulder as he was wont to do, and said with his customary gravity:

"It's time for me to assure you, my son, that I have accompanied Mosaïde for nothing else than this. I see you cruelly tormented by the goblins. Those little spirits of the earth have attacked you, deceiving you with all sorts of phantasmagoria, seducing you by a thousand lies, and finally forcing you to fly from my house."

"Alas! sir," I replied, "it's quite true that I left your house in apparent ingratitude, for which I beg your pardon. But I have been persecuted by the constables, and not by goblins. And my dear tutor has been murdered. That's not a phantasmagoria."

"Do not doubt," the great man answered, "that the unhappy abbé has been mortally wounded by the Sylphs, whose secrets he has revealed. He has stolen from a sideboard some stones, which were the work of the Sylphs, and which they left unfinished, and still very different from diamonds in brilliancy as well as in purity.

"It was that avidity, and the indiscreet pronouncing of the name of *Agla,* which has angered them. You must know, my son, that it is impossible for philosophers to arrest the vengeance of this irascible people.

"I have heard from a supernatural voice, and also from Criton's reports, of the sacrilegious larceny M. Coignard committed by which he flattered himself to find out the art by which Salamanders, Sylphs, and Gnomes ripen the morning dew and insensibly change it into crystals and diamonds."

"Alas! sir, I assure you he thought of no such thing, and that it was that horrible Mosaïde who stabbed him with a stiletto on the road."

My words very much displeased M. d'Asterac, who urged me in the most pressing manner never to repeat them again.

"Mosaïde," he further said, "is a good enough cabalist to reach his enemies without going to the trouble of running after them. Know, my son, that, had he wanted to kill M. Coignard, he could have done it easily from his own room by a magic operation. I see that you're still ignorant of the first elements of the science. The truth is that this learned man, informed by the faithful Criton of the flight of his niece, hired post-horses to rejoin her and eventually carry her back to his house, which he certainly would have done, had he discovered in the mind of that unhappy girl the slightest idea of regret and repentance. But, finding her corrupted by debauchery, he preferred to excommunicate and curse her by the globes, the wheels and the beasts of Ezekiel. That is precisely what he has done under my eyes in the calash, where he lives alone, so as not to partake of the bed and table of Christians."

I kept mute, astonished by such dreams, but this extraordinary man talked to me with an eloquence which troubled me deeply.

"Why," he said, "do you not let yourself be enlightened by the counsels of philosophers? What kind of wisdom do you oppose to mine? Consider that yours is less in quantity without differing in essence. To you as well as to me nature appears as an infinity of figures, which have to be recognised and classified, and which form a sequence of hieroglyphics. You can easily distinguish some of those signs to which you attach a sense, but you are too much inclined to be content with the vulgar and the literal, and you do not search enough for the ideal and the symbolic. And withal the world is comprehensible only as a symbol, and all you see in the universe is naught but an illuminated writing, which vulgar men spell without understanding it. Be afraid, my son, to imitate the universal bray in the style of the learned ones who congregate in the academies. Rather receive of me the key of all knowledge."

For a moment he stopped speaking, and then continued in a more familiar tone:

"You are persecuted, my son, by enemies less terrible than Sylphs. And your Salamander will not have any difficulty in freeing you from the goblins as soon as you request her to do so. I repeat that I came here with Mosaïde for no other purpose than to give you this good advice, and to press you to return to me and continue your work. I quite understand that you want to assist your unhappy master till the end. You have full license to do it. But afterwards do not fail to return to my house. Adieu! I'll return this very night to Paris with that great Mosaïde whom you have accused so unjustly."

I promised him all he wanted, and crawled into my miserable bed, where I fell asleep, weighed down as I was by fatigue and suffering.

CHAPTER XX

Illness of M. Jérôme Coignard

THE next morning, at daybreak, I returned to the surgeon's house, and there found Jahel at the bedside of my dear tutor, sitting upright on a straw chair, with her head wrapped up in her black cape, attentive, grave and docile, like a sister of charity. M. Coignard, very red, dozed.

"The night was not a good one," she said to me in a whisper. "He has talked, he sang, he called me Sister Germaine, and has made proposals to me. I am not offended, but it is a proof that his mind wanders."

"Alas!" I exclaimed, "if you had not betrayed me, Jahel, to ramble about the country in company with a gallant, my dear master would not lie in bed stabbed in his breast."

"It is the misery of our friend," she replied, "that causes me bitter regrets. As for the rest, it is not worth while to think of it, and I cannot understand, Jacques, how you can occupy your mind with it just now."

"I think of it always."

"For my part, I hardly think of it. You are the cause of three-fourths of your own unhappiness."

"What do you mean by that, Jahel?"

"I mean, my friend, that I have given the cloth, but that you do the embroidery, and that your imagination enriches far too much the plain reality. I give you my oath that the present hour I cannot remember the quarter of what causes you grief, and you meditate over it so obstinately that your rival is more present to your mind than I am myself. Do not think of it any more, and let me give the abbé a cooling drink, for he wakes up."

At this very moment M. Coquebert approached the bed-side, his instrument-case in hand, dressed the wound anew, and said aloud that the wound was on the best way to heal up. But taking me aside he said:

"I can assure you, sir, that the good abbé will not die from the wound he has received, but to tell the truth I am afraid it will be difficult for him to escape from a pleurisy caused by his wound. He is at present the prey of a heavy fever. But here comes the vicar."

My good master recognised him without any difficulty, and inquired after his health.

"Better than the grapes," replied the vicar. "They are all spoiled by *fleurebers* and vermin, against which the clergy of Dijon organised this year a fine procession with cross and banners. Next year a still finer one will have to be arranged, and more candles burnt. It also will be necessary for the official to excommunicate anew the flies which destroy the grapes."

"Vicar," said my good master, "it is said that you seduce the girls in your vineyards. Fie! it is not right at your age. In my youth, like you I had a weakness for the creatures. But time has altered me very much, and quite lately I let a nun pass without saying anything to her. You do otherwise with the damsels and the bottles, vicar. But you do worse by not celebrating the masses you have been paid for, and by trafficking the goods and chattels of the Church. You are a bigamist and a simoniac."

Hearing this discourse the vicar was painfully surprised; his mouth remained open, and his cheeks dropped wistfully on both sides of his big face. And at last, with eyes on the ground, he sighed:

"What an unworthy attack on the character of my profession! What talk for a man so near the tribunal of God! Oh, Monsieur l'Abbé, is it for you to speak in that way, you who have lived a holy life and studied in so many books?"

My dear master raised himself on his elbows. The fever gave him, unhappily, that jovial mien of his that we had always liked so much.

"It is true," he said, "that I have studied the ancient authors. But I have read much less than the second vicar of the Bishop of Séez, for, as he had the look and the mind of an ass, he was able to read two pages at the same time, one with each eye. What do you say to that, you villain of a vicar, you old seducer, who runs after the chicks by moonlight? Vicar, your lady friend is built like a witch. She has hairs on her chin, she's the barber-surgeon's wife. He is fully a cuckold, and well he deserves it, that homunculus, whose whole medical science consists in the art of blood-letting and giving a clyster."

"God Almighty! What does he say?" exclaimed Madame Coquebert, "for sure he has the devil in him."

"I have heard the talk of many delirious patients," said M. Coquebert, "but not one has said such wicked things."

"I am discovering," said the vicar, "that we'll have more trouble than we expected to conduct this unhappy man to a peaceful end. There is a biting humour in his nature and impurities I did not find out at first. His speech is malicious, and unfit for a priest and a patient."

"It's the effect of the fever," said the barber-surgeon.

"But," continued the vicar, "that fever, if it's not stopped, will bring him to hell. He has gravely offended against what is due to a priest. But still, I'll come back to-morrow and exhort him, for I owe him, by the example of our Lord, unlimited compassion. But I have my doubts about it. Unhappily there is a break in my wine-press, and all the labourers are in the vineyard. Coquebert, do not fail to give word to the carpenter, and to call me to your patient if he should suddenly get worse. These are many troubles, Coquebert!"

The following day was such a good one for M. Coignard that we hoped he would remain with us. He drank meat broth, and was able to rise in his bed. He talked to each of us with his accustomed grace and sweetness. M. d'Anquetil, who dwelt at Gaulard's, came to see him, and rather indiscreetly asked him to play piquet. Smiling, my good master promised to do so next week. But in the evening the fever returned. With pale eyes swimming in unspeakable terror, and shivering and chattering teeth, he shouted:

"There he is, the old fornicator. He is the son of Judas Iscariot begot on a female devil, taking the form of a goat. But hanged he will be on his father's fig-tree, and his intestines will gush out to earth. Arrest him. . . .He kills me! I feel cold!"

But a moment later he threw the blanket off and complained of the heat.

"I'm very thirsty," he said. "Give me some wine! And let it be cool! Madame Coquebert, hasten to cool it in the fountain: the day will be a burning one."

It was night-time, he confounded the hours in his head.

"Be quick," he also said to Madame Coquebert, "but do not be as simple as the bell-ringer of the Cathedral of Séez, who, going to lift out of the fountain some bottles he had put there to cool, saw his own shadow in the water and shouted: 'Hello, gentleman; come and help me. There are on the other side some Antipodeans, who'll drink our wine if we don't take good care.'"

"He is jovial," said Madame Coquebert. "But just now he talked of me in a manner quite indecent. Should I have deceived Coquebert I certainly would not have done it with the vicar, out of regard for his profession and his age."

This very moment the vicar entered the room and asked:

"Well, abbé, what are your dispositions now? What is there new?"

"Thank God," answered M. Coignard, "there is nothing new in my soul, for, as said Saint Chrysostom, beware of new things. Don't walk in untrodden ways, one wanders without end when one commences to wander. I have had that sad experience, and lost myself for having followed untrodden roads. I have listened to my own counsels, and they have conducted me to the abyss. Vicar, I am a poor sinner, the number of my iniquities oppresses me."

"These are fine words," said the vicar. " 'Tis God Himself who dictates them to you. I recognise His inimitable style. Do you want to advance somewhat the salvation of your soul?"

"Willingly," said M. Coignard. "My impurities rise against me. I see big ones and small. I see red ones and black. I see infinitesimals which ride on dogs and pigs, and I see others which are fat and naked, with breasts like leather bottles, bellies in great folds, and thighs of enormous size."

"Is it possible," said the vicar, "that you can see as distinctly as that? But if your faults are such as you say, it would be better not to describe them and to be content to detest them in your own mind."

"Would you, then, vicar," replied the abbé, "that my sins were all made like an Adonis? Don't let us speak

of it any more. And you, barber, give me a drink. Do
you know M. de la Musardière?"

"Not that I know of," said M. Coquebert.

"Then know," replied my dear master, "that he was
very taken with the ladies."

"That's the way," interrupted the vicar, "by which
the devil takes his advantage over men. But what subject do you follow, my son?"

"You'll soon know," said my good master. "M. de la
Musardière gave an appointment to a virgin in a stable.
She went, and he let her go away just as she entered it.
Do you know why?"

"I do not," said the vicar, "but let us leave it."

"Not at all," continued M. Coignard. "You ought to
know that he took good care to have no intercourse with
her as he was afraid of begetting a horse, on which
account he would have been subject to criminal prose-
cution."

"Ah!" said the barber, "he ought rather to have been
afraid to engender an ass."

"Doubtless," said the vicar. "But such talk does not
advance us on the road to heaven. It would be useful
to retake the good way. But a little while ago you spoke
so edifyingly!"

Instead of giving reply, my good master began to sing,
with rather a strong voice:

> "Pour mettre en goût le roi Louison
> On a pris quinze mirlitons
> Landerinette
> Qui tous le balai ont rôli
> Landeriri."

"If you want to sing, my son," said the vicar, "you'd
better sing a fine Burgundian Christmas carol. You'd
rejoice your soul by it and sanctify it."

"With pleasure," replied my dear tutor. "There are some by Guy Barozai which, I think, in their apparent rusticity, to be finer than diamonds and more precious than gold. This one, for example:

> 'Lor qu'au lai saison qu'ai jaule
> Au monde Jésu-chri vin
> L'âne et le beu l'échaufin
> De le leu sofle dans l'étaule.
> Que d'âne et de beu je sai
> Dans ce royaume de Gaule,
> Que d'âne et de beu je sai
> Qui n'en a rien pas tan fai.'"

The surgeon, his wife and the vicar sang together:

> "Que d'âne et de beu je sai
> Dans ce royaume de Gaule,
> Que d'âne et de beu je sai
> Qui n'en a rien pas tan fai."

And my good master replied in a weaker voice:

> "Mais le pu béo de l'histoire
> Ce fut que l'âne et le beu
> Ainsin passire tô deu
> La nuit sans manger ni boire
> Que d'âne et de beu je sai
> Couver de pane et de moire
> Que d'âne et de beu je sai
> Que n'en a rien pas tan fai!"

Then he let his head fall on the pillow and sang no more.

"There is good in this Christian," said the vicar, "much good, and a while ago he really edified me with his beautiful sentences. But I am not without a certain apprehension, as everything depends on the end, and nobody knows what's hidden at the bottom of the basket.

God in His kindness wills that one single moment brings us salvation, but this moment must be the last one, so that everything depends on a single minute, in comparison with which the whole life does not count. That's what makes me tremble for the patient, over whom angels and devils are furiously quarrelling. But one must never despair of divine mercy."

CHAPTER XXI

Death of M. Jérôme Coignard

TWO days passed in cruel alternations. After that my good master became extremely weak.

"There is no more hope," M. Coquebert told me. "Look how his head lies on the pillow, how thin his nose is."

As a fact, my good master's nose, formerly big and red, was nothing now but a bent blade, livid like lead.

"Tournebroche, my son," he said to me in a voice still full and strong but of a sound quite strange to me, "I feel that I have but a short time to live. Go and fetch that good priest, that he may listen to my confession."

The vicar was in his vineyard. There I went.

"The vintage is finished," he said, "and more abundant than I had hoped for; now let's go and help that poor fellow."

I conducted him to my master's bedside and we left him alone with the dying.

An hour later he came out again and said:

"I can assure you that M. Jérôme Coignard dies in admirable sentiments of piety and humility. At his request, and in consideration of his fervour, I'll give him the viaticum. During the time necessary for putting on my holy garments, you, Madame Coquebert, will do me the favour to send to the vestry the boy who serves me at mass every morning and make the room ready for the reception of God."

Madame Coquebert swept the room, put a white coverlet on the bed, placed a little table at the bedside, and

covered it with a cloth; she put two candlesticks on the
table and lit the candles, and an earthenware bowl wherein
a sprig of box swam in the holy water.

Soon we heard the tinkling of the little bell, saw the
cross coming in, carried by a child, and the priest clad in
white carrying the holy vessels. Jahel, M. d'Anquetil,
Madame Coquebert and I fell on our knees.

"*Pax huic domui,*" said the priest.

"*Et omnibus habiantibus in ea,*" replied the servitor.

Then the vicar took holy water and sprayed it over the
patient and the bed.

A moment longer he meditated and then he said with
much solemnity:

"My son, have you no declaration to make?"

"Yes, sir," said M. Abbé Coignard, with a firm voice,
"I forgive my murderer."

Then the priest gave him the holy wafer:

"*Ecce Agnus Dei, qui tollit peccata mundi.*"

My good master replied with a sigh:

"May I speak to my Lord, I who am naught but dust
and ashes? How can I dare to come unto you, I who
do not feel any good in me to give me courage? How
can I introduce you into me, after having so often wounded
your eyes full of kindness?"

And the Abbé Coignard received the holy viaticum in
profound silence, interrupted by our sobs and by the great
noise Madame Coquebert made blowing her nose.

After having received, my good master made me a sign
to come near him, and said with a feeble but distinct
voice:

"Jacques Tournebroche, my son, reject, along with the
example I gave you, the maxims which I may have proposed to you during my period of lifelong folly. Be
in fear of women and of books for the softness and pride

accords the little ones a clearer intelligence than the wise
one takes in them. Be humble of heart and spirit. God
can give them. 'Tis He who gives all science. My boy,
do not listen to those who, like me, subtilise on the good
and the evil. Do not be taken in by the beauty and
acuteness of their discourses, for the kingdom of God
does not consist of words but of virtue."

He remained quiet, exhausted. I took his hand, lying
on the sheet, and covered it with kisses and tears. I told
him that he was our master, our friend, our father, and
that I could not live without him.

And for long hours I remained waiting at the foot of
his bed.

He passed so peaceful a night that I conceived a
quite desperate hope. In this state he remained part of
the following day. But towards the evening he became
agitated and pronounced words so indistinctly that they
remained a secret between God and himself.

At midnight he fell into a kind of swoon, and nothing
could be heard but the slight scratching of his finger nails
on the sheet. He no longer knew me.

About two o'clock the death rattle began. The hoarse
and rapid breathing which came from his breast was
loud enough to be heard far away in the village street, and
my ears were so full of it that I fancied I heard it long
after that unhappy day. At daybreak he made a sign with
his hand which we could not understand, and sighed long
and deeply. It was his last. His features took in death
a majesty worthy of the genius that had animated him,
and the loss of which will never be repaired.

CHAPTER XXII

Funeral and Epitaph

THE Vicar of Vallars prepared a worthy funeral for M. Jérôme Coignard. He chanted the death mass and gave the benediction.

My good master was carried to the graveyard close by the church; and M. d'Anquetil offered supper at Gaulard's to all the people who had assisted at the funeral. They drank new wine and sang Burgundian songs.

Afterwards I went with M. d'Anquetil to the vicar to thank him for his good offices.

"Ah!" he said, "that priest has given us a grand consolation by his edifying end. I have seldom seen a Christian die in such admirable sentiments, and I think it fit to fix his memory by a suitable inscription on his tombstone. Both of you, gentlemen, are learned enough to do that successfully, and I engage myself to have the epitaph of the defunct engraved on a large white stone, in the manner and style wherein you compose it. But remember, in making the stone speak, to make it proclaim nothing but the praise of God."

I begged of him to believe that I should apply all my zeal to this work, and M. d'Anquetil promised to give the matter a gallant and graceful turn.

"I will," he said, "try to write French verse in the style of M. Chapelle."

"That's right!" said the vicar. "But are you not curious to look at my winepress? The wine will be good this year,

240

and I have made enough for my own and my servants' use. Alas! save for the *fleurebers* we should have had far more."

After supper M. d'Anquetil called for ink, and began the composition of his French verses. But he soon became impatient and threw up in the air the pen, ink and paper.

"Tournebroche," he said, "I've made two verses only, and I am not quite sure that they are good. They run as follows:

> 'Ci-dessus gît monsieur Coignard
> Il faut bien mourir tôt ou tard.'"

I replied that the best of it was, that he had not written a third one.

And I passed the night composing the following epitaph in Latin:

D. O. M.
HIC JACET
IN SPE BEATÆ ÆTERNITATIS
DOMINUS HIERONYMUS COIGNARD
PRESBYTER
QUONDAM IN BELLOVACENSI COLLEGIO
ELOQUENTIÆ MAGISTER ELOQUENTISSIMU
SAGIENSIS EPISCOPI BIBLIOTHECARIUS SOLERTISSIMUS
ZOZIMI PANOPOLITANI INGENIOSISSIMUS
TRANSLATOR
OPERE TAMEN IMMATURATA MORTE INTERCEPTO
PERIIT ENIM CUM LUGDUNUM PETERET
JUDEA MANU NEFANDISSIMA
ID EST A NEPOTE CHRISTI CARNIFICUM
IN VIA TRUCIDATUS
ANNO ÆT. LII°
COMITATE FUIT OPTIMA DOCTISSIMO CONVITU
INGENIO SUBLIMI
FACETIIS JUCUNDUS SENTENTIIS PLENUS
DONORUM DEI LAUDATOR
FIDE DEVOTISSIMA PER MULTAS TEMPESTATES
CONSTANTER MUNITUS
HUMILITATE SANCTISSIMA ORNATUS
SALUTI SUÆ MAGIS INTENTUS

QUAM VANO ET FALLACI HOMINUM JUDICIO
SIC HONORIBUS MUNDANIS
NUNQUAM QUÆSITIS
SIBI GLORIAM SEMPITERNAM
MERUIT

which may be translated:

HERE SLEEPS
In the hope of a happy eternity
THE REVEREND JEROME COIGNARD
Priest
Formerly a very eloquent professor of eloquence
At the college of Beauvais
Very zealous librarian to the Bishop of Séez
Author of a fine translation of Zosimus the Panopolitan
Which he unhappily left unfinished
When overtaken by his premature death
He was stabbed on the road to Lyons
In the 52nd year of his age
By the very villainous hand of a Jew
And thus perished the victim of a descendant of the murderer
Of Jesus Christ

He was an agreeable companion
Of a learned conversation
Of an elevated genius
Abounding in cheerful speech and in good maxims
And praising God in his works
He preserved amid the storms of life an unshakable faith
In his truly Christian humility
More attentive to the salvation of his soul
Than to the vain and erroneous opinions of men
It was by living without honour in this world
That he walked towards eternal glory

CHAPTER XXIII

Farewell to Jahel—Dispersal of the Party

THREE days after the demise of my good master, M. d'Anquetil decided to continue his journey. The carriage had been repaired. He gave the postboys the order to be ready on the following morning. His company had never been agreeable to me; in the state of sorrow I was in, it became odious. I could not bear the idea of following him and Jahel. I resolved to look for employment at Tournus or at Mâcon, and to remain hidden till the storm had calmed down sufficiently to enable me to return to Paris, where I was sure to be received with outstretched arms by my dear parents. I imparted my intention to M. d'Anquetil, and excused myself for not accompanying him any farther. He tried to retain me with a gracefulness I was not prepared for, but soon willingly gave me leave to go where I wished. With Jahel the matter was more difficult, but, being naturally reasonable, she accepted the reasons I had for leaving her.

On the night before my departure, while M. d'Anquetil drank and played cards with the barber-surgeon, Jahel and I went to the market place to get a breath of air. It was embalmed by the scent of herbs and full of the song of crickets.

"What a night!" I said to Jahel. "The year cannot produce another like it, and perhaps all my life long I shall never see one so sweet."

The flower-decked village graveyard extended before our eyes its motionless turf, and the moonlight whitened

243

the scattered graves on the dark grass. The same thought
came to both of us to say a last farewell to our friend.
The place where he was put to eternal rest was marked
by a tear-sprinkled cross planted deep in the mellow
earth. The stone whereon the epitaph was to be engraved
had not yet been placed. We seated ourselves very close to
the grave on the grass, and there, by an insensible but
natural inclination, we fell into one another's arms without
fearing to offend by our kisses the memory of a friend
whom deep wisdom had rendered indulgent to human
weakness.

Suddenly, Jahel whispered in my ear, where her mouth
was already placed:

"I see M. d'Anquetil, who, from the top of the wall,
looks eagerly towards us."

"Can he see us in this shadow?" I asked.

"He certainly sees my white petticoat," she said; "it's
enough, I think, to tempt him to look for more."

I first thought to draw my sword, and was quite decided
to defend two existences, which were at this moment still
very much mixed. Jahel's calm surprised me, neither her
movements nor her voice showed any fear.

"Go," she said to me, "fly, and don't fear for me. It's
a surprise I have rather wished for. He began to get
tired of me, and this encounter is quite efficacious to
reanimate his desires and season his love. Go and leave
me alone. The first moment will be hard, for he is
of a very violent disposition. He'll strike me, but after,
I shall be still dearer to him. Farewell!"

"Alas!" I exclaimed, "did you take me then, Jahel, for
nothing but to sharpen the desires of my rival?"

"I wonder that you also want to quarrel with me.
Go, I say!"

"What! leave you like this?"

"It's necessary. Farewell! He must not meet you here. I want to make him jealous, but in a delicate manner. Farewell! Farewell."

I had hardly gone a few steps between the labyrinth of tombstones when M. d'Anquetil, having come forward to enable him to recognise his mistress, began to shout and to curse loud enough to awaken the village dead. I was anxious to tear Jahel away from his rage; I thought he would kill her. I glided between the tombstones to her assistance. But after a few minutes, observing them very closely, I saw M. d'Anquetil pulling her out of the cemetery and leading her towards Gaulard's inn with a remainder of fury she was easily capable of calming, alone and without help.

I returned to my room after they had entered theirs. I could not sleep the whole of the night, and looking out at daybreak, through an opening in the window curtains, I saw them crossing the courtyard apparently the best of friends.

Jahel's departure augmented my sorrow. I stretched myself full length on my stomach on the floor of my room, and with my face in my hands cried until the evening.

CHAPTER XXIV

I am pardoned and return to Paris—Again at the *Queen Pédauque*
—I go as Assistant to M. Blaizot—Burning of the Castle of
Sablons—Death of Mosaïde and of M. d'Asterac

FROM now onwards my life loses the interest which
events had lent it, and my destiny, having again become in conformity with my character, offers nothing but
ordinary occurrences. If I should prolong my memoirs my
narrative would very soon become tiresome. I'll bring it to
a close with but few words. The Vicar of Vallars gave
me a letter of introduction to a wine merchant at Mâcon,
with whom I was employed for a couple of months, after
which my father wrote to me that he had arranged my
affair and that I was free to return to Paris.

I took coach immediately and travelled with some re-
cruits. My heart beat violently when I again saw the
Rue Saint Jacques, the clock of Saint Benoît le Bétourné,
the signboard of the *Three Virgins* and the *Saint Catherine* of M. Blaizot.

My mother cried when she saw me; I also cried, and
we embraced and cried together again.

My father came in haste from the *Little Bacchus* and
said with a moving dignity:

"Jacquot, my son, I cannot and will not deny that I
was very angry when I saw the constables enter the *Queen
Pédauque* in search of you, or, in default of you, arresting
me. They would not listen to any sort of remonstrance,
alleging that I could easily explain myself after being
taken to jail. They looked for you on a complaint of M.
de la Guéritude. I conceived a most horrible idea of

246

your disorders. But having been informed by letter that it was a question only of some peccadillo I had no other thought but to see you again. Many a time I consulted the landlord of the *Little Bacchus* on the means to hush up your affair. He always replied: 'Master Léonard, go to the judge with a big bag full of crown pieces and he will give you back your lad as white as snow.' But crown pieces are scarce with us, and there is neither hen nor goose nor duck who lays golden eggs in my house. At present I hardly get sufficient by my poultry to pay the expenses of the roasting. By good luck, your saintly and worthy mother had the good idea of going to the mother of M. d'Anquetil whom we knew to be busy in favour of her son, who was sought after at the same time as you were, and for the identical affair. I am quite aware, my Jacquot, that you played the man about town in company with a nobleman, and my head is too well placed not to feel the honour which it reflects on our whole family. Mother dressed as if she intended to go to mass; and Madame d'Anquetil received her with kindness. Thy mother, Jacquot, is a holy woman, but she has not the best of society manners, and at first she talked without aim or reason. She said: 'Madame, at our age, besides God Almighty nothing remains to us but our children.' That was not the right thing to say to that great lady who still has her gallants."

"Hold your tongue, Léonard," exclaimed my mother. "The behaviour of Madame d'Anquetil is unknown to you, and it appears that I spoke to her in the right way, because she said to me: 'Don't be troubled, Madame Ménétrier; I will employ my influence in favour of your son; be sure of my zeal.' And you know, Léonard, that we received before the expiration of two months the assurance that our Jacquot could return unmolested to Paris."

We supped with a good appetite. My father asked me if was my intention to re-enter the service of M. d'Asterac. I replied that after the lamented death of my kind master I did not wish to encounter that cruel Mosaïde in the house of a nobleman who paid his servants with fine speeches and nothing else. My father very kindly invited me to turn the spit as in former days.

"Latterly, Jacquot," he said, "I gave the place to Friar Ange, but he did not do as well as Miraut or yourself. Don't you want to take your old place at the corner of the fireside?"

My mother, plain and simple as she was, did not want common-sense and said:

"M. Blaizot, the bookseller of the *Image of Saint Catherine,* is in want of an assistant. This employment, Jacquot, ought to suit you like a glove. Thy dispositions are sweet, thy manners are good, and that's what's wanted to sell Bibles."

I went at once to M. Blaizot, who took me into his service.

My misfortunes had made me wise. I did not feel discouraged by the humbleness of my employment, and I fulfilled my duties with exactitude, handling the duster and broom to the satisfaction of my employer.

One of my duties was to pay a visit to M. d'Asterac. I went to the great alchemist on the last Sunday of November, after the midday dinner. It's a long way from the Rue Saint Jacques to the Croix-des-Sablons, and the almanac does not lie when it announces that in November the days are short. When I arrived at the Roule it was quite dark, and a black haze covered the deserted road. And sorrowful were my thoughts in the darkness.

"Alas," I said to myself, "it will soon be a full year since I first walked on this road, in the snow, in company with my dear master, who now rests in a small village in Burgundy encircled by vineyards. He sleeps in the hope of eternal life. And it is but right to have the same hope as a man as wise as he. God preserve me from ever doubting of the immortality of the soul! But, one must confess to oneself, all that is connected with a future existence and another world is of those verities in which one believes without being moved and which have neither taste nor savour of any kind, so that one swallows them without perceiving it. As for me I find no consolation in the idea of meeting again the Abbé Coignard in Paradise. Surely I could not recognise him, and his speeches would not contain the agreeableness which he derived from circumstances."

Occupied with these reflections, I saw before me a fierce light covering one-half of the sky; the fog was reddened by it, and the light palpitated in the centre. A heavy smoke mixed with the vapours of the air. I at once became afraid that the fire had broken out at the d'Asterac castle. I quickened my steps, and very soon ascertained that my fears were but too well founded. I discovered the calvary of the Sablons, an opaque black on a background of flame, and I saw nearly all the windows of the castle flaring as for a sinister feast. The little green door was broken in. Shadows gesticulated in the park and murmured the horror they felt. They were the inhabitants of the borough of Neuilly, who had come for curiosity's sake and to bring help. Some threw water from a fire engine on the burning edifice, making a fiery rain of sparks arise. A thick volume of smoke rose over the castle. A shower of sparks and of cinders fell round me, and I soon became aware that my garments and my hands were blackened. With much mortification I thought that all that burning dust in the air was the end of so many fine books and precious manuscripts, which were the joy of my dear master, the remains, perhaps, of Zosimus the Panopolitan, on which we had worked together during the noblest hours of my life.

I had seen the Abbé Jérôme Coignard die. Now, it was his soul, his sparkling and sweet soul, which I fancied reduced to ashes together with the queen of libraries. The wind strengthened the fire and the flames roared like voracious beasts.

Questioning a man of Neuilly still blacker than myself, and wearing only his vest, I asked him if M. d'Asterac and his people had been saved.

"Nobody," he said, "has left the castle except an old Jew, who was seen running laden with packages in the direction of the swamps. He lived in the keeper's cottage on the river, and was hated for his origin and for the crimes of which he was suspected. Children pursued him. And in running away he fell into the Seine. He was fished out when dead, pressing on his heart a cup and six golden plates. You can see him on the river bank in his yellow gown. With his eyes open he is horrible."

"Ah!" I replied, "his end is due to his crimes. But his death does not give me back the best of masters whom he slew. Tell me again; has nobody seen M. d'Asterac?"

At the very moment when I put the question I heard near me one of the moving shadows cry out:

"The roof is falling in!"

And now I recognised with unspeakable horror the great black form of M. d'Asterac running along the gutters. The alchemist shouted with a sounding voice:

"I rise on wings of flame up to the seat of life divine!"

So he said, and suddenly the roof fell in with a tremendous crash, and the flames as high as mountains enveloped the friend of the Salamanders.

CHAPTER XXV

THERE is no love will stand separation. The memory of Jahel, smarting at first, was smoothed down little by little, and nothing remained but a vague irritation, of which she was no longer the only object.

M. Blaizot aged quickly. He retired to Montrouge, to his cottage in the fields, and sold me his shop against a life annuity. Having become in his place the sworn bookseller of the *Image of Saint Catherine,* I took with me my father and mother, whose cookshop flourished no more. I liked my humble shop and took care to trim it up. I nailed on the doors some old Venetian maps and some theses ornamented with allegorical engravings, which made a decoration old and odd no doubt, but pleasant to friends of good learning. My knowledge, taking care to hide it cleverly, was not detrimental to my trade. It would have been worse had I been a publisher like Marc-Michel Rey, and obliged like him to gain my living at the expense of the stupidity of the public.

I keep in stock, as they say, the classical authors, and that is a merchandise in demand in that learned Rue Saint Jacques of which it would please me one day to write an account of its antiquities and celebrities. The first Parisian printer established his venerable presses there. The Cramoisys, whom Guy Patin calls the kings of the Rue Saint Jacques, published there the works of our his-

torians. Before the erection of the College of France,
the king's readers, Pierre Danès, François Votable,
Ramus, gave their lectures there in a shed which echoed
with the quarrels between the street porters and the wash-
erwomen. And how can we forget Jean de Meung, who
composed in one of the little houses of this street the
Roman de la Rose?[1]

I have the whole house at my disposal: it is very old,
and dates at least from the time of the Goths, as may be
seen by the wooden joists crossed on the narrow front and
by the mossy tiles. It has but one window on each floor.
The one on the first floor is all the year round garnished
with flowers, strings are attached, and all sorts of climbers
run up them in springtime. My good old mother takes
care of this.

It is the window of her room. She can be seen from
the street, reading her prayers in a book printed in big
letters over the image of Saint Catherine. Age, devotion
and maternal pride have given her a grand air, and to
see her wax-coloured face under her high white cap one
could take his oath on her being a wealthy citizen's wife.

My father, in getting old, also acquired some dignity.
As he likes exercise and fresh air I employ him to carry
books about town. First I employed Friar Ange, but he
begged of my customers, made them kiss relics, stole their
wine, caressed their servant girls, and left one-half of my
books in the gutters. I soon gave him the sack. But my
good mother, whom he makes believe that he is possessed
of secrets for gaining heaven, gives him soup and wine.

---

[1] Jacques Tournebroche did not know that François Villon also
dwelt in the Rue Saint Jacques, at the Cloister Saint Benoît, in a
house called the *Porte Verte*. The pupil of M. Jérôme Coignard
would no doubt have had great pleasure in recalling the memory
of that ancient poet, who, like himself, had known various sorts
of people.

He is not a bad man, and in the end I became somewhat attached to him.

Several learned men and some wits frequent my shop. And it is a great advantage to my trade to be in daily contact with men of merit. Among those who often come to look at new books and converse familiarly among themselves there are historians as learned as Tillemont, sacred orators the equals of Bossuet and Bourdaloue in eloquence, comic and tragic poets, theologians who unite purity of morals with solidity of doctrine, the esteemed authors of "Spanish" novels, geometers and philosophers capable, like M. Descartes, of measuring and weighing the universe. I admire them, I enjoy the least of their words. But not one, to my thinking, is equal in genius to my dear master, whom I had the misfortune to lose on the road to Lyons; not one reminds me of that incomparable elegance of thought, that sweet sublimity, that astonishing wealth of a soul always expanding and flowering, like the urns of rivers represented in marble in gardens; not one gives me that never-failing spring of science and of morals, wherein I had the happiness to quench the thirst of my youth, none give me more than a shadow of that grace, that wisdom, that strength of thought which shone in M. Jérôme Coignard. I hold him to be the most amiable spirit who has ever flourished on the earth.

MODERN LIBRARY OF THE WORLD'S BEST BOOKS

COMPLETE LIST OF TITLES IN

THE MODERN LIBRARY

For convenience in ordering please use number at right of title

AUTHOR	TITLE AND NUMBER
RENAN, ERNEST	The Life of Jesus 140
RODIN	64 Reproductions 41
ROSTAND, EDMOND	Cyrano de Bergerac 154
RUSSELL, BERTRAND	Selected Papers of Bertrand Russell 137
SALTUS, EDGAR	The Imperial Orgy 139
SCHNITZLER, ARTHUR	Anatol, Green Cockatoo, etc. 32
SCHNITZLER, ARTHUR	Bertha Garlan 39
SCHOPENHAUER	The Philosophy of Schopenhauer 52
SCHOPENHAUER	Studies in Pessimism 12
SCHREINER, OLIVE	The Story of an African Farm 132
SHAW, G. B.	An Unsocial Socialist 15
SMOLLETT, TOBIAS	Humphrey Clinker 159
SPINOZA	The Philosophy of Spinoza 60
STENDHAL	The Red and the Black 157
STERNE, LAURENCE	Tristram Shandy 147
STRINDBERG, AUGUST	Married 2
SUDERMANN, HERMANN	Dame Care 33
SUDERMANN, HERMANN	The Song of Songs 162
SWINBURNE, CHARLES	Poems 23
SYMONDS, JOHN A.	The Life of Michelangelo 49
TCHEKOV	Rothschild's Fiddle, etc. 31
TCHEKOV	Sea Gull, Cherry Orchard, Three Sisters, etc. 171
THOMPSON, FRANCIS	Complete Poems 38
TOLSTOY, LEO	Anna Karenina 37
TOLSTOY, LEO	Redemption and Other Plays 77
TOLSTOY, LEO	The Death of Ivan Ilyitch and Four Other Stories 64
TOMLINSON, H. M.	The Sea and The Jungle 99
TURGENEV, IVAN	Fathers and Sons 21
TURGENEV, IVAN	Smoke 80
VAN LOON, HENDRIK W.	Ancient Man 105
VAN VECHTEN, CARL	Peter Whiffle 164
VILLON, FRANCOIS	Poems 58
VOLTAIRE	Candide 47
WALPOLE, HUGH	Fortitude 178
WLLLS, H. G.	Ann Veronica 27
WHISTLER, J. McNEIL	The Art of Whistler with 32 Reproductions 150
WHITMAN, WALT	Leaves of Grass 97
WILDE, OSCAR	An Ideal Husband, A Woman of No Importance 84
WILDE, OSCAR	De Profundis 117
WILDE, OSCAR	Dorian Gray 1
WILDE, OSCAR	Poems 19
WILDE, OSCAR	Fairy Tales, Poems in Prose 61
WILDE, OSCAR	Salome, The Importance of Being Earnest, etc. 83
WILDER, THORNTON	The Cabala 155
WOOLF, VIRGINIA	Mrs. Dalloway 96
YEATS, W. B.	Irish Fairy and Folk Tales 44
YOUNG, G. F.	The Medici 179
ZOLA, EMILE	Nana 142